Alison has a busy family life in Edinburgh. After running her own Mexican food business for 25 years while her five kids grew up, she then took a counselling diploma and worked as a bereavement counsellor before moving back to Edinburgh. She has currently written two other novels, the first, 'Seal Lodge of Kintyre', also a Scottish historical ghost story released in July 2018. The second, 'Road to Lag', will be released soon. Alison spends a lot of her time researching Scottish history and legends, which are the basis for her books. She is often found walking in the Pentland Hills most afternoons with her two dogs, finding inspiration in the ever-changing scenery.

Here's tae us

Wha's like us

Damn few

And they're aw deid

Mair's the pity!

Thank you to my parents, for all your stories of the Highlanders that fed my imagination as I grew up.

Alison Hill

THE GHOST OF GLENCOE

AUSTIN MACAULEY PUBLISHERS™

LONDON · CAMBRIDGE · NEW YORK · SHARJAH

A CIP catalogue record for this title is available from the British Library.

ISBN 9781528907699 (Paperback)
ISBN 9781528907705 (E-Book)

www.austinmacauley.com

First Published (2019)
Austin Macauley Publishers Ltd
25 Canada Square
Canary Wharf
London
E14 5LQ

I'd like to thank the friendly people of Glencoe and Kinlochleven who unknowingly helped me create this story. Also the fantastic book about the Glencoe Massacre by John Prebble, simply titled 'Glencoe', that told me the story in such detail.

The Massacre of Glencoe

(Written by Jim McLean 1963, performed by the Corries)

Oh, cruel is the snow that sweeps Glencoe, and covers the grave o'
Donald
Cruel was the foe that raped Glencoe, and murdered the house o'
MacDonald

They came in the blizzard, we offered them heat
A roof o'er their head, dry shoes for their feet
We wined them and dined them, they ate of our meat
And they slept in the house o' MacDonald

Oh, cruel was the snow that swept Glencoe, and covered the grave
of Donald
And cruel was the foe that raped Glencoe, and murdered the house
of MacDonald

They came from Fort William wi' murder in mind
The Campbells had orders King William had signed...
Put all to the sword, these words underlined
And leave none alive called MacDonald

Oh, cruel was the snow that swept Glencoe, and covered the grave
o'Donald
And cruel was the foe that raped Glencoe, and murdered the house
o'MacDonald

They came in the night when the men were asleep, this band o'
Argyll's through snow soft and deep
Like murdering foxes amongst helpless sheep, they slaughtered the
house o'MacDonald

Oh, cruel was the snow that swept Glencoe, and covered the house
o'MacDonald

And cruel was the foe that raped Glencoe, and murdered the house o'MacDonald

Some died in their beds at the hand of the foe, some fled in the night and were lost in the snow
Some lived to accuse him who struck the first blow, but gone was the house o'MacDonald

Oh, cruel was the snow that swept Glencoe, and covered the grave o'Donald
Cruel was the foe that raped Glencoe, and murdered the house o'MacDonald

Prologue

In April 1689, William of Orange and his wife Mary were proclaimed King and Queen of Scotland. There would no longer be a Stuart king on the Scottish throne, which did not sit well with many of the highlanders, who caused many a skirmish throughout the country against the English soldiers.

In August of 1691 William offers a full pardon to all the Clan's if their Chieftains sign an Oath declaring allegiance to William and Mary, recognising them as their sovereigns. Those who did not sign the Oath by the 1st January 1692, would be dealt with 'the upmost extremity of the law'.

By December the MacDonalds of Glencoe had still not signed the oath, waiting along with many other clans for a message from James 11, who was in France. The message from James arrived mid-December, giving permission for the Clans to do as they saw fit, stating he was too exhausted to travel farther. Meanwhile the King's troops were ordered to march from the lowlands to Fort William, where the Cameron's, the Stuarts and the Macdonald's resided.

MacIain, the old chief of the Glencoe MacDonalds travelled to Fort William to take the Oath at the garrison stationed there. It was the 30th December. The Governor, John Hill, told MacIain that he was not authorised to take the Oath, and that he must travel to Inveraray and swear the Oath to the Campbells. There was a great deal of bad blood between these two old feuding Clans, nevertheless MacIain agreed and left straight away for Inveraray. John Hill gave him a letter to carry, assuring the Sheriff Clerk of Argyll that MacIain had attempted to sign the Oath within the allotted time frame. Unfortunately, MacIain was captured on route and held up for another twenty-four hours before he could continue on his journey. He was now an old man, and it was a cold, harsh winter. He did not arrive at Inveraray until the 2nd January, only to find that Sir Colin Campbell, the Sheriff, was away enjoying the New Year celebrations with his family.

MacIain MacDonald spent three more uncomfortable days, hiding out in the heart of Campbell country, awaiting Sir Colin's return. It was not until January 6th, that the Sheriff Clerk of Argyll finally accepted MacIain's Oath. The old MacDonald returned to Glencoe able to tell his people that they were safe from reprisals and the Oath had been sworn.

By the middle of January, the Master of Stair heard that MacIain was five days late in signing the Oath, and refused to accept it, scratching MacIain's name from the list of those who had signed. He issued orders for the soldiers to descend on Glencoe.

On the first of February, under the command of the Campbells of Glenlyon, Argyll's regiment marched into Glencoe asking for shelter, as the garrison at Fort William was already full. It was Highland tradition to offer hospitality and the MacDonald's were no exception. They housed the men, three to five in each cottage, fed them and entertained them for nearly two weeks. MacIain, although wary at first, was still under the belief that his Oath had been accepted, and that they were able to become good, friendly hosts to the Campbell Soldiers.

At five o'clock in the morning of February 13th, as a blizzard blew through the mountains of Glencoe, the Campbell's soldiers awoke and began their slaughter. They killed many of the MacDonald's as they lay in their beds. MacIain MacDonald was slaughtered as he tried to get dressed, his wife, the Lady MacDonald, was stripped naked, relieved of her jewellery, and thrown out into the snow to perish.

Men battled, as women and children ran for their lives in disbelief that their houseguests would turn on them this way. Another Regiment of four hundred soldiers came over the Devil's Staircase to join in the massacre. It was a perfectly coordinated attack, but the blizzard blew hard, allowing many of the MacDonald's to escape into the snow, including MacIain's sons.

The slaughter was brutal, the cottages were burned to the ground as the MacDonald's fled. Women and children were cut down and thrown onto a heap of bloody bodies. It was reported that thirty-eight of MacIain's men were killed on that morning, though it does not account for the women and children, nor those who perished in the freezing winter storm with nowhere to hide.

The repercussions of the massacre were felt as far as London and Paris, leaving William of Orange distancing himself from any blame. News of the vicious attack was circulated around Scotland,

and became a hugely significant turning point in the history of Scotland It is still known worldwide as 'The Massacre of Glencoe'.

Chapter One

"Why the hell did I come out at this time of day?" Anna muttered to herself. It was nearly five on a Friday. Not surprisingly, they were stuck in back to back traffic, but for once the boys sat quietly in the back of the car. Ollie still had the occasional tear drip silently down his cheek from his distraught brown eyes whilst James just sat, staring out of the window towards the sky, his face pale and miserable. It was making it all the more difficult for Anna not to soften and offer some form of forgiveness.

They had been shopping at the Gyle Centre in Edinburgh, picking up a few final items to take on their trip up north that was planned for the next day. Anna had called into a supermarket on their way home, and the boys, Ollie aged four-and-a-half and James who was six, had been acting up as usual around the store. Anna's mind had switched off and she managed to ignore their persistent arguing whilst she concentrated on picking up a few supplies for their first day or two in the Highlands.

Her mummy radar was obviously switched off, as she should have twigged something was up when the boys suddenly stopped squabbling and became very quiet. They continued around the store, but it wasn't until after she had gone through the checkout that her mummy senses started tingling when, out of the corner of her eye, she saw James hand Ollie a small plastic toy with a wrapper on it.

"Where did that come from?" Anna demanded. "Hand it over!"

James burst into tears. "Ollie made me do it!" he cried, immediately turning on his brother as he put the small packet in his mother's outstretched hand.

Ollie sat wide eyed, with tears beginning to form.

"What do you think you were doing? That's stealing!" said Anna in a sort of shouty whisper, aware that people were looking over their shoulders at them.

"Ollie said it was okay?" James sobbed.

"No, I didn't!" Ollie cried.

"James, you're the oldest, so you knew it was wrong!" said Anna, unmoved by their tears. She narrowed her eyes as she looked at Ollie. "This has your name all over it; you two are coming with me."

Anna marched the boys along with the shopping trolley to the customer service desk where a rather bewildered-looking woman, with a fixed smile, stood watching as Anna stomped up to the counter.

"I'm terribly sorry but the boys seem to have taken this without paying for it," Anna announced to the woman, whose fixed smile slipped into a look of horrified confusion. James and Ollie were both crying now as they stared woefully at the woman behind the counter. Anna stood behind them, frantically flapping her arms at the woman, who clearly had no idea what she was expected to do. After what seemed an age, she finally made eye contact with Anna who, by this time, was gathering quite an audience as she stood gesturing with her hands like a mad woman.

In desperation, Anna pointed to the back of the boys' heads, then pulled her finger across her throat, nodding frantically at the same time.

At last, recognition lit up in the shop assistant's face, and she changed her demeanour, looking at the boys with a stern frown as she said, "Now boys, you have to remember to pay for things when you come to a shop, don't you?"

"Yes!" both boys answered at once through floods of tears.

"What do you say to the lady?" Anna asked them.

"Sorry," they both cried, distraught. "Will the police put us in jail?" sobbed Ollie.

"Aww, how sweet," said a shopper behind them. Anna turned to glare at her and the lady moved away quickly.

The shop assistant almost broke, but somehow managed to keep the firm look on her face. "Not this time, I think that you will probably never do it again, so I'm going to give you this chance," she told them, then looked up at Anna and gave her a half smile as if to say, "Is that what you wanted?"

Anna nodded gratefully at the shop assistant, then marched the boys out to the car. They both climbed quietly into their car seats, still sniffling. They were so upset, and Anna found she was trying to resist the urge to scoop them both up to tell them it was okay. But she remained resolute, and now, here they were, stuck in Friday night traffic, making the punishment seem incredibly long. "What would you say if we went to McDonald's, where we can pay for a toy in a happy meal?" she asked eventually, caving in.

"Yes, please," said Ollie in a small voice, while James just nodded quietly, still looking like he had the weight of the world on his small shoulders. The queue at the McDonald's drive-through was so long, it took them another forty minutes to get through. By then, the earlier incident was forgotten and both boys were almost back to normal by the time Anna swung the car into her driveway. James and Ollie ran straight into the house, Happy Meal boxes already explored by the time they plonked themselves at the kitchen table. They pulled out their toys, squealing with delight as they both had a small plastic torch in the shape of a Minion.

Dexter, their huge mutt of a dog, recognising the McDonald's scent immediately, placed himself strategically under the table awaiting the fries that would inevitably be dropped on the floor as they pulled them from their wrappers. He was a cross between a chocolate Labrador and a Cockapoo, which made him a rich reddish-brown colour with a huge shaggy head, long legs and a lithe, lean body.

Anna unloaded the bags of shopping while the boys were eating, taking the shopping inside, only to repack it all into boxes for their journey, then reload it back into the car, ready for the next day. Everything was more or less sorted now; the rest of the stuff she would do when the boys were in bed.

Anna Ferguson still lived in the family home she had once shared with her husband, Alex. That was until he went on one of his many business trips to Dubai but had accidently been caught on a social media post in a French ski resort with some mysterious blonde. Anna's best friend Clare had seen the post, bringing the devastating news to her door.

Anna felt betrayed, angry, humiliated, but if she were to be honest, she was neither completely devastated nor as surprised as she should have been. When she confronted him, Alex did them both a favour by not trying to deny it, then he moved out almost immediately afterwards.

Anna found that she had actually breathed a sigh of relief; there had been something wrong in their marriage ever since Ollie had been born so quickly after James. Alex had distanced himself from their family life, whilst Anna threw herself into being a full-time mother to two baby boys. It was a strange kind of irony, seeing as Alex had been the one wanting to start a family so quickly after they had married.

Anna met Alex when she worked as an accountant for her father's investment firm. Alex was the head of the sales department, tall, athletic with closely cropped strawberry blonde hair, pale skin and pale blue eyes. It was in complete contrast to Anna, who had inherited her grandmother's Celtic islander colouring, with olive skin, dark brunette hair, beautiful brown eyes and a small, slim but shapely figure.

Alex was dynamic, aggressive and full of confidence, and he set his sights on Anna, sweeping her off her feet before she really knew what was happening. She had never come across anyone like him, and before her feet had time to hit the ground, they were getting married. Everything had been organised for her, from the venue to the catering. Alex had even chosen her dress; perhaps that alone should have flagged some warning signal, but her father seemed to really like Alex and was paying tooth and nail for the wedding.

It had been a large, extravagant affair, more to Alex's taste than hers. Anna never liked being the centre of attention, but Alex was an enterprising, forceful character, on a mission to prove he was the golden boy of her father's company.

Looking back, the whole romance had been such a whirlwind that Anna really didn't have time to think it through properly; even then, their differences were very apparent. Perhaps Anna should have realised that marrying the boss's daughter was a step up the ladder for her very ambitious husband. Anna wished she had listened more to her mother who was not shy in expressing her misgivings. She had told Anna it was all happening too fast, that she needed to take a step back and make sure Alex was what she really wanted in life.

A year after their wedding, things changed dramatically in their relationship. James was born; then soon after, Anna's father decided to retire from the business he had built from scratch. Anna was beginning to realise the potent confidence that had attracted her so much to Alex when they first met was in fact nothing more than self-obsessed arrogance. Alex seemed to have her father wrapped around his finger, especially with the birth of his first grandchild. And so, without much deliberation on her father's part, he handed the reigns of his business over to Alex. From then on, their marriage was on a downwards spiral, and she may have left then, had she not discovered she was pregnant again.

They were financially secure, with a large, gated house near Crammond Beach, with a view of the Firth of Forth. On Alex's insistence, Anna had given up her job at the firm to take on the role of full-time mother as soon as James was born. This was a step she was unsure of initially, but she soon found she loved being with her baby. Luckily, Anna had many friends with young children, so she didn't feel isolated in the way some young mothers do.

After Ollie was born, Alex began to take more and more business trips away, or so he had said. Anna was so busy with two young toddlers, she never really noticed, until Clare appeared with the tell-tale Facebook post. Clare had never really liked Alex, but the intention of showing Anna was not out of any sort of malice. She knew Anna was not on Facebook herself, so it was unlikely that she would see it. Clare had sat on it for weeks, trying to decide what to do, but when others in their group started to talk about it, she finally approached Anna. It was the kick up the bum Anna needed to get out of her sham of a marriage.

The mysterious blonde had turned out to be a new employee at their firm, ironically in Anna's old role. Anna's father had been furious, but there was not much he could do as contracts had been signed. Alex was now CEO of the company.

Anna got herself a lawyer; as far as she was concerned, the more distance she could put between herself and Alex was a good thing. The divorce went through with no hiccups. Alex signed the house over to her, agreeing to pay the mortgage along with a healthy maintenance payment every month.

Anna changed her surname from Hammond back to Ferguson, which gave her the closure she needed. She had no intention of being idle, but until the boys went to school full time, she had no plans to go back to work.

Alex had tried to be the weekend father for a while but had no patience for toddlers, with the mess and the sleepless nights. The visits became less regular, much to Anna's disgust, but the boys hardly mentioned him anymore. He would occasionally appear to take them on some trip or another, throw lots of money and toys at them, then disappear for another few weeks.

The boys had accepted these impromptu visits without much thought, but Anna felt it was an intrusion. Alex always chose what was convenient and easy for him. If it suited his needs to become the doting father, then he would appear, sometimes without prior warning. Anna soon had her lawyer put a stop to that, and Alex's visits were now a rarity.

James had inherited his father's colouring, with fair skin and rose blonde hair, although he had Anna's deep brown eyes. Ollie had brown eyes also, but his hair was as dark as hers and his skin

18

had the same olive hue, giving him that Mediterranean sun-kissed look.

Anna was thirty-two now. She had let her dark hair grow long since she had left work, making her look younger than that. She needed little make up, preferring jeans and tee shirts to the high fashion and labels of Edinburgh society. Alex had been the wrong choice for her from the start. He was all about appearances, priding himself on having a beautiful wife at his side, dressed in the latest designer gear. Anna guessed that his arriving home to find baby sick down the front of her shirt on a regular basis was probably one of the reasons he strayed. But in all honesty, Alex was not the sort of man who needed an excuse to stray. Fatherhood was not as glamorous as he had initially thought, and he was certainly not prepared for changing dirty nappies whilst babies drooled over his nice Gucci shoes.

Although her friends had tried to convince her otherwise, Anna was not looking for another man in her life. She was enjoying the freedom her single status was giving her, much to her mother's disappointment. Admittedly, Bea Ferguson, Anna's mother, had not managed to hide her 'told you so's' from Anna after the news of Alex's affair became common knowledge. However, she still wanted her daughter to find the right husband. Anna's mother was old school, not accepting that a young woman's life could possibly be complete, without a good husband by her side. She pointed this out frequently on her visits, then would drop the guilt bomb by saying that the boys needed a good father figure. Anna loved her mother, but these last few years with Alex had given her a strength she hadn't known she possessed. She had no intention of replacing the boys' father.

What made it worse for Anna was that her brother, Glen, had come out as gay when he was in his late teens. Her parents had really struggled with that, although they had become more accepting during the last few years. Glen moved away, leaving Anna the main focus of her mother's attention.

In her desperation for her daughter to meet someone new, Anna's mother had offered to take the boys for a couple of weeks to their villa in Tenerife over the summer, leaving Anna free to socialise. Grandma Bea was great with the boys and they loved her dearly, but Anna had no intention of spending her first summer as a free woman away from her children. She had gratefully declined the offer, instead hiring a large cottage near to Glencoe village in the Highlands for a month. She planned to use the cottage as a base from where she could take the boys boating, fishing, hiking and exploring.

She had let Alex know in an email that she was planning to be away for the summer with their sons, to which his one-word response was, 'Cool'.

***

It was now the night before their trip and she put the boys to bed, then finished packing up the car before she phoned Clare. Her best friend was excited for her to go, though disappointed she couldn't get any time herself to visit them up there. Glen and his husband, Rob, were coming to stay for the second week they were there. Anna was beginning to feel excited about the first trip she had ever made on her own steam. She had always been the daughter or the partner or the wife; she had never done anything like this on her own before. She said goodbye to Clare then let her thoughts drift to what they could get up to over the next few weeks.

Her parents had taken them up to the Highlands many times when they were children. She had some of her best ever memories in these hills and lochs. They had taken an old battered caravan with them back in those days. Anna choked back a giggle as she thought of how her mother wouldn't be seen dead stepping foot in one of those nowadays. All four of them with their dog, Shep, squashed into a tiny box, sitting around the table eating Scotch pie with baked beans with Oxo gravy whilst the summer rain hammered onto the roof. She and Glen had slept in a tent outside the caravan if it wasn't too wet. If it was wet, they had to curl up on the floor at the foot of their parents' fold-down bed. She wondered how James and Ollie would feel about doing that; they would probably love it, but she would never let them sleep alone in a tent nowadays.

She took herself off to bed, drifting off quickly into a dreamless sleep. The next thing she knew was that daylight had filled her room and James was lying on his stomach next to her, staring at her hard. He had crept in bed beside her along with Buzz, his toy rabbit with one ear missing. James was a quieter child than Ollie, always worrying and over thinking things.

Anna pulled him to her. "Are you okay, little man?" she asked as she kissed his forehead.

"Buzz doesn't want to go to the new house," whispered James.

"Why doesn't he want to go?" Anna whispered back.

"Because his friends will miss him," said James.

"Just think of all the exciting adventures Buzz will have to tell all his friends about when he gets back. He will have done things no other rabbit will have done, he'll be a hero," whispered Anna.

"But what if they aren't here when he gets back? What if his bed and his room and all his friends have gone?" James asked, looking at her with big, worried eyes.

"You can tell Buzz that they aren't going anywhere. He will have the same bed with all his cuddly toy friends when he gets back. They will miss him, but they want him to go so that they can hear about all his adventures," Anna assured him, kissing him again on the forehead.

"But Benji doesn't want us to go. He doesn't like the new house," said James, still frowning.

"Well, why don't you ask Benji to stay here, and he can look after all the other toys?" said Anna. Benji was the latest of James's imaginary friends. He had been around for a few weeks now.

"But he's my friend," sighed James, as if Anna should know this.

"Well, you can tell Benji that I have checked the new house from top to bottom; it is going to be really fun. You and Buzz are going to have a great time there, and Benji can come if he wants to," said Anna.

James seemed to accept that, snuggling into her just as the door suddenly flew open, announcing the tornado that was Ollie, hair everywhere, one eye stuck shut, with only his pyjama bottoms on. He dived in the bed between them, "Why didn't you wake me? Is it time to go?" he demanded excitedly.

"As soon as we're dressed and have had some breakfast," said Anna, laughing. "Come on, let's get going."

Chapter Two

An hour later, Anna was driving onto the M9 to take her to Stirling, where she could get onto the A84 to take her up through Callander and into the highlands. The A84 was already overloaded with caravans and coach tours; it was the holiday season, and she guessed it was going to be slow going on the one lane road into the mountains.

She had rented an old seventeenth-century converted cottage named Kirstin's Cot, just through the Glencoe Gorge, before you reached Glencoe village. She was near enough to Loch Leven but had decided against a waterside lodge because of the midges, which could be a nightmare at this time of year. Kirstin's Cot was located high above the road, as far as she could tell from the description online, with its driveway off a one-track lane that ran from the Clachaig Inn to Glencoe village.

The photos of the cottage looked fantastic; 'a building of two halves' was how it was described on the website. The front of the cottage was made of old grey stone, with small square windows dotted unevenly in the build. The photos had shown that the huge kitchen was in the old part of the building, with the stone walls a feature on the inside also. There was a fireplace with a wood burner set inside it, and an AGA oil-burning stove that would keep the room permanently warm. The windows seemed quite high up in the kitchen, so there was not a lot of natural light, though the soft lighting from overhead spotlights made it look very cosy.

There were two bedrooms in the old part of the cottage, both quite large and gothic looking. One of the rooms had a four-poster bed; Anna had already decided she was sleeping there. The other had a newer-looking king-size bed, but that room seemed quite dark and foreboding.

The new part of the cottage was built onto the back, looking more like a wooden ski chalet than an old cottage. There was a narrow wooden hallway, with a glass roof leading from the older part of the cottage through to the new build. This part of the cottage had another two bedrooms, all fresh looking and brightly lit, with large windows showing off panoramic views of the mountains. There was also a lounge area in this part of the cottage, complete with all the mod cons, a giant screen TV facing a huge, comfortable looking sofa.

There were French doors from the lounge that led out onto a decking area that surrounded most of the cottage at the back. What really sold the property to her was the secluded, matured garden for the boys to play in, with a pool house complete with its own hot tub and sauna. Both the boys could swim now; they had no idea about the pool house and she knew they would love it, especially as the weather could be so unpredictable. It always rains in Scotland; that's why you always take your umbrella!

The drive was flat and uneventful until they drove through the busy tourist town of Callander. Then they started heading up the hills, along the side of Loch Lubnaig. There was a low mist blocking the views of the mountains and Anna hoped the sun would burn it off soon—she wanted her boys to experience all the excitement of travelling through the mountains. Dexter was seated shotgun in Anna's car as usual, as the boys were in their car seats in the back. Dexter loved travelling in the car, making sure he sat in the front seat next to her; he'd done that ever since he was a puppy. It became increasingly difficult to drag him off the seat as he grew bigger, so, the front seat became known as 'Dexter's seat'. He would sit upright the whole way, staring at the scenery or into other people's cars depending on what held more interest for him.

It was slow going through these roads during tourist season. Anna reckoned it would probably take half the time during the winter, when coaches weren't stopping every couple of miles so hundreds of tourists could get out and take photos of the mountain views.

Anna left the A84 at Lochearnhead, then followed the signs to Fort William. When they reached Tyndrum, she decided to stop at The Green Welly for lunch. It was heaving, but she managed to find a parking spot, then luckily a picnic table at the front of the café and shops. It was a popular place to stop in the Highlands, situated on the junction of the A85 that would take you to Oban and the Western Isles and the A82 which went north to Fort William, then eventually leading you up the side of Loch Ness. For that reason, the place was always busy throughout the year had great food, ample parking and lots of shops for the hikers who were about to embark on the West Highland Way.

Anna left Dexter sitting at a wooden picnic table with the boys, then bought some sandwiches, crisps and drinks in the shop just next to where they were seated, so she could keep one eye on them. Ollie had already managed to collect two sticks by the time she returned to the table. Ollie liked to collect sticks; her back garden at home was full of them. They were his stick people and he had names for them, but unfortunately, Dexter liked to eat sticks, so it was not unusual to hear Ollie scream bloody murder, sending her running into the garden to find Dexter and Ollie playing tug of war with one of Ollie's stickmen.

Anna always had to have a large supply of plasters at hand for Ollie to put on his sticks after Dexter had tried to destroy them. Luckily, today, Dexter was too interested in the food that had just been deposited on the table to notice the new stick arrivals.

As Anna bit into her tuna sandwich, a blue Porsche sports car spun onto the loose stones of the car park at speed, making everyone look up with a start.

"What a jerk, people with their children everywhere and he's driving at that speed!" said an American man from the table behind them.

It was just what Anna had been thinking, and as she looked over at the car to see who the jerk was that was driving it, a thin blonde woman, with ridiculous high heels, stepped out of the driving seat. The woman turned, shouting something to someone inside the car, before slamming the door shut forcefully. The passenger side of the Porsche swung open as two long legs appeared, followed by a very tall man, who had to curl his way out the little car. The vehicle was clearly not built for a man of his stature.

He must have been at least six feet four, stretching his limbs uncomfortably as he also slammed the door of the Porsche shut. He was dark haired, handsome in a rugged way, and he looked really angry.

Anna avoided looking at the woman as she marched past their table in her heels that looked incredibly out of place here in the mountains. The woman had perfectly styled hair, a lot of makeup and a disdainful expression on her face. Anna thought she looked ridiculous amongst all the hill walkers and cyclists and resisted the urge to giggle as she made eye contact with the American man seated behind them who winked at her and pulled a comical face.

"Is she from Daddy's work?" asked Ollie in a loud voice just as the disgruntled man from the Porsche reached their table.

Anna choked back a laugh. "No, I don't think so," she replied.

"She looks like she's from Daddy's work," James joined in.

The man looked down at Anna as he passed, his anger fading from his face as he gave her a commiserative smile. He was dressed in jeans, sneakers and a light sweater, which made him look like he fitted comfortably in their surroundings. He followed the woman, whom Anna assumed was his wife, into the restaurant. *Poor bloke*, she thought. *That's why I'm so much better off without a relationship.*

They didn't see the couple again as they finished their sandwiches, then headed back to the car. They carried on up the mountains until the road finally levelled out as they drove through Rannoch Moor—a flat marshland high in the hills, dotted with glistening glass pools of turquoise water, framed with clumps of deep pink and purple heather. Not a safe place to hike across but picturesque nonetheless.

The mountains of Glencoe and Glen Etive got closer as they drove through; the mist had burnt away by now leaving a clear, blue sky. Eventually, they reached the entrance to Glencoe gorge, with the mountains named the Three Sisters dwarfing them on their left and the Devil's Staircase looming on the right-hand side. It always made Anna feel really small and insignificant when she drove through Glencoe. It had been a few years since she had last been there, but the view still took her breath away. Anna told the boys to look out of the windows at the mountains they would be climbing.

"No way could we climb them!" cried Ollie. "They're too high!"

"Well, I could," said James.

She finally got to the sign that took them off the main road and onto a narrow, one-track road running along the side of a small river, then eventually up past the infamous Clachaig Inn.

She had spent some wild nights there when she was younger. As they drove past, Anna noticed the inn was a lot larger than she remembered it from last time; it looked like they had built a hotel onto the back of it.

She carried on past the inn, eventually finding the sign for Kirstin's Cot at the side of the road. She drove through the gates, up a steep hill through some trees, and there in front of them was the cottage. The boys, whose excitement had peaked, had already undone their buckles on their car seats and were throwing themselves around the back of the car trying to see what was to be their home for the next month. Dexter still managed to sit straight up, completely unimpressed, staring straight ahead.

There was an ancient-looking pickup truck parked up next to the front entrance, Anna saw an elderly man wave at her from one of the windows inside the cottage. She got out of her car, then let the boys out, Ollie still clutching his two sticks.

"Well, ye made it in good time," said the man as he came out the front door. He had long white hair tied back from his face in a pony-tail and a short white beard. His face was weather-worn but younger than Anna had first thought when she had seen him through the window.

"I'm Angus MacDonald, the cottage caretaker. I've come tae help ye settle in," he said, shaking her hand, then shaking each one of the boys' hands in turn.

"Hallo Angus, I'm Anna, these two are James and Ollie, and somewhere sniffing around is Dexter," she introduced herself.

"Let me help ye with yer car. Ye didnae pack that all yerself, did ye?" said Angus, pulling open the boot of her car.

"No, the boys helped," she said, laughing as Angus rolled his eyes.

"Aye, I bet they were a big help," he said.

Fifteen minutes later, the entirety of the car had been unloaded. Anna was grateful; sometimes a man did come in useful, she conceded to herself. Once everything was inside, Angus then showed her around the cottage which looked much larger than it had done in the photos.

It was without a doubt a building of two halves, with the older building at the front of the property and the modernised extension at the back. The front entrance led directly into the large kitchen. It seemed quite dim, as it was only lit by three small windows set high on the stone walls, but when Angus switched the lights on it transformed the whole room into a warm, farm-style kitchen. The old part of the cottage was very much in keeping with its original features; the interior was quite dark, and the ceilings were low. There were a few old portraits and paintings hung on the stone walls of the dark hallway that led through to the bedrooms.

Anna hoped James wouldn't get too frightened as it did seem to have the potential to be quite eerie, especially at night, she imagined. The boys had already run off exploring; she could hear them squeal and shout every time they found something new.

"This is the main bedroom," Angus told her, taking her into a large room in the old part of the cottage. The walls were grey stone apart from the back wall, which was covered in wooden panels.

There was a large four-poster bed against that wall, with bedside tables on either side. In the corner of the room was an old free-standing wardrobe, then next to that was a dressing table with a chair. The windows were small, so the room was dark, but again, when Angus turned on the main light switch, it turned on four lamps which transformed the room into a warm, cosy chamber. Anna loved it.

"Will ye be staying in here?" Angus asked, smiling at her reaction to the room.

"Yes, I think so. I saw the picture of this room online; I loved the Gothic design," said Anna. "Who's that in the painting?" she asked, pointing to the only picture in the room. It was of a young woman, dressed in blue with a tartan plaid around her shoulders. She was standing on a hillside with her fair hair blowing in the wind and her blue eyes shining with happiness. Anna could see that set on top of the hillside in the distance was a cottage similar to this one.

"That's Kirstin MacDonald, the wife of Rab Macdonald. She lived here in Glencoe, just before the massacre. She was actually a lowlander by birth, she came frae Ayrshire and she wisnae used tae the harsh highland way of life. But she met and fell in love wi' young Rab MacDonald during a trip tae Glasgow, then against her family's wishes, ran away wi' him here tae Glencoe," explained Angus.

Anna appreciated the impromptu history lesson but was distracted by the cries and squeals of the boys as they explored their way around. She wished she was with them to see their reactions, so she just smiled and said, "So that's why the cottage is called Kirstin's Cot; wait till I tell the boys."

Just then, there was a blood-curdling scream coming from Ollie. Anna raced out the room towards its direction just as the boys came running straight into her.

"There's a pool! There's a pool!" screamed Ollie with excitement.

"Can we go swimming now?" James asked, jumping up and down at her feet.

Anna laughed at their delighted faces.

"There's rules about the pool," Angus butted in. "Firstly, can ye swim?"

"Yes!" cried the boys in unison.

"Can they?" Angus looked at Anna.

"Yes, they both can swim well. I taught them when they were babies," said Anna.

"Well then, there's no rules except tae have fun. Here's the key tae the pool," said Angus, handing it to James. "Dinnae lose it."

The boys had already chosen to share a room in the modernised part of the cottage. It was brighter than the rest with huge windows, decorated in warm gold and yellows and with two single beds. They had already put their toys on the bed they had each chosen. Anna pulled out their swimming shorts, and within minutes, they were both in the pool.

"Thank you, Angus; I think we'll love this place," said Anna.

"Aye, well there's a wee shop in Glencoe village; that's probably yer closest for basic supplies. Of course, there's a supermarket in Fort William, it's nae that far, but if yer stuck for anything then just call me. Here's my number, I have a wee cottage nae far frae here. I'll leave ye tae it then, enjoy yer time here, cheerio for now," he said, waving as he set off.

Anna sighed heavily, glad to be left to her own devices. She made her way back to the pool house to watch the boys, but when she arrived, she found Dexter was in the water with them, and thanked her lucky stars that Angus hadn't seen that. She hauled Dexter out of the pool and towelled him dry then opened the huge glass patio doors that surrounded the pool to let the soggy dog out to explore.

The boys were busy throwing themselves off the side of the pool into the water, squealing with laughter and joy. Anna collapsed onto one of the soft sunbeds around the pool, relaxed and happy for the first time in what seemed like forever.

The boys had exhausted themselves in the pool by early evening. Anna had them showered, in their PJ's and sitting in front of the TV by seven o'clock. She made a simple meal of mac and cheese, allowing them to wolf it down hungrily on their laps as they watched SpongeBob. Ollie fell asleep on the sofa, and James wasn't far behind him, so she carried Ollie, as she half dragged James, to their beds. They were both fast asleep as their heads hit their pillows.

Daylight was still in charge outside, so Anna poured herself a glass of wine, then headed out to the garden to sit and gaze at the spectacular views of Meall Mor. She remembered her father telling Glen and her about the massacre on their first visit to Glencoe. He had pointed out Meall Mor, telling them that was the mountain that many of the surviving Macdonald's had fled to, to escape the Campbell soldiers.

Further down the Glen, facing the back of the cottage, was the Devil's Staircase. It is the steepest part of the West Highland Way, a popular hiking track for thousands of hikers every year. Anna promised herself one day she would do the ninety-six mile trek, but she would have to wait until the boys were a little older. She sat enjoying the majesty around her as she sipped her white wine, trying to ignore the midges that were starting to bite. These little blighters could be incredibly annoying, but she had tough Scottish skin, so they rarely bothered her. She smiled when she remembered how Alex had swelled up in a mass of itchy lumps when she had brought him to the highlands. He had refused to put on any midge spray so suffered the consequences. He then made them cut their trip short because of it.

Thinking of Alex triggered a hidden emotion in her she did not expect. As the sun went down, the mountain shadows stretched hauntingly over the valley, Anna was struck suddenly by a complete sense of loneliness. For the first time since the breakdown of her marriage, Anna began to feel the heartache that she had kept hidden from everyone, including herself. She had kept herself so busy with the boys, the house and sorting out her divorce, that she hadn't given herself time to grieve. It wasn't as if she missed Alex; she was glad to be rid of him, but sitting here, drinking alone with these majestic, ancient giants looming all around her just emphasised how alone she really felt.

It was just like her to soldier on as if nothing affected her; a stiff upper lip was the British way, wasn't it? But the mountains were telling her she was a fake and tears filled her eyes as she allowed herself to let go.

She sat crying quietly until the last bit of light disappeared, then realising she was sitting alone in the dark, she snapped out of her misery, feeling foolish. Her eyes were red and swollen, yet somehow, her heart felt lighter. She went back inside the cottage, locking the door behind her and leaving her wine glass and empty bottle on the side, then headed straight for her bed.

Anna realised she had been right about the house; it did have that spooky feeling in the dark. All the old portraits were watching her with their frozen eyes as she walked through to the new part of the cottage to check on the boys.

They were both sound asleep still, so Anna went to her room, threw off her clothes, brushed her teeth, then clambered into the four-poster bed. Sleep came easily, helped by the wine, and she sank into a deep, dreamless void of darkness.

She awoke with a start. The room was still very dark, and it took her a minute to remember the black-out curtains that held back the sunlight, as the sun rose on her bedroom's side of the cottage. She reached over to turn on the bedside lamp to find there was another little body in bed with her. As she flicked on the light, she recognised the Spider-Man pyjamas that James always wore. He was curled up in a small ball, with his head buried under the pillow. It wasn't unusual for James to sneak into her bed at night, but it was unusual that he hadn't woken her.

Anna slipped out of bed; going to the window, she opened the thick curtains slightly. She was instantly blinded by the bright sunlight that blasted through the gap; it was going to be a nice day. She checked her phone and saw it was nearly nine o'clock. She couldn't believe that Ollie had slept so late. Then, as if she had willed it, her bedroom door was flung open and Ollie came charging in with Dexter at his heels.

"Can I go in the pool?" he cried, diving onto her bed with Dexter following.

"Why don't you wait until James is awake, then we can go together?" said Anna, pushing Dexter back down.

"I am awake!" mumbled James, pulling his head out from under the pillow, his eyes narrow slits and his hair indescribable. "I didn't get a wink of sleep all night."

"Really?" said Anna, laughing. "Every time I checked on you, you were snoring your little socks off."

"I wasn't wearing any socks," said James, puzzled.

"It's just a saying, I meant you were fast asleep when I saw you," replied his mum. James took everything so literally.

"Well, I wasn't asleep all night; ask Corri," said James crossly.

"And who's Corri?" asked Anna.

"She's my friend; I thought you knew that," replied James.

"Well, you haven't introduced me to Corri. I thought your friend was called Benji? Where is Corri from?" said Anna, pulling James onto her knee.

"I didn't bring Benji, he's guarding the toys at home. Corri came instead, but she's not here just now," said James, rolling his eyes. "She woke me up and told me to go and sleep with you because you were sad."

Anna felt a chill race through her body for an instant, but she shook it off. "Well, I'm not sad," she said. "I'm excited because we are going on a boat trip today!"

"Yes!" cried Ollie, diving on top of her. Within a second, she had both boys and the dog all wrestling on her bed with excitement. Anna laughed at herself. This was all she needed in her life; what had she been thinking the night before?

Chapter Three

Ollie and James were allowed to go for a quick half hour swim while she showered and made their breakfast. There was a Seal Watchers' boat tour that sailed around Loch Linnhie for three hours, leaving from Fort William at eleven o'clock. Anna also wanted to stock up with groceries for the rest of the week, so she planned to take the boys on the boat tour, then hit the supermarket on the way back to get their supplies. She hadn't been able to pack a lot of food, as there was not enough room with the rest of their gear.

After breakfast, they got in the car, leaving a very sad looking Dexter staring mournfully out of the window at them. Ollie had left him two of his sticks for company, on the understanding that Dexter wouldn't eat them. Anna didn't hold out much hope, having no doubt they would find them in pieces when they got home, so she added extra plasters to her shopping list.

The sun was blazing down, evaporating the last of the mountain dew which covered the mountains in a shimmering blue haze as they drove out of the gorge. Fort William was already alive with the buzz of summer tourists making the most of the sunshine. Many were off to climb Ben Nevis, the highest mountain in the UK, a popular destination for dedicated mountain climbers. Anna parked at the harbour carpark, checking the time on her watch. It was twenty minutes before the boat sailed, so they walked quickly to the ticket counter to collect their tickets, then straight onto the boat. As soon as they were off the gang plank and onto the deck, Ollie and James ran off towards the front of the boat.

This wasn't their first boat trip and they wanted to get to the bow of the ship. As Anna rushed after them, she heard the captain on the PA system, "Would the two wee boys leaning over the front bars of the boat, please get doon and come and see me! I'm the captain in the cabin behind ye!"

Oh God, thought Anna, as she spun around the corner to find James and Ollie standing on either side of the tall man she had seen in Tyndrum the day before. He was grinning at her, his eyes full of humour as he pushed both boys gently to stand in front of him.

"Boys, I told you not to run off!" Anna reprimanded them.

"No, you didn't," said James, frowning.

"You didn't, Mummy," confirmed Ollie.

"Well, you know by now you're not allowed to run off, especially on a boat!" Anna snapped at them.

"Why especially on a boat?" James asked looking puzzled.

Anna groaned, "Will you stop answering me back, James?" Then, seeing that James was going to interrupt again, "Not another word, we have to go see the captain now; he will be cross."

"I'm sure he's used to it," said the man offering some support. "They won't be the first young boys that want to hang over the edge of his boat," he laughed.

"I hope so," Anna smiled at him, finding herself blushing. "Thank you for rescuing them."

"Perhaps if you watched them closer, they wouldn't need rescuing" came a sarcastic female voice from behind them. Anna turned to see the scornful blonde woman who had been accompanying the man yesterday. The first thing Anna noticed was the bright red lipstick on the woman's smug lips. It seemed to take over her face completely. The woman was still dressed as if she was on a night out in some club rather than on a fishing boat. She had a glass of sparkling wine in her hand, compliments of the cruise being served as a freebie in the bar below deck, and she was glaring daggers at Anna.

"Calum, give her kids back; we're not here to babysit brats," the woman demanded.

The man, Calum, looked furious and was visibly embarrassed. "I'm sorry," he turned to Anna. "She got out of bed on the wrong side this morning."

The woman looked like she was going to explode, but they were interrupted by the ship captain who appeared out of nowhere and who thankfully wore a big, friendly grin on his face.

"Right youse two rascals, dae you want tae help me steer the boat?" he said.

"Yes!" cried both the boys at once.

"Well, trainee captains need tae wear these life jackets, because they dae dangerous jobs only captains can dae," said the captain, winking at Anna as he helped the boys put their life jackets on.

"Thank you," Anna said gratefully, then turned, ready to give the poisonous woman a piece of her mind. Thankfully, the woman and Calum had gone back down to the bar.

The captain kept the boys busy as he took the boat along the coastline, so Anna sat up on the deck towards the bow, letting the warm sun and cool wind beat down on her in equal measure. Thankfully, she didn't see Calum or that awful woman, assuming they must still be down in the bar, which seemed like a waste on a day like this. The captain knew his stuff, relaying many highland stories to his captive audience through his PA system. For a seal tour, there was a noticeable lack of seals, but he covered it well with his commentary.

As the boat started to turn back towards Fort William, Anna saw Calum with the woman appear back on deck and she couldn't help but wonder why they had come on a boat trip on a nice sunny day, if all they wanted to do was sit in a bar. The woman looked slightly worse for wear and it seemed that Calum was having to hold her steady as the boat bounced over the choppy waters.

Ollie came running over to Anna. "Mummy, there's seals, come and see," he cried, dragging her off her seat. She followed him up to the captain's cabin, where James was sitting staring out some binoculars.

The captain grinned at her, "Ye've got a fine pair of interesting wee laddies here."

"I'm grateful the term you used was 'interesting'," Anna laughed. "It gives me a lot of scope to work with."

"Aye, they're right wee characters, they told me all aboot yer cottage with its pool. Must be Kirstin's Cot yer staying at," said the captain.

"Yes, we're up from Edinburgh. We've rented the cottage for a month; it's a great location," replied Anna.

"So ye must have left yer husband at the cottage tae come on this boat trip. Does he nae like boats?" he asked.

Anna looked at the captain. He seemed harmless enough, with a thick mop of reddish blonde hair with a handsome but weather-worn face, a bit too old for her, but he was definitely flirting, and her own personal hazard lights started flashing in her head. "No, he doesn't," she replied.

"Daddy does like boats!" said James, still staring out of the binoculars.

"Erm, not today he doesn't, that's why he stayed at the cottage," reaffirmed Anna, feeling herself go pink.

"Daddy's at the cottage?" Ollie asked, eyes wide. "Why has he come?"

The captain burst out laughing. "My name is Murdo. Apologies if I made ye uncomfortable."

Anna smiled with embarrassment. "I'm Anna. You know the old rule, you never tell a strange man you're alone."

"Well, I'm quite safe, everyone kens me roond here. I have a hoose in Ballachulish near tae Glencoe, so if yer stuck wi' anything ye can gie me a call. We're all happy tae help up here in the wilds. And ye may want tae try tae find a babysitter so ye can experience a good night oot at the Clachaig Inn while yer here," said Murdo, handing her a card with his number on it.

Anna found herself relaxing and spent the remainder of the trip chatting happily to Murdo. She found out that he and his brother, Craig, owned the boat together; they had been running the tours now for over twenty years. They took it in turns, taking the boat out.

"It's a great way tae pick up lassies," he teased. "They all love a boat captain."

"I can imagine," laughed Anna, rolling her eyes. She was really enjoying herself.

Just then, there was a clatter from the deck, they looked down to see Calum lifting the blonde woman to her feet. She had obviously lost her balance in her high heels, smashing her wine glass at the same time.

"They're nae allowed tae bring glasses frae the bar on deck, fir that very reason," said Murdo with disgust. "I dinnae ken what Calum is daeng wi' her; she is some piece of work."

"You know him?" Anna asked.

"Aye, that's Calum MacAlistair, he grew up here, but he lives doon in your part of the country noo. Made it big in some sort of export/import business doon at Leith in Edinburgh. He's up visiting his parents quite often, but I dare say Fiona MacAlistair won't be tae impressed wi' that Barbie doll. I thought he had better taste than that," said Murdo.

"Well, I hope he gets her home in one piece; she looks like she is going to be sick," said Anna.

"James, take that lady this bucket, make it quick and dinnae stand on any glass," said Murdo.

"Aye, Captain," said James, running down the step, a bright yellow bucket in hand with Ollie following.

Anna watched, trying not to laugh as the boys ran up to the woman. "Captain says to give you a bucket," James announced so the whole deck could hear.

There was muffled laughter as Calum, who was picking up the pieces of broken glass, looked up towards the cabin with a wry smile of his face. Murdo waved at him while Calum took the bucket from James.

"Tell the captain thank you very much, and I'm going to kick his ar...backside later," Calum told them.

The delighted boys instantly ran off back to Murdo to give him the message.

Anna thanked Murdo when they got back to the dock. He made her promise to call him so he could take her to the Clachaig Inn. He played a fiddle there at the ceilidh they held in the Boot Bar, on a Thursday evening, so Anna promised she would see what she could do for babysitters.

After leaving the boat, they jumped in the car and she drove to the local supermarket where she filled her trolley with enough food to last them for at least a week. She could see the boys were getting tired from their day on the boat, and sure enough, once they were back in the car, they both passed out in their car-seats on the drive back to the cottage. Anna drove past all the huge hotels situated at the side of the Loch, then rounded the bend at Onich where she saw Calum standing with his thumb out, opposite the Onich hotel. Her curiosity got the better of her, so she pulled over to pick him up.

Calum pulled the passenger door open, smiling instantly when he saw who it was. "We haven't been formally introduced, so I really appreciate you picking me up."

"I feel like we're old friends," said Anna, returning his smile.

"I'm only going to the other side of Ballachulish if you don't mind. I've had to leave Helena with her car at the hotel. Hopefully, she will sleep it off, then go home to Edinburgh," said Calum.

"Sure, we go past that way. Sounds like you've had a tough day?" she replied as she pulled back onto the road not daring to look at him again. His blue eyes were way too inviting.

"I dinnae ken what I was thinking," said Calum. "I should never have agreed to bring her here."

"Funny, that's what Murdo said on the boat," Anna laughed.

"Did he now? I already owe him an arse kicking, oh sorry!" Calum turned, then breathed a sigh of relief when he saw both boys were asleep.

"They look like they had a good day. Are ye on your own here with them?" he asked.

"I've been asked that a lot today," said Anna. "Yes, I'm on my own with my sons. We have a cottage at Glencoe for the summer. My brother and his other half are coming at the end of the first week, so I won't be alone for long."

"Really, what cottage are you staying at?" Calum asked.

"I'm not sure I should give away our whereabouts," she laughed. "I'm not used to people being so direct with their questions."

"People round here don't have anything to hide, so we kind of just ask," Calum explained.

"I heard you now live in Edinburgh," said Anna.

"So, you've been talking about me," said Calum grinning.

"No, not like that, it was only when your girlfriend made a bit of a scene on the boat that Murdo told me who you were," said Anna.

"Well, I can assure you Helena is not my girlfriend. We have been seeing each other on and off, but nothing serious; she insisted on coming up here with me. I don't know why I let her talk me into it, and I realised very quickly en route that I couldn't introduce her to my mother, so I booked her in at the Onich Hotel. I've just left her a note, telling her to go home," said Calum.

"A note! That's not very nice," cried Anna, but couldn't help laughing.

"I ken, I'm a wee bit of a rat," said Calum shamelessly.

"Well, you said that, I didn't," replied Anna. "Now we're in Ballachulish, where to?"

"Just over the other side of the Loch, then you can drop me and I'll walk the rest," said Calum. "What's the name of yer cottage again, I forgot?"

Anna pursed her lips, pretending to think about whether she should tell him or not. She drove over the long bridge across Loch Leven then when she crossed it, she pulled over. She turned to look directly at Calum who was sitting there expectantly.

"Kirstin's Cot," she said.

"Thank you," said Calum, winking at her as he got out of her car.

Chapter Four

Despite the sunny day, the old part of the cottage had a chill to it, the sunshine unable to penetrate the thick stone walls. Anna unloaded the shopping while the boys played outside with Dexter, who had not appreciated being locked in for most of the day. She lit the wood burner to bring some warmth into the kitchen, then took a pile of sausages, buns and sweetcorn outside to the BBQ at the rear of the cottage. The sun was still high in the sky and very warm, so she lit the coals, then warned the boys to stay clear of the BBQ while she went back inside to collect the plates, ketchup and mustard. As she stepped back into the kitchen, she felt a breeze of icy air rush by her. She stopped dead, feeling chilled with the hairs on her body all standing on end. She could have sworn there was someone in there with her.

"Hello!" Anna called out, feeling a little ridiculous. Of course, there was no reply; she quietly laughed at herself for getting spooked about nothing. She started walking towards the fridge, still feeling slightly tense with a strong feeling there was some sort of menacing presence in the room with her. As she leaned across to pull the ketchup from the fridge, she felt another cold blast of air rush by her. She turned just in time to see the plates she had stacked ready on the large wooden table suddenly fly off across the room of their own accord. There was a huge smash as they all hit the stone wall simultaneously. Anna stood motionless, her mind not taking in what she had just witnessed.

"Mummy, what did you do?" asked Ollie, appearing wide eyed in the doorway.

Anna snapped herself back to reality. "Erm, I dropped the plates," she said slowly. "Ollie, go wait outside while I clear this up. I don't want you getting cut."

"Wow, that's a lot of mess," said James as his head appeared around the door frame. "Corri says you need to be more careful."

Dexter then came running in at that moment, "Right! All of you out, take Dexter with you, he is going to cut his paws. I will be out in a minute," Anna shouted at them in frustration.

They all disappeared instantly as she took a deep breath. She couldn't figure out what the hell had just happened; the plates had literally flown across the room in front of her. It wasn't her imagination; she was sure she felt someone in the room with her. Anna didn't want to scare the boys, or herself for that matter, but she couldn't help but wonder if the cottage was haunted.

Collecting the broom from the utility room, she swept up the broken crockery into a dustpan. The room felt warm again thankfully, so she began to relax. This must be connected to all the trauma she had been through the last few months; she was just imagining things, surely? Crying alone last night for hours, now seeing things fly off a table. She would have to get a grip, and snap out of it. She grabbed the condiments and some paper plates from the cupboard, then went back outside into the warm sunshine.

The boys were building a sort of structure with some old bricks and stones they had found. Ollie, who had amassed a huge collection of sticks already, was trying to make them stand around the structure, only to have Dexter appear every now and then and steal one.

Anna threw the corn and the sausages on the grill, then opened a cold can of diet coke, sitting herself down on one of the garden chairs. James came over to steal a sip of her coke.

"Is Corri here?" Anna asked suddenly, remembering what James had said in the kitchen.

"No, she went away when you came back outside," said James. "She says she's going to keep us safe."

"Safe from what?" asked Anna.

"Don't know," said James shrugging. "She didn't tell me."

"I'd like to meet all your friends, James. I haven't met Corri. Do you think she would come and talk to me?" Anna asked, frowning slightly. This was making her a little uncomfortable. James had had imaginary friends before but never a woman. Usually, he conjured up a child of his own age.

"She says she doesn't want to talk to you and that your sausages are burning!" said James, pointing at the BBQ.

Anna jumped up. Sure enough, flames were leaping up from the grill, the sausages had caught fire, so she rushed over to try to save them, conversation forgotten. Half an hour later, the boys were finishing off their sausage buns. As most of the sausages were slightly blackened, to say the least, Dexter had scored big time, sitting at their feet, awaiting any last bits likely to come his way.

It was already eight o'clock, so after they had eaten, Anna put them to bed, reading them only one story before Ollie was fast asleep. She kissed James on his forehead as she snuck out of their room. It was after nine when she locked up the cottage, going to her room to read. The day on the boat had tired her out as well as the boys, so she was only a chapter in when she drifted off to sleep.

***

The red coats were smashing through the door as Kirstin grabbed her young son, Jamie, hauling him from his cot. She didn't have time to understand what was happening. The soldiers had been their guests for weeks; why would they attack them?

The door of the cottage flew open with a crash. Kirstin screamed as her husband shouted at her to escape through the back entrance. He had already unsheathed his claymore and he turned to face the redcoats with his giant sword drawn. Kirstin threw a plaid over her small son, then squeezed through the rear door that had been almost jammed shut with the weight of the snow compacting against it.

She could hear musket fire and screaming all around her as she ran, holding Jamie close to her chest. In her blind panic, she did not know where she was running to; the snow was swirling around her thick and fast; she couldn't make out who was friend or foe. Her eyes were stinging from the smoke of the muskets, the biting wind and the burning cottages of her friends and family. The soldiers were all around her. She hadn't noticed that her feet were bare in her terror to get out of her cottage. They had been roused from their bed by the screams of their neighbours, then everything seemed to happen at once. Suddenly, a strong arm grabbed her; she started to scream.

"Hush, Kirstin, it's me. We must heed up tae Meall Mor, the others are heading there. Gi'e me the bairn, stay close tae me," said her husband, Rab. She clung on to him, terrified still but relieved that he was alive.

Rab took Jamie from her arms, pulling her forwards through the snow, out of the MacDonald's compound, then up the slope towards the mountain. There was a loud bang and flash from a musket close by. Rab let go of her hand, forcing Jamie back in her arms, then charged at the soldier who had fired on them, before the young red

40

coat could reload his musket. Kirstin screamed after her husband, but she lost sight of him blinded by the snow, so she turned and kept on running towards the mountain, crushing Jamie to her chest once more.

Kirstin couldn't feel her feet now; she then realised she had left her shoes in the cottage; there had been no time to think clearly. The pain of the burning snow had faded to numbness which was a blessing, though probably not in the days to come when the frostbite would set in. She would lose some toes for sure. The slope rose as Kirstin was suddenly under cover of thick pine trees. She knew instinctively where she was now, at the foot of Meall Mor, the gunfire and shouting from below becoming more muffled because of the blizzard.

She gave herself a minute to stop and catch her breath, turning to see the misty orange glow from their burning homes down below. Jamie had been very quiet, his little arms tight around her neck. He was watching her face with huge, terrified eyes. Kirstin bent forward and kissed his brow. "Ye'll be alright wee man," she whispered to him.

There was a rustle from some of the trees, followed by a voice she recognised, "Mistress Kirstin, is that you?"

Kirstin turned to see Flora, her nursemaid, hiding in the tree. "Flora, yer safe, did the others get oot?" she asked as the girl ran over to her.

"I dinnae ken if they all did. Alisdair and Wil tried tae get their dirks when the soldiers came in, but they were cut doon before they could turn tae fight. I just ran," Flora sobbed. "Why are they doing this, mistress?"

"I dinnae ken Flora, the devil must have possessed them. Come noo, we have tae get tae the cover of the rocks on Meall Mor, the others are heading there," said Kirstin, praying that her husband would find her soon.

"De ye want me tae take Jamie? He's heavy for ye," said Flora, wiping her eyes.

"Aye, hold him for a wee bit Flora," said Kirstin, passing her little boy over to the nurse. Jamie started to scream; she had to prise his fingers from around her neck. "Hush noo, it's all right wee man, it's only Flora," she told him.

Flora pulled the small boy to her chest and threw the plaid around him. The two women both started to climb through the snow. Kirstin noticed that Flora had her boots on, but she made no comment about her own ruined feet.

***

Anna jumped awake, all her senses on alert. It took her a minute to realise she had been dreaming. She was still shivering from the cold of the snow; her feet were burning with agony. She leaned over to put the bed side lamp on, then pulled back the duvet. Her feet were bright red. She reached down to touch them; they felt like ice. What on earth? She had heard of people getting psychosomatic symptoms before, but surely not from a dream. She checked her phone, it was 5.45 am, but she was now wide awake, so Anna decided to go for a swim. The pool would warm her feet up without the agonising burn of stepping into a hot shower or bath.

The sun had come up an hour before, shining through the glass of the pool room, bathing it in warmth and light. The water was warm, and her painful feet stung as she entered the water, but soon enough, they were back to normal. Anna swam around lazily, looking out the huge glass windows at the mist that sat nestled to the base of the mountains around her.

Her mind went back to the dream. It had been so terrifyingly real, almost as if she was living it. Had Anna dreamt of something that had actually happened to Kirstin or was it just her imagination running away with itself? She was here in Glencoe after all, with its brooding mountains and bloody history.

Ollie appeared in the doorway with a cross look on his face. "Mummy, why didn't you wake us? We want to come in the pool with you!" he demanded.

"I wanted the pool all to myself," laughed Anna. "Why are you up so early?"

"James kept waking me up, talking to Corri," said Ollie. "I'm going to get my shorts on!" he cried, then ran off in the direction of the cottage.

Anna frowned; did that mean Ollie could see Corri too? She would have to ask them about it later.

Less than a minute later, both the boys came tearing into the pool room, swimming shorts on, with Dexter at their heels. They threw themselves in the water, while Dexter followed suit. Anna gave up; the dog clearly thought he was one of the boys.

An hour later, Anna was cooking bacon and eggs for them all. The boys were getting themselves dressed into the clothes she had left out, though she was sure Ollie would be wearing everything back to front.

She had planned a day hillwalking, not too far from the cottage. She wanted to get the boys acclimatized to the outdoors before her brother and Rob arrived next week. They were keen hillwalkers, so she had no doubt they had some hiking planned. She was looking forward to seeing them. Anna always enjoyed their company, but unfortunately did not get to see them that often as they lived down in Devon. It would be good for her brother to spend some time with his nephews, as he hadn't seen them much when she was with Alex. He had not got on with Alex particularly well.

She and Glen were two years apart, though they were close when they were growing up. Glen had moved down to London just after he came out to his family, giving his parents 'the space' they needed to come to terms with it. He met Rob soon after arriving in the city; they had been a couple ever since.

Two years ago, they left London, buying a hotel in Devon, near to Sidmouth. Rob was a chef, and it had been a dream of his for years. Glen ran the hotel side of things while Rob ran the restaurant which was excellent, making it a popular destination for the locals and people visiting Devon alike. Anna was happy for them, but it meant her brother was always busy. She had taken the boys down there for a few days after she had first split from Alex. Glen and Rob were great with the boys; it had been a nice break for Anna. She missed Glen, wishing he didn't live so far away.

Glen and Rob had managed to get themselves a break for a couple of weeks, opting to spend the first week lying around a pool in Greece before they headed up to Highlands to visit Anna for their second week off.

Glen was worried about Anna. Even though she had told him over the phone that she was doing fine, he had known by her voice that she was struggling. He had thought Alex was an arrogant money grabber from the moment they met. Alex, in turn, had disliked Glen, and Anna found it difficult to maintain a good relationship with her brother, so they had drifted apart slightly. But as soon as Glen heard about the separation, he had been on the phone almost daily. His support had been invaluable, making Anna feel like she had her brother back.

Ollie and James were munching their way through their eggs when Anna brought her coffee to the table to join them.

Ollie's tee shirt was on backwards, his shoes were on the wrong feet, but all in all, it wasn't a bad attempt for him.

"So, who's Corri?" Anna asked as soon as she sat.

"She's James's friend. She doesn't talk to me much," said Ollie, dropping his bacon into Dexter's open mouth.

"I told you who she was!" cried James and explained again. "She's my friend and she's going to help us."

"But I haven't met her," said Anna. "Can you introduce me?"

"She only wants to talk to James," said Ollie, smearing ketchup up the side of his face.

"Have you seen her too?" Anna asked.

"Yes, she looks scary, she wears funny clothes and has long red hair," replied Ollie. "Can I go outside now? I need to feed the stick men."

"She's not scary, she's nice!" said James. "I think she's pretty."

Anna thought for a short while then said, "James, come and look at the painting in my bedroom, would you?"

"Why?" asked James, his mouth full of eggs.

"Just come with me," said Anna, not giving him wiggle room to argue.

James followed her out of the kitchen and into her bedroom. Anna pointed at the painting of Kirstin on her wall. "Is that Corri?" she asked.

James screwed up his face. "No, that's not her," he said. "She's not in a painting."

"I didn't mean she was in a painting. I meant did it look like her?" said Anna.

"No, Corri had red hair," said James.

It was a long shot; Anna didn't really know why she thought it might be Kirstin. She was relieved to find it wasn't.

"Can I go out now?" James asked.

The boys ran out of the door into the garden. Anna sighed, sitting back down at the kitchen table as she nursed her coffee. Was this an imaginary friend or were they seeing ghosts? She decided that she would start to try to find out a little bit more about the cottage. History was not really her strong point, which is why she had become an accountant, but perhaps it was time to investigate why all these strange things seemed to be happening. She would call on Angus later to see if he knew anything about the place.

The front doorbell rang; it was a delivery service with an enormous bouquet of flowers.

"Someone is sending ye a message wi' these," said the driver, grinning.

She thanked him as she tried to squeeze the huge bunch through the narrow doorway. They would fill three vases at least; she hoped the cottage had enough of them.

"Wow, they're huge! Are they from Daddy?" James asked as he trotted down the hallway towards her.

"I don't think so," replied Anna, searching for the card. She tore it open.

'Thanks for the lift, Calum' the card read.

Anna smiled to herself. She liked Calum, but he was barking up the wrong tree if he thought she was interested in him. She had seen his choice of women and she wasn't impressed. Still, it was flattering receiving such a big bunch of flowers.

"C…a…l…u…m," James spelt out as he read the card. "Who's that, Mummy?"

"We gave him a lift back from the boat yesterday," explained Anna.

"We did?" said James, frowning, trying to remember.

"You and Ollie were asleep."

"Why did he give you flowers?" James asked, still frowning.

"To say thank you," replied his mum.

"Does he want to love you?" Ollie asked.

Anna feigned outrage. "No, absolutely not! He was just saying thank you. Now why the twenty questions?"

"It wasn't twenty; it wasn't anywhere near twenty," James pointed out.

"I give up. Ollie, come here, let me put your shirt on straight, change your shoes around to the right feet please, then let's get out of here," she said.

Soon, Anna was driving her car back through Glencoe gorge, then she turned right onto another one-track road that led through Glen Etive.

She parked by a small waterfall, grabbed their backpacks, then they set off on foot following the river through the mountains. Corri and the strange happenings at the cottage were long forgotten as they spent the day exploring the glen.

Chapter Five

They got back to the cottage around 4 pm. The boys were still charged with energy. The lovely day turned into a lovely evening, so after they had their dinner, Anna decided to drive over to find Angus to ask him about the cottage. The house of Angus MacDonald was set about 500 metres from the main road, just outside Ballachulish, hidden in a shallow dip surrounded by pine trees. It was a quaint little building, covered in flowers, which Angus was out watering when Anna and the boys pulled up into his drive.

"Well, hallo there! So ye managed tae find me then," he said, putting down his watering can as he opened the door of Anna's car to let the boys out. Dexter jumped out, running immediately into the trees, ignoring Anna who was frantically calling after him.

"Dinnae worry, he cannae get in much trouble roond here," said Angus. "Would ye like a cup of tea or something a wee bit stronger?"

"No, thanks Angus, we're fine honestly. I just had a couple of questions about the cottage," replied Anna.

"Aye well, I'll get the wee ones some lemonade. I have some in the cupboard left over from Christmas, then we can have a chat," he said, walking towards his house. "Take a wee seat," he pointed to the round wooden garden table with matching chairs before disappearing, only to appear a minute later with a half full bottle of lemonade and two glasses. He poured the boys a glass each and they both picked up their drink, each taking a large gulp; it was warm and flat. Ollie pulled a face and put his glass down on the table. James raised his hand, obviously wanting to say something, leaving Anna in no doubt that he was going to tell Angus that his lemonade was flat. She glared at her son and he caught the warning look in his mother's eye, so he put his hand down again, biting his lip, managing to stay silent, much to Anna's relief.

"Why dinnae ye laddies go explore my garden. See if ye can find the wee burn wi' the bridge I built over it," Angus suggested.

The boys didn't need to be asked twice; they ran off immediately, with Dexter suddenly appearing from under cover of the trees to chase off after them.

"Noo, is there a problem wi' the cottage?" asked Angus. "I can fix most things, except the television; I havnae a clue aboot these things."

"No, Angus, there's nothing wrong with the cottage; it's very comfortable. It's just that…" Anna felt foolish now she was sitting here with him. How on earth was she going to ask if the place was haunted without sounding like a paranoid idiot?

"It's just that a few strange things I can't seem to explain have happened. I wondered if anyone else had ever come across anything when they stayed there," she finally asked.

"You're the first family that have stayed there for any length of time. There was a couple that stayed, but only for a few days," said Angus. "The auld cottage used tae be owned by a local lady called Nelly Hill. She lived in Kirstin's Cot for over sixty years, a lovely, gentle wee woman she wis. She never married, but everyone roond here kent her. She was a church elder at St Mary's church in Glencoe, with a lovely singing voice in the choir. Nelly was a very private'dy but it wasnae as if she didnae have friends, everyone liked Nelly, but she just didnae want them aroond her cottage. I dinnae really ken why, as we do live in an open-door community roond here, but everyone just kent not tae bother Nelly at her cottage."

"So who owns the cottage now?" asked Anna.

"Well, it's a wee bit strange," said Angus. "I wis probably the only one who visited the cottage regularly, as I mowed the lawn for Nelly, and did odd jobs aroond the place when she needed it. It wis me that found her when she died. She wis just sitting there, at her kitchen table. I saw her frae the window, but she didnae move when I knocked on. I let myself in tae find she had passed away. One strange thing though, that I never bothered tae tell anyone, wis that she wis holding a smooth stone in her hand. I wis curious so I took it frae her and saw it had an old Rune marking on it. I wouldnae have thought Nelly would have been intae anything like that, being a good church-going woman. So, I just hid it away before the ambulance came tae take her away."

Anna gave an involuntary shiver. "How long ago did that happen?" she asked.

"Och, only about eighteen months ago. Her only relative was a nephew who lived doon south in Bristol somewhere. She had never mentioned him tae me before, but she left the cottage tae him. He and his wife appeared not long after she had died; they never had any interest in poor old Nelly when she wis alive. They decided tae extend the cottage, then let it oot as a holiday home. They were looking for someone tae manage it for them, so I took the job. They didnae even bother tae stay aroond tae see how the extension went. He wis a weasley, big streak o'nothing that nephew, I wis glad when he went. He gave me the heebie jeebies. I think he wis just more interested in the money it would bring them."

"So, this is the first time it's been let out?" asked Anna.

"No, no, I told you a couple came in May, for just a week. Funny thing, they didnae stay fir a week. He said that they had tae get home, some sort of emergency. They were only there three days in the end, but they didnae complain about the cottage, or any strange happenings there," said Angus.

"We certainly don't have any complaints; it's a lovely cottage, just what we needed. There's just been a couple of strange incidents over the last couple of days," said Anna. "The plates went flying off the table and smashed by themselves last night. I will, of course, replace them, but it was very strange. Then James keeps talking to someone called Corri, who apparently is a woman with long red hair. Ollie has seen her also, but not me. She doesn't want to talk to me."

Angus was silent for a moment, as he appeared to be deep in thought. His eyes glanced over at the boys who were playing in the burn that trickled through his garden. "I'll be back in a minute," he said, getting to his feet to go back inside his house.

He reappeared moments later, carrying a small book in his hands. He laid it on the table so that Anna could see it was quite old, with a frayed blue hard cover, entitled 'The People of Glencoe'.

He flicked through the pages until he got to the 'C' section, turning a page to reveal a black and white drawing of a wild-looking woman in Highland dress, carrying a knife in one hand and a small pouch in the other. The drawing was detailed, showing the woman's face contorted with anger as her long, wild hair flew loose around her in the wind. There was a mark on one of her cheeks that looked like a 'w', and she was pointing with her knife to cottages all ablaze in the valley below her. Underneath the drawing was written 'Corrag, Witch of Glencoe'.

"Are you saying that James is speaking to an old witch?" Anna asked incredulously.

"Aye, well it's just a possibility. Corrag is well known here in the Glen. She tried tae warn the MacDonald's of the Campbell's soldiers' betrayal before the massacre. They didnae believe her, so she fled tae the hills tae escape. There are a lot of local people who say they have seen Corrag wandering the hills aroond here over the years. So, it wouldnae surprise me if young James was talking wi' her," said Angus seriously.

"You're serious, aren't you? It's a bit scary, Angus, to be honest," replied Anna, beginning to regret coming over.

"Aye, it's scary all right. Boys!" he shouted over to Ollie and James. They both came running over to the table. "Dae ye ken who this is?" Angus asked them.

"That looks like Corri," said Ollie immediately.

"No, Corri's much prettier than her," James pointed out with a frown.

"No, she's not!" argued Ollie. "She's carrying that pouch of stones she always has with her."

"But it's a horrible drawing," said James. "She's always happy when she comes, not angry like that."

"That's probably how the artist just drew her, laddie. She wisnae happy when the soldiers came tae kill her kin," said Angus.

"What soldiers?" asked Ollie, his eyes suddenly brightening with curiosity. "Who did they kill?"

Anna decided enough was enough at that point. "Okay boys, you can go back and play now; we'll be going soon."

When the boys had gone, Angus turned to Anna. "I would hazard a guess that yer laddies have been talking with Corrag. I dinnae ken why she'd be bothering them, but they seem happy enough."

"I'm more worried about the fact they are actually seeing ghosts, never mind who they are," said Anna, slightly exasperated. "Do you think Corrag knew Kirstin?"

"Aye, I'm sure she did. The Macdonald's were a very close-knit community in these days. Everyone would have kent everyone who lived in the Glen and beyond. Kirstin no doubt would have met Corrag often; perhaps they were friends," said Angus.

"It just seems strange to me. James has had lots of imaginary friends and I just thought she was another one at first. If it is Corrag, why do you think she would come tae James?" said Anna thoughtfully.

"Well, maybe yer wee laddie is a sensitive. Some people can talk wi' the spirit of the deed. I cannae explain why she has come to

James, but I wouldnae have thought she means any harm," said Angus, then shut up when he saw the look on Anna's face. "Yer nae thinking of leaving, are ye?" he asked suddenly.

"No, of course not," said Anna, deciding to ignore Angus's comment about James being sensitive. "If it is Corrag haunting the place, then from the way she threw the plates across the room, she obviously doesn't like me very much. But my brother is arriving in a few days, and I'm sure he will find all this fascinating. The boys don't seem in the least bit bothered, and we do love the cottage."

"I'll dae a wee bit of investigating in toon. If there is any more information on Corrag, Kenneth will ken aboot it. He's a good friend of mine who lives in Fort William, a local historian, and believe me when I say there is nothing he disnae ken aboot this area," said Angus. "It's strange though, if there wis any reason tae haunt this place, I would have guessed it would have been haunted by one of the MacDonald's, ye ken the story?"

"I've heard of the Glencoe massacre; everyone in Scotland learnt about it in history lessons. It's a Scottish legend, the MacDonalds killed by the treacherous Campbells after playing host to them for a couple of weeks. We must be near to the massacre sight, then?" said Anna.

"Aye, that cottage you're in, is built on top of the foundations of Rab MacDonald's hoose. He was murdered that night. His wife, Kirstin and their son, Jamie, disappeared intae the snow, fleeing frae the Campbells. Kirstin died frae frostbite and exposure a couple of weeks later, but her son disappeared that night; she never saw him again. Their cottage wis burnt tae the ground wi' all the other MacDonald cottages, but the foundations remained, so the surviving MacDonalds rebuilt new cottages ontae them," explained Angus.

Anna felt herself chilled once more. Angus had just described what had happened in her dream the night before. She decided against mentioning it to him, he seemed to relish in old scary stories, and she didn't want to give him another opportunity.

"That's such an amazing story, I'll have to tell the boys. They are going to love the history about this place," said Anna, putting on a cheery smile to hide the fact that she had no intention of telling the boys that murderous tale at their age. "You should have some sort of plaque up, telling the story of the cottage."

"We dae, it's on the wall by the front door," said Angus with a frown.

"Oh, I'm sorry, I'm so blinkered these days running around after the boys," said Anna, embarrassed.

"Aye, it's hard on yer own. When ye get the time, ye should have a look at the old pictures in the hallway in the old part of the cottage. There are some interesting characters there, including MacIain himself. I found them all packed away in a cupboard after Nelly had died. There's a wee book in the drawer of the dresser in yer bedroom that explains who they all are," said Angus.

"Thanks Angus, you've been really helpful," said Anna, looking around to see where the boys had got to. She could see them running through the trees at the end of the drive, so she shouted at them to get ready to go.

"I'll come roond with some information after I've spoken wi' Kenneth. Meantime, I'm sure if it is Corrag who is haunting ye, then she's just looking out for ye," said Angus.

Anna laughed at how ridiculous it all sounded, thanking Angus again for listening to her mad ramblings about ghosts and hauntings.

Ollie and James appeared, with Dexter close on their heels. Ollie had collected another five sticks to take back to the cottage with them. Anna headed back up to Kirstin's Cot, realising it was nearly nine o'clock as the sun was beginning to disappear over the mountains when they arrived back at the cottage. The boys got themselves out of their car seats, running towards the cottage to be first to get some snacks before bedtime.

Anna opened the front door and the boys pushed past her as she hung back, looking around the door frame. Sure enough, about a foot off the ground at the side of the door was a small grey plaque. It read, "These foundations were once the home of Rab and Kirstin MacDonald, victims of the Glencoe Massacre 1692."

Anna stood for a minute frowning at the plaque. What had actually happened to Kirstin? In her dream, Kirstin had escaped the soldiers and was running towards the safety of the mountain.

"Mum, where are you?" James called, interrupting her thoughts. "Ollie got the last Jaffa cake; he knew I wanted it. He doesn't even like them!"

She went into the cottage to sort out the 'Jaffa cake' battle, then got them ready for bed. It only took one story before they were both in the land of nod. The fresh mountain air was doing its job in getting them to sleep; she usually struggled getting Ollie down at night when they were at home.

Anna went to her room to put on her bikini under her dressing gown, then slipped out of the cottage to the pool house. It was nearly dark outside now, so she put the poolside lights on, then sunk into the warm water.

Anna loved swimming but very rarely got a chance to swim on her own these days. She cleared her mind from the conversation she had had earlier with Angus, then started to front crawl through the water, soon feeling her energy levels rise. She swam length after length, then after a while started to float on her back, enjoying the feeling of all her muscles relaxing. Suddenly, everything went dark.

She stood upright, blinking to let her eyes adjust to the darkness. The pool house would have been in complete blackness if not for the huge windows allowing the moonlight to drift in, making it possible to see. There was a splash from the far end of the pool; Anna froze for a moment trying to see what was there. There was another splash, and she struck out frantically to get to the side of the pool. Her heart was hammering in her chest as she hauled herself out of the water. Getting to her feet, she called out, "Who's there?"

There was no reply; the only sound Anna could hear was her heart beating loudly in her eardrums.

She turned to pick up a towel, suddenly feeling very cold. There was another splash, this time more distinct, like something heavy had fallen in the water.

She turned back around quickly; this time, she could make out a dark shape floating towards her under the surface of the water. It looked almost human in shape as it drifted slowly towards her. Anna could feel herself begin to tremble; the pool house was getting colder.

"Corri, is that you?" Anna said firmly, trying to stop her voice from shaking.

"Jaaamiiimmieee," a woman's voice whispered the name in a long, drawn-out cry filled with pain.

Anna was rooted to the spot in fear, unable to speak.

The shape below the surface had stopped moving now, but the water began to bubble all around it. Soon, the whole pool was bubbling and churning violently, as if it were boiling water. Then, just as abruptly as it started, everything went quiet, the pool house started to warm up and the lights came back on.

Anna didn't hang around; she grabbed her bathrobe, then fled from the pool house, running back to the safety of the cottage and her room. She threw herself onto her bed, pulling the covers around her like a child hiding from her nightmares. She was breathing rapidly, her head was pounding and she knew she had to find a way to calm down. Anna had experienced a panic attack once before and it had really frightened her, so she concentrated on slowing down her breathing as she had been taught, focusing on wiggling her toes to stop her heart from racing. It worked, her shaking started to subside and she could take proper breaths of air again without gasping.

She couldn't wrap her head around what the hell had just happened in the pool. She had never felt so terrified, and now she was sure the cottage was haunted. Thank God her brother and Rob were arriving soon, otherwise she may have had to rethink staying in Kirstin's Cot. At least the boys didn't seem troubled, which was a blessing. The voice had been calling out for Jamie; that must be Kirstin's son. Was it Corrag or Kirstin that was haunting the place? Knowing her luck, it would be both of them.

Dexter suddenly pushed the door of Anna's bedroom open, padding in quietly, thinking she didn't notice him. He crept up onto her bed, lying down beside her, then snuggling up into the crook of her back. For once, Anna was grateful of the big lump taking advantage of her weakness, so she allowed him to stay. She curled up under the covers next to him, praying she would fall asleep soon.

Chapter Six

The next morning Anna awoke early, finding herself hanging off the edge of the bed, with something preventing her from rolling over. She sat up, switching on the lamp, to find Dexter lying fully stretched out on her bed, snoring loudly, with his head on her pillow.

"Dexter!" she shouted at him.

The dog jumped up, looking at her quizzically. Anna swore this was the last time she would allow the dog to get on the bed with her, even though she had been grateful for his company the night before. She opened the curtains and was met by a thick white mist that made it impossible to see more than a few yards. *Damn it*, she thought, then conceded that they had been lucky with the weather so far, and this was more typical of a morning in the mountains of Scotland.

She went and made herself a pot of coffee, letting Dexter outside to do his business. As she sipped on the steaming black liquid, she began to feel more grounded, allowing her mind to drift back to the events in the pool the night before. It had been real, she was sure of it. She had heard a woman's voice call out for Jamie. Could it be Kirstin? Was she there looking for her son? Was that just a coincidence or was her mind really playing tricks on her? All that talk of ghosts with Angus had maybe triggered it.

James came into the kitchen, dragging Buzz along by his remaining ear. "Mum, we can't see anything out the window."

"I know, it's exciting isn't it, being trapped in the mist," replied Anna, picking James up and giving him a kiss.

"Can we go outside?" said Ollie, running in the kitchen with four sticks in his hands.

"You might get lost in the mist," said Anna, pulling Ollie over for his morning snuggle. "Ollie, I told you to leave these sticks outside. I don't want them in the cottage."

"I did, but Corri brought them in for me," he said indignantly. "I didn't ask her to."

Anna frowned, then called out to the back of the kitchen, "Corri, no more sticks in the house please!"

"She's not here," said James.

"Oh, where has she gone?" Anna asked.

"She's gone to speak with Kirstin," said James, attempting to pour himself some Golden Nugget cereal into a bowl and managing to miss so that they poured onto the floor where Dexter was waiting.

Anna stared at her son, her mind racing and her heart beating faster. "James, have you seen Kirstin?"

"No, I haven't seen her," said James. Anna breathed a sigh of relief. "But Corri says if I do see her, I have to call for her. She doesn't want me to talk to Kirstin."

"Do you think I could talk to Corri?" Anna asked, trying to keep her voice light and airy.

"I'll ask her," said James, now trying to hold up the milk carton. Dexter had already demolished the spilt cereal and was waiting in anticipation as James tried to tip over the milk carton. Anna stepped in just in time, grabbing the carton and adding the milk to his bowl before he spilt that also. Dexter gave a loud sigh, then went to lie sadly down on his bed in the corner.

Once the boys had eaten their cereal, they both wanted to go to the pool. As the thick mist limited their choices of things to do, the pool was a blessing. They were all in the water half an hour later, playing with a ball. Anna decided not to question the boys any further about Corrag or Kirstin. She hoped that things would settle down, then she could discuss it with Glen when he arrived. He and Rob had texted to say that they would be there with them a day earlier than expected, much to her relief. She could definitely hold out until then; she didn't want to over react as the boys were really enjoying themselves here.

Anna had been nominated Marco in the game of Marco Polo that they were playing in the pool. The boys were shrieking and squealing as they splashed to get away from her. "Marco!" Anna shouted. "Polo!" the boys yelled back before both diving away in different directions. With so much noise, Anna didn't hear the knocking at the door, nor Dexter barking.

"Marco!" she shouted with her eyes squeezed shut, but the boys had gone quiet.

"Polo," Calum's voice echoed across the pool.

Anna's eyes flew open, to see Calum standing there grinning at her. "I did knock," he said, holding his hands up. "I was out walking, and as I was passing I just thought I'd pop round to check you were okay with all this fog around. It's a bit hazardous out on the roads, but I know them well enough, so if you needed anything?"

Anna knew she was blushing. She felt like she had been caught out, standing there in her bikini, albeit in the water, with her hair sticking to her head and not a stitch of makeup on. Before she could answer, Ollie piped up, "I saw you on the boat with that angry lady."

Calum laughed with embarrassment. "Yes, I confess that was me."

"Ollie, that was rude," said Anna. "You don't know if she was angry. This is Calum; he is a friend."

"She was angry, Mummy, and she was drunk. That's what Captain Murdo said," interrupted James.

"Is she here?" asked Ollie.

"No, she has gone home to Edinburgh now. She didn't much like it here," replied Calum.

"You sent Mummy flowers!" Ollie suddenly shouted over everyone, the realisation dawning on him. "Is my mummy your girlfriend now?"

"Your mummy is a really nice lady, but she is not my girlfriend. She gave me a lift when I needed one; you two were asleep in the back of the car," Calum expertly replied.

Meanwhile, Anna was desperately trying to find the location of her bath robe and working out approximately how long she would be in full view with just her bikini on, if she got out the pool now. "Would you like a coffee, Calum?" she asked, hoping he would make his excuses and leave.

"Yea, that would be nice, is the cottage open? How about I go put the pot on while you get out the pool?" he suggested. "Will the boys be okay here on their own? I can see they can swim well."

"Yes, they'll be fine. I won't be long," she said gratefully, admiring his quick thinking to save her embarrassment. Calum left the pool house, leaving Anna wondering if there was some sort of chemistry going on between them, but she shoved that thought angrily to the back of her mind.

That was definitely not going to happen. She pulled on her bath robe; then, due to a lack of a hair brush, she ran her fingers through her dark hair, hoping it didn't look too bad. Leaving Dexter in charge of the boys, (no doubt the hairy hound would be in the water as soon as her back was turned anyway) she went over to the cottage. Calum already had the coffee on as she entered the kitchen.

"I see you found your way around," she commented with surprise. "So, you were just out walking, in the fog?"

"I like walking in the fog. I have this super power; I can see through fog," said Calum with a grin. "Actually, truth be told, I recommended a couple of friends of mine to stay here in May, so I have been in Kirstin's Cot before. I spent a day with them, so I guess I know my way around quite well."

"Why did they not stay the full week?" asked Anna, regretting the abrupt question as soon as it left her lips.

"You're jumping ahead of me here. How do you know they didn't stay for the whole week?" said Calum, looking puzzled.

"Angus MacDonald told me. They were the first couple to stay in the cottage before us," she explained. "He told me that they had left early." She didn't want to scare Calum off with her directness, but after last night in the pool, she really wanted some answers.

"What reason did they give Angus for why they left?" Calum asked before Anna could speak. She could see he was guarded.

"Family emergency or something like that, I think," she replied. "Why, was there some other reason?"

Calum sighed, knowing he would have to come up with some sort of explanation. He decided to skip over what his friends had told him actually happened, playing it down for Anna's benefit. He didn't want to scare her, though he suspected Anna might have something to hide also. It was blatantly obvious that neither one of them wanted to be the one who stuck their neck out first.

"Philip and Amber are a nice couple I know from Manchester. They hadn't been to the Highlands before, so, as I knew Angus was getting the cottage ready to let, I gave them his number. I drove up from Edinburgh to spend a day or two with them. Amber has always said she is a bit psychic, and when I got here she was really quite disturbed, by what she thought was an angry ghost haunting the place. Philip and I teased her about it, but I think it really got to her, so they decided to go home early."

"Did anything happen? Did she see a ghost?" Anna asked.

"Erm, I don't really know," replied Calum, wishing Anna would just drop it now. "Right, coffee is made; shall we go and see what the boys are up to?"

Calum carried their mugs as Anna got a couple of boxes of juice out of the fridge. The fog was beginning to clear as they stepped back outside and walked back over to the pool house. They pulled up some chairs at the side of the pool and sat down drinking their coffee in what seemed like a slightly awkward silence. Anna desperately wanted to quiz Calum some more but didn't know how to broach the subject. Her eyes flickered over Calum, who was watching the boys with a smile on his face. He looked so handsome in a simple tight-fitting navy sweater with dark blue jeans. He had that rough unshaven look that was so ruggedly attractive on men, a complete contrast to her clean shaven, immaculately dressed ex-husband. Calum suddenly glanced in her direction, catching Anna staring at him. She looked away, blushing furiously, turning her attention towards her sons.

They were still in the water, playing a new game diving down for stones on the bottom of the pool. Anna frowned, wondering where the stones had appeared from; then, her question was answered as Dexter arrived at the door with a huge rock in his mouth, trotted over to the pool then dropped it in.

"Okay, that's enough of that," said Anna, getting up and grabbing Dexter by the collar, dragging him over to the door to lock him outside the pool house. There was a couple of dismayed barks, then silence as he obviously had found something else to keep him occupied.

Anna came back to sit down to an amused looking Calum. "When you said you didn't really know if your friend saw a ghost, did that mean that you do know, but don't want to tell me?" asked Anna, deciding to take the plunge.

"Well, it's a bit awkward talking about ghosts when you're staying at the cottage," said Calum, staring at her with some confusion. "Why are you so curious? Have you seen any spectres flying around?"

"No, not me. But the boys have. They keep talking about a woman called Corri," Anna finally admitted, dropping her eyes to the floor. "It's beginning to worry me."

"Amber never mentioned seeing anyone by that name, but she did hear a woman crying out for someone during the night," Calum told her. "Philip didn't hear anything, but it really must have freaked Amber out. She wouldn't stay another night."

"I think I know what she meant. Something similar happened to me while I was swimming here last night. The lights went out, then I heard a woman's voice crying out for someone called Jamie," said Anna. "I was terrified, then the lights just came back on. I'm not sure what to think, but the boys don't seem in the least bit bothered by anything here, least of all ghosts. This Corri person they are talking to seems to be a friend. I asked Angus and he thought it might be the ghost of Corrag the Witch that apparently everyone knows about around here."

"Aye, we've all heard of Corrag, that's for sure. The kids dress up as her on Halloween, but I wouldn't take much stock in old Angus's stories. He's a lovely old soul, but he does like to tell a good tale. He and that friend crazy old friend of his, Kenneth Macfie, used to scare the pants off us all, when we were kids, with all their wild stories," said Calum.

He was appreciating the way Anna had bent her body over in her chair so she could get closer to him. She looked so tempting with her dark, serious eyes watching him intently, while her wet hair flowed loose down the back of her white bath robe. The robe had come slightly loose, so that Calum could see the curve of her cleavage; God, he really wanted to kiss her badly. If the boys had not been here, he might well have chanced it.

"Angus said he was going to try to find out more for me about Corrag. He mentioned a Kenneth in Fort William; he said he was a historian," said Anna, unaware of Calum staring at her.

"Aye, well I suppose Angus would call him that, though officially I can't be sure. Kenneth Macfie did used to teach history here sometimes at the school in Glencoe when I was a boy, though I don't think he was officially a teacher either," said Calum.

"Mummy, come back in the water," shouted James.

"Why don't you boys get all the rocks out the pool, I'll stay with you, so we can let your mummy get dressed. Then how's about I take you all out to lunch at the Clachaig Inn. There's a play park there," suggested Calum.

The boys immediately roared, "Yes!" So, Anna shrugged her shoulders. "It seems like I'd be outvoted anyway. I'll just go and get dressed then," she said, leaving Calum with the boys who were already at the bottom of the pool collecting the stones that lay there.

She switched on the shower, stepping into the steaming water. Her heart was beating more rapidly than normal as she allowed herself to feel excited about going out with Calum. Had she imagined the signals she was reading from him while they were talking about the ghosts, or had she been out of the dating game so long now, she was reading it wrong? Anyway, surely the last thing she wanted was another relationship just now, wasn't it? But he was incredibly attractive, and the boys were very much at ease with him.

She blow-dried her hair, so it was shiny and straight, then applied some mascara and eyeliner. She pulled on some jeans, with a light, pale pink sweater, then finally she put on her sneakers before she gave herself one final check in the mirror. She looked good for a change; it was amazing what a bit of makeup could do.

Anna collected some clothes for the boys and headed back to the pool house. Calum's eyes met hers as she walked in; she noticed he smiled approvingly.

"You look pretty, Mummy," said Ollie.

"Thank you, Ollie. Now the two of you out the water; let's get you dressed," she said.

They walked from the cottage down to the narrow road. The fog that had lingered was now slowly climbing up the mountain slopes, then melting away into the sky. There was a faint warmth in the air as the sun just about managed to shine through the haze, but it was still on the chilly side. Anna regretted not bringing her jacket. As if he read her mind, Calum suddenly put his jacket over her shoulders. "It's a wee bit nippy in the fog; it will warm up in a bit."

It didn't take them long to reach the Clachaig Inn and Calum took them into the Bidean Lounge as the Boot Bar didn't allow children. The boys immediately spotted the outside play area and were soon clambering over it.

"Do you want to sit outside? I think the sun will break through any minute now," said Calum.

"Sure, I'll get us a table," Anna replied, grabbing one of the menus and bringing it out with her for the boys.

Calum ordered a beer for himself, a glass of wine for Anna and two lemonades. It was a strange feeling, being out with a family; he had to admit he kind of liked it. The boys were rascals, full of energy and imagination, as boys should be. He'd got so used to seeing his friend's kids glued to some tablet screen or PlayStation that it was a refreshing change to see them play. He never thought about having his own children before; he was too wrapped up in his business. Now, he had a strong feeling that he had been really missing out. Who could have guessed that a chance meeting with Anna would have made him feel that way?

Calum took the drinks outside to find Anna sitting at a table, watching her sons, his jacket still around her shoulders. His heart skipped a beat when he saw her; she was everything a woman should be, as far as he was concerned.

They took their time ordering food, while the boys played with limitless energy. Anna chatted a little about her home life in Edinburgh, though she didn't mention her divorce or ex-husband.

Calum told her a little about his business, though he never mentioned Helena or how he knew her. Both of them were being a little cagey and Calum couldn't quite work out why. He really liked Anna. She was so easy to be around; he was determined not to blow it.

The food arrived. The boys both had spaghetti, while Anna had ordered the soup with a baguette and Calum a man-size portion of fish and chips. They all sat, chatting happily as they ate their meals. The sun had just infiltrated through the mist, flooding them with its warm rays, leaving them all relaxed and happy.

Halfway through their meal, there came the furious sound of a revving car engine and they all turned around to see Helena's Porsche spin haphazardly into the Clachaig car park. Anna didn't register who it was at first, but when she saw the look on Calum's face, it then dawned on her.

The leggy blonde stepped out of the car, wearing a short skirt, high heels and a tight, red leather jacket. The handbag and designer sunglasses made her look like she should be in Monte Carlo, not the mountains of Scotland.

"Darling, I've been looking for you. Your mother said you might be here," said Helena, walking towards their table.

Calum's mouth was hanging open in shock as she approached. "You spoke to my mother?" he said, looking completely bewildered.

"Yes, darling, lovely woman. She was surprised that you hadn't introduced me already. I told her I was your fiancé," replied Helena, casting a spiteful glance at Anna.

"You did what!" roared Calum, suddenly snapping out of his confusion. "You're not my fiancé!"

"Really darling, just how would you describe me then?" replied Helena, completely unflustered.

The boys had stopped eating their spaghetti and were watching the exchange curiously, both with red pasta sauce spread around their faces, from their noses to the bottom of their chins. Anna could see Ollie was itching to say something, so she tapped him under the table with her foot, giving him a wink and a look of warning. It didn't go unnoticed by Helena, who rounded on Anna.

"Nice jacket. It doesn't suit you, but it's always a good tactic, isn't it? Were you cold?" Helena snarled sarcastically.

"It's not Mummy's jacket, it's Calum's," said James, immediately jumping to his mother's defence.

"Oh, I knew that darling; your mummy is very clever," said Helena with the same nasty smile.

Before Anna could say anything, Calum got to his feet, and Anna could see he was shaking with anger. He grabbed Helena under the arm and marched her away from their table back towards her car.

"I don't like her, Mummy," said Ollie with a mouthful of the spaghetti he had resumed eating.

"Me neither," agreed Anna.

The door of the bar swung open, and Murdo appeared carrying a pint, grinning from ear to ear, "Hello boys and Mummy."

"It's Captain Murdo!" cried Ollie. "Come and sit with us?"

"Aye, I can dae that," laughed Murdo, winking at Anna, who had to admit she was relieved to see him. "I can see oor Calum's has got himself intae a wee bit of bother," he chuckled.

"Erm yes, you could say that," Anna smiled as she looked over to the Porsche. Whatever was being said was very heated; Calum's face was red with anger, while Helena was being extremely animated. The next thing the pair of them got into the car, and Anna watched in amazement as they sped off.

"Has Calum gone?" asked James, clearly puzzled. "He didn't say goodbye."

"No, he didn't," said Anna, whilst thinking that he hadn't paid for lunch either. It was a good job she had her bank card in her jeans pocket.

"He forgot his jacket," James pointed out.

Anna threw the jacket off her shoulders as if it was infected with something nasty. "So he has," she said. "Well, I suppose you two better eat up, then we can head back to the cottage." She felt slightly foolish; she was clearly a bad judge of character where men were concerned.

"I'm sure Calum wouldnae have left withoot good reason. She's a bit of a handful that yun," said Murdo, still looking amused.

"You're telling me. Where on earth did he find her?" replied Anna, laughing in spite of herself.

"Well, his bad luck. He's left the door wide open for me to swoop in," grinned the captain. "Let me pay for yer lunch."

"Certainly not, Murdo, and there is no door to be opened," said Anna firmly, laughing again as Murdo clasped his hands to his chest, feigning heartbreak.

They stayed for a little while longer, the boys playing while Anna and Murdo chatted about Glencoe and things to do. She paid for lunch, then she and the boys left an hour later. Murdo said he would drop Calum's jacket off at his mother's house for him; it was on his way home. He couldn't wait to hear what Calum's mother had thought about her unexpected visitor. Anna thanked him, relieved as she didn't want to see Calum again; she'd had quite enough of playboy men and their fake women.

Chapter Seven

Calum was beyond furious. Helena had embarrassed him, not only in front of Anna and the boys, but she had also visited his mother. He had known if he didn't remove her from Anna there and then, there would have been trouble, and Anna would never forgive him if anything happened in front of her boys. She certainly didn't deserve to deal with this crazed bitch of a woman when she was here for a quiet holiday. He felt like a fool.

Helena was trouble, and he kicked himself for not realising it sooner. He had met her six months before but had never really taken her seriously. She was an attractive woman and the sex was good, but Calum had never considered her for a serious relationship. He was lazy when it came to relationships, and Helena was nothing more than a distraction whilst he built his business. He had never thought for a minute that she had thought differently, and he just hadn't noticed how involved she had become in his life, though if he was honest, he hadn't really cared. He had let her organise their nights out, and had footed the bill without much thought. Yet he couldn't have seen her more than once a week and sometimes not even that. He never phoned her, she always contacted him, and he had just accepted it.

Now he was in this situation and he knew it was his own stupid fault. Helena had somehow managed to persuade him to take her with him when he came home to visit his family. His parents were old school, hardworking and straight talking. They certainly wouldn't have approved of Calum bringing some woman they didn't know to their house and sharing a bed with her. Calum had never had any intention of putting his parents through that, and he had told Helena, as they were driving up, that he had booked her into the Onich Hotel.

It hadn't occurred to him that she had wanted to meet his parents, and she was absolutely furious that he had intended to leave her at the hotel and stay with his family. Their row was in full force when Helena had spun her car into the Green Welly carpark at

Tyndrum. Calum had suggested that she drive home if she wasn't happy with the arrangements; he could get a bus to Ballachulish from Tyndrum. Helena had sulked but calmed down, insisting that they carry on together.

Calum cringed at what his mother would have thought about Helena if she met her. Fiona MacAlistair was an intelligent woman, who did not suffer fools lightly. And now Helena was telling him that she had introduced herself to his mother as his fiancé. This whole situation was now a bloody mess, she was obviously crazy, why hadn't he seen that before? Calum had a horrible feeling in the pit of his stomach that it wasn't going to be that easy to get rid of her.

They drove back to the Onich Hotel in silence. Once they pulled into the carpark, Calum hauled himself out the little car. "Right Helena, pack your bags and leave," he said in as calm a voice as he could muster. "I will settle the hotel bill; it's my own stupid fault for bringing you here."

"You don't mean that," said Helena, suddenly throwing her arms around his neck.

Calum wrenched her arms from him and held her at arm's length, taking a step back. "Look at me, Helena, do I look like I'm joking? I want you gone; you have completely humiliated me!" he said more harshly than he intended.

"You can't just dump me!" cried Helena, her voice attracting the attention of many holiday makers who were sitting enjoying their drinks in the sunny beer garden.

"Keep your voice down. You've embarrassed us enough these last couple of days. I thought you had enough sense to leave already, but clearly I was wrong. How much clearer do I have to be? I don't want you here; we are finished!" snapped Calum, losing his patience.

"I will not keep my voice down! You can't just bring me here, then dump me when you think you have had a better offer! Who the hell do you think you are, Calum MacAlistair? I helped make you in Edinburgh," screamed Helena.

Calum grabbed her arm and marched her down to the beach, away from the onlookers. "What are you on about? You are crazy; we've dated a few times over the last few months. I've never led you to believe it was anything else than a casual dalliance, and I really don't have to be 'made' in Edinburgh. You were always free to date who you wanted."

"You're a liar! You said you loved me!" cried Helena.

"When! When did I ever say that? I don't even say that to my mother!" shouted Calum, his hands trembling with rage.

"Wait till I tell your mother how you've treated me! I can't imagine she is going to be very proud of her son!" shouted Helena.

"You will not go anywhere near my family! You don't know them, and believe me, my mother has probably worked out how crazy you are by now. She knows I would never get engaged without telling her first. You need to leave, Helena, go back to Edinburgh and leave me alone," said Calum, trying to keep his voice at a normal level.

"What? Leave you alone so you can pursue that frumpy little mumsy? What the hell do you see in her?" said Helena, glaring daggers at him.

"That's none of your business. And she is just a friend!" he groaned.

"Oh, believe me, it is my business. And I am not leaving, Calum. You think you can walk all over me? Me! No, you are going to regret every word you have just said to me; now get out my way," she hissed at him as she started to leave.

Calum grabbed her arm. "What is that supposed to mean?"

"Let go of me or I will scream bloody murder," she replied, and he could see the madness in her eyes.

Calum let go of her arm, and she stormed off towards the hotel. He watched her go, aware the hotel guests were looking at him, and he felt completely helpless. How the hell did he get mixed up in all this? He always considered himself a nice, happy-go-lucky sort of guy. Now he was shaking with shock and rage as he turned and started to stroll towards the main road. What a mess he had made of things. He only hoped that Helena would calm down, see sense and head back to Edinburgh.

Then, his thoughts turned to Anna. He must have blown it with her now; she wouldn't give him the time of day again. He could hardly blame her; if the shoe had been on the other foot he would have definitely scarpered. It was in a mess; he had never felt so infatuated before. Anna was incredibly attractive, as well as calm and intelligent, everything Helena was not. He knew the last thing she needed in her life was complications.

Suddenly, a car horn made him jump. He turned to see Murdo grinning in his pickup. "Looks like ye need a lift."

"Aye, I need a lift but not a lecture!" said Calum, jumping in the passenger side. "Tell me you saved my life and paid for lunch for them."

"I tried tae, but she wouldnae let me," laughed the captain. "That's some mess ye've got yerself in. By the way, yer jacket's in the back there. I'd love tae see how yer gonnae get yerself oot of this one. Am I taking ye home?"

"Aye, I've got some explaining to do to my mother," sighed Calum.

"I'd have loved tae have seen Fiona's face when that nutjob told her she wis yer fiancé," said Murdo still laughing.

"Shut up, Murdo," groaned Calum. "I really know how to pick 'em, don't I? I don't suppose Anna is going to want to see me again either."

"Ye've definitely blown that one. She wanted me tae bring yer jacket as she doesnae want to clap eyes on ye. I'd stay away frae that one fir a while," Murdo suggested.

"Aye, I'll have to give her a few days. I need to make sure that crazy bitch heads back to Edinburgh first." Calum sighed. How had his life gotten so complicated?

Chapter Eight

The next few days were gorgeous. The sun broke through the mist every morning as Anna and the boys made the most of exploring the glens, the lochs and rivers. Every day was spent outdoors and every evening playing in the pool or the garden. Anna was relieved when Calum didn't show up to try to explain, and she simply refused to think about him. There was no room in her life for someone like that. Thankfully, she was also sleeping well, without any dreams or ghostly disturbances. She had been a little uneasy being on her own at night, though. It seemed the house creaked a lot more at night than she had first noticed.

Anna had also discovered the little book Angus had told her about in the old dresser in her bedroom. Sure enough, in Nelly's handwriting were descriptions of each painting hanging in the hallway. MacIain MacDonald was pictured standing in a battle pose with his sword and the Glencoe skyline behind him. He was dressed in the modern MacDonald tartan, with his hair blowing loose behind him in the wind. Nelly had said the picture was painted by a local artist named Edith Macfie in 1989. Anna wondered if she was any relation to Kenneth Macfie, Angus's historian friend.

The next picture was much older, painted in 1862 by a name Anna couldn't make out. It was a head and shoulder portrait of Lady MacDonald, MacIain's wife. She was a beautiful woman, with porcelain skin and bright, opaque blue eyes that followed you around the room. The same artist had painted a similar picture of MacIain's daughter, who just looked a younger version of her mother.

There was also another older oil painting of a group of women working outside, harvesting some sort of crop in the glen. This painting really did look dated, and Nelly had written that she did not know how old it was or who had painted it. She had inherited it along with the cottage back in 1953. As Anna stood staring at, it she realised one of the women she was looking at was Kirstin. She looked the same as she did in the picture in her bedroom, but it was the woman standing behind Kirstin that drew her eyes. She stood a short distance from the other women, with them, but somehow apart from them. She was tall, with striking long red hair and a scarred cheek. Her eyes were fixed on Kirstin with what seemed to be a look of recrimination. Anna felt herself tense as she realised she was looking at Corrag.

James was still talking with Corri, which made Anna uneasy, but as he was quite happy, she didn't pursue questioning him too much. She was looking forward to her brother arriving, as she had to admit she was beginning to really miss adult company.

Saturday arrived finally and Glen and Rob arrived around four o'clock. Their Range Rover pulled up onto the stone drive as the boys and Dexter came charging out of the cottage, followed by Anna.

"Uncle Glen, we've got a pool!" were the first words out of their mouths.

"A pool! That's fantastic!" cried Glen, picking them both up at the same time and swinging them around as Rob jumped out the driving seat.

"Hey, where's my hug?" he said, and they threw themselves at him.

"Hey, you," said Glen, hugging his sister. "What a fantastic place; how on earth did you find it? We had a great drive here. Rob hasn't been to Glencoe before; it blew him away driving into the gorge."

Anna was so pleased to see him she could feel her eyes welling up. She shook her head slightly, trying to hide them. "It was really foggy this morning, I was worried it wouldn't clear. I'm so glad you're here."

"I can see that," said Rob hugging her. "Are you okay, darling?"

Anna gazed into the sincere blue eyes filled with concern as Rob looked down at her. "Oh, it's just been all go with the boys and my emotions, and I think we have a ghost," she blurted out, trying to hold back the hot tears that threatened to spill down her cheeks.

"A ghost?" said Glen, his eyes sparkling with interest. "Of course we have a ghost! It is MacDonald country, after all. How could we not?"

"Will you come in the pool with us?" Ollie asked.

"Ollie, they've just arrived," scolded his mum.

"As soon as I find my trunks," said Glen, laughing.

After a quick tour of the cottage, with the boys jumping around with excitement, they all went to the pool. Glen and Rob made an attractive looking couple, both of them in good shape and suntanned from their recent trip abroad. Glen was dark like Anna, but in contrast, Rob was the ultimate Nordic, blue-eyed blonde.

Anna went and made a pitcher of margaritas as Glen and Rob played with the boys in the pool. She arrived back, pouring them all a glass, then she sat on the sun lounger sipping away at hers. Rob came and sat with her.

"Have you found it hard on your own?" he asked gently.

"Harder than I thought I would. I think that was why I was so emotional when you arrived. It's been a difficult year, I guess, and I kind of buried it. Somehow being here, it all bubbled to the surface. I feel loads better now you're here though," she admitted.

"We should have been there for you more," said Rob sadly. "I feel guilty, but we were so busy with the hotel. You must come down and stay with us. We have some very nice single gentlemen down in Devon."

"You sound like my mother," groaned Anna.

"Oh God, no! If I do that again, slap me please," he laughed.

Anna had got some fresh crab in for their dinner, so after the pool they sat in the low evening sunshine, drinking cold white wine and eating crab, with lemon wedges, garlic mayonnaise and fresh, crusty bread.

She hadn't felt so happy for a long time, and they talked and laughed until she finally put the boys to bed. Ollie had told them about Calum and the horrible lady, as Anna cringed; she knew she would have some explaining to do.

When the boys were finally down, she went back out and filled Glen and Rob in on her meeting and then the disastrous lunch with Calum.

"Oh no, my skin is literally crawling with embarrassment for him," laughed Rob. "He probably left to protect you from some sort of scene."

"Yea, left her with the bill, very classy!" said Glen. "He's not going to come back from that one. Unless… Is he gorgeous?"

"He's quite good looking," said Anna, in spite of herself.

"So, will you give him a second chance then?" asked Rob.

"No, absolutely not. He's blown it," she said firmly.

"Little liar," laughed Glen. "I can see in your face you like him."

"Maybe, but I can do without the crazy ex-girlfriend appearing out of nowhere," she smiled.

"I cannot wait to meet him," said Rob.

"You're not going to. I can't imagine he would dare show his face here again. Anyway, it was days ago. He hasn't made any effort to apologise," Anna laughed.

"Probably trying to sort out the ex. If he's keen, darling, he will show up, trust me," Glen winked at her.

The conversation then turned to the ghost the boys were seeing and the strange happenings around the cottage.

"When you said the word ghost, I didn't really take it seriously. It sounds a little scary to be honest," Glen said.

"Rubbish, she hasn't done them any harm. As Anna said, the boys are not in the least bit bothered about her. If it is the ghost of Corrag, then she sounds quite friendly," said Rob.

"Do you mean like Casper?" replied Glen rolling his eyes.

"I just mean that if she was going to do them any harm, wouldn't they be more frightened of her?" said Rob.

"Maybe we should see what this historian friend of Angus's comes up with. By all accounts, there is not much information about Corrag, other than she tried to warn the MacDonalds of the massacre before it happened. It's strange she's here talking with James, if it is her," said Anna.

"Well, I think the whole thing sounds very exciting," said Rob, pulling a face at Glen. "It wouldn't be a trip to the Highlands without a good ghost story would it?"

The mist had started to blanket the mountains again and it was getting cold. They decided to call it a night, planning to go into Fort William the next day. Anna felt so much more relaxed now her brother was here, she got ready for bed, falling straight to sleep as soon as her head hit the pillow.

***

The snow was relentless, she was soaked through and her hair was frozen to her shoulders. Kirstin had never been this cold in her life. Highlanders never went out in blizzards; they knew better. It was something she learnt quickly when Rab first brought her to the mountains. Now here she was with no shoes, trying to scramble up the side of the mountain. She could still hear musket fire and screaming from down below her, and she had no idea if Rab was alive still.

Why had the soldiers turned on them? They had been excellent hosts to them over the last couple of weeks. She and Rab had housed Sergeant Walter Purdie and young Archie and Wullie Tweedy, both newly appointed foot soldiers in the Earl of Argyll's red coat regiment. Rab had told her it was the Highland way, to grant hospitality to those who ask for it.

Kirstin fed them with porridge every morning and a rich meat broth with freshly made bread every evening. The soldiers had played with Jamie, then chatted and shared ale with them late into the evenings. No matter how cold Kirstin was feeling now, she suffered more from the sickening level of betrayal that these young men had dealt them.

"Mistress Kirstin, ye must keep walking. We're nearly at the ledge" came Flora's voice through the snow. Kirstin hadn't realised she had fallen that far behind. She was moving as if in a dream; her body was numb along with her heart. She had been happy here in Glencoe. She loved her husband and their son. Her family had told her she would regret her marriage to a savage highlander. She was from Tarbolton in Ayrshire, a well-bred young lady, daughter to a well-respected and prosperous farmer. She met Rab whilst visiting Glasgow with her father. He had won her heart in less than a week, and they eloped. Kirstin never regretted a day living with Rab; he treated her like a queen.

"Kirstin! Are ye wi' us lassie?" said someone shaking her roughly. It was John MacDonald, son of MacIain. He lifted her up and carried her to the shelter under some trees and a rocky overhang.

"Eibleen, she needs attending tae. Fir the love o' God, the lassie has nae shoes, her feet are ruined," he called over to the others.

Kirstin felt herself being moved gently, then covered with plaids; she had no feeling in her feet or hands and could not focus. Her last thought before she passed out was of Jamie, her son.

***

"Mummy, why are you crying?" said James.

Anna awoke to find James sitting on top of her cupping his little hands around her face. She blinked for a moment, not sure where she was. Her feet were numb and she felt cold. She smiled at James who was looking at her with a frown, and she reached out to touch his face.

"Mummy, your hands are freezing!" he shouted, leaping back away from her.

Anna reached over to switch on the bedside lamp with tingling fingers. It was 5 am. Her hands were red and cold, but the feeling was coming back to her feet. She looked at James, who was sitting cross-legged on her bed, looking at her intently.

"What are you doing up so early, little man?" she asked him.

"Corri told me I had to come and wake you. She doesn't like it when you dream about Kirstin. She says Kirstin needs to go away," said James.

Anna sat stunned, looking at her child's questioning expression. She felt a wave of anger wash over her. Why the hell was this Corri talking to her son? "James, is Corri still here?" she asked.

"No, she went when you woke up. She said you would be angry with her," said James watching her. "Are you angry, Mummy?"

"I just wish Corri would come and talk to me. She shouldn't be waking you in the middle of the night," said Anna sternly.

"But it's daylight," said James, jumping off the bed and pulling the curtains open. The light poured into her room, though all she could see outside was a thick white fog.

"James, it's just really early in the morning. We should both be asleep. Let's get back into bed," she said, pulling the curtains to again. Her door opened slowly, and Ollie appeared, rubbing his eyes.

"I can't find James," he whined, then saw his brother in bed with his mum.

Anna lifted Ollie into the bed with them. Shortly after, Dexter, having heard their voices, appeared and sneaked up onto the bed quietly, still under the illusion that no one was noticing him.

They all snuggled down for a couple more hours' sleep, but as the boys drifted off, Anna lay awake going over and over the dream in her head.

With all the other strange happenings, she had forgotten to tell Glen and Rob about her strange dreams and the physical effect they had on her when she awoke.

She was reliving the nightmare as Kirstin, feeling the cold and the fear of the soldiers. What was worse was the anguish she was feeling at the thought of Kirstin losing her son, Jamie.

The more Anna thought about it, the more she realised that it had to be Kirstin who was haunting the cottage. But that still didn't explain what Corri was doing here, or even if she was actually Corrag, the Glencoe witch. This Corri had attached herself to James for some reason, and Anna was worried. She lay awake until around seven, then slipped out of the bed, leaving the boys to sleep. Dexter half lifted his head as she moved quietly across the room, then plonked it back down again. She went to put on some coffee; her body was now crying out for some caffeine.

Chapter Nine

Everyone else was up and dressed by nine thirty. The mist was already clearing by then so they decided to skip Fort William and take Glen's new Land Rover to Ben Nevis. Anna knew her brother was probably itching to do some outdoor hiking, and it was going to be a beautiful day in the Highlands. They all had their walking boots on, but didn't bother carrying anything more than some bottled water, deciding to stop somewhere for lunch when they were out.

The boys and Dexter were in the back with Anna. It was a nice change for her not to be doing the driving, though it had been a bit of a battle with Dexter trying to stop him getting in the front seat. She had decided not to mention her dream until later, but it had darkened her mood for sure, making her feel more subdued than normal. She relaxed with her head leaning on the car door window as her brother drove across Loch Leven onto the B863 that went along the side of the loch, taking them to Glen Nevis visitor centre. As Anna gazed absentmindedly at the loch, her eyes suddenly focused on the small islands still shrouded by the mist in the water. They looked deserted and overgrown from this side of the shore. She had never really noticed these islands before, they seemed so small and insignificant, and she wondered if anyone ever went there.

"Are you okay, Anna? You're very quiet," said Rob, disturbing her thoughts.

"Yes, fine, just enjoying being chauffeured around for a change. I was just wondering about these islands in the middle of the loch there," she replied.

"They're the clan-burial islands," said Glen. "I remember visiting them with some friends a few years ago. The biggest island is St Munda's Island; it's the burial place for Clan Donald. The MacDonalds massacred at Glencoe were buried there, including MacIain MacDonald himself. The Camerons and Stewarts also used St Mundo's to bury their dead in the past. It's quite an eerie place to visit; it was all overgrown when we went. There aren't any actual tours to the islands, so we sneaked across on my friend's dad's boat.

We were about seventeen at the time. I remember we picked mussels from the beach and cooked them on a fire we made. One thing we did discover though, as we made our way across the island, were some really old graves. They were so worn that we could see some human bones lying around the surfaces. Scared the shit out of us back then."

"I want to go to the island!" cried Ollie, closely followed by, "Uncle Glen just said a bad word."

"Me too," said James. "I want to see some human bones."

"Oh God, we'll never hear the end of that now," groaned Anna, glaring at the grinning face of her brother in the rear-view mirror. "We are not going to look at dead people's bones. Absolutely NO WAY!"

"Can we pick mussels and cook them on a fire then?" said Ollie, defiant to the last.

"Yes, we can definitely do that," said Anna. Then, before Ollie could speak, "But not on the island! See what you've done, Glen?"

They turned off the road and headed up to the visitor's centre to park their car and then spent the rest of the morning exploring the Ben Nevis trail. The seventeen kilometre all-round trek to the summit was not doable with the boys, so instead they crossed the bridge from the visitor's centre at the east side of the mountain to join the mountain track, known locally as Pony Track, that was situated on the western side.

Even though the boys were small, they managed the steep path without any complaints. It was nice to be out in the open again, and Anna could see Glen and Rob were really enjoying the walk. The breeze was getting fiercer the higher they climbed, and soon Anna could see Ollie was beginning to flag. Against the odds, as there were not many trees around, he had managed to collect a small bundle of sticks. He was chatting away to them as he walked further and further behind the rest of them. Dexter kept running back to him, trying to make him hurry up.

Anna took pity on her son and said to her brother, "Look, why don't you two carry on up and get some good photos of the mountain? I'm going to take the boys back down, it's getting a bit much for them now. We can get some sandwiches at the visitor's centre and go down for a picnic beside the river." She didn't want to spoil the climb for Glen and Rob.

"No, don't be silly, we're here to see you guys. We can climb Nevis another day, you're not worried, are you Rob? It's just lovely being out in the Scottish fresh air again," said Glen.

"To be honest, I'm getting hungry anyway. I haven't had enough food to climb a mountain. Let's all go explore the river, we can get some ice creams and then we'll go out for lunch," replied Rob.

The boys didn't need to be asked twice; they turned and started to make their way down the track, reinvigorated. They were certainly finding the descent a lot easier, and Anna was sure it had something to do with the promise of ice cream. Ollie had given up on his sticks, deciding it was best to leave them to sleep by a rock as they were very tired from climbing.

Anna watched them run down the mountain. There were quite a few walkers out attempting the summit, and in the distance, she saw them stop to talk to a man who was making his way towards them. She couldn't quite make out his face, but her heart began to beat as she recognised his stance. As he approached, flagged on either side by James and Ollie, she began to see his face more clearly.

"Well, hallo, I didn't expect to see you today," said Calum, trying to keep his voice light, but smiling uncomfortably.

"We're here exploring Ben Nevis," said Anna, keeping her voice equally as light.

Glen and Rob shared a look. "Are you going to introduce us?" said Glen.

"This is Calum," said James, taking control of the situation. "He likes my mummy."

Rob choked back a laugh, then regained his composure quickly. "This is Anna's brother, Glen, and I'm his husband, Rob. It's nice to put a face to the name. We heard all about you," said Rob, grinning like a Cheshire cat while Anna cringed in her shoes.

"Yes, I bet you have," said Calum, feeling completely trapped. "I'm so sorry about the other day, Anna. I have no idea why Helena was behaving like that. I've made it clear that I want nothing more to do with her. I know I left abruptly, but I thought it would be best to get her out the way. I didn't want her to cause a scene with your children there. I know I owe you a lunch, and a massive apology, but I wanted to leave it a few days just to make sure that Helena had actually left the area. She has been a nightmare."

"Apology accepted," said Glen before Anna could speak, then he turned to Anna. "It is, isn't it?"

"Yes, of course, I'm sure you did the right thing," she said, wishing she was anywhere else but here at this moment. "Are you going up the mountain?" she asked.

"I needed a day out in the fresh air after this disastrous trip. I'm just hoping I finally got through to Helena and she is back in Edinburgh. I don't understand what she was thinking. I thought I'd climb my old friend here; it's been some years since I've been up on the summit," said Calum, looking at Anna trying to see if he could read her. She wouldn't make eye contact with him and seemed as uncomfortable as he felt.

"Why don't you come around for a BBQ with us later? Rob's cooking, he does an amazing butterfly lamb's leg on the grill, and we can all have a good laugh at this episode," suggested Glen, completely out of the blue. Anna glared at him.

"Yes, come round, Calum," said Ollie, backed up immediately by James. "We want to show you our den."

"Erm... okay, sure, that will be nice," replied Calum, still unable to see Anna's face clearly; she was deliberately avoiding him, pretending to stare out at the view. "I'll see you later then," he said, giving them a half-hearted wave as he started his hike back up the mountain.

They walked until they were out of earshot before Anna turned on her brother. Glen was ready for it and was already chuckling to himself. "What the hell, Glen! I told you I didn't want to see him again!"

"Aw, he's nice, Anna. Really good looking, quite a catch I'd say," he replied, still laughing.

"I think he's nice, Mummy. Why don't you like him?" asked James. frowning.

"I do like him!" cried Anna. "Would you guys stop ganging up on me?"

"We're not ganging up on you," said James with a worried expression.

"I know, I just didn't want there to be any complications. He has a crazy girlfriend, remember," said Anna, realising suddenly that she was trying to explain to a six year old.

"She's horrible," said Ollie. "Dexter doesn't like her and neither do my stick people!"

"Well, she's not coming," said Glen. "Calum says she has gone home."

"I don't think she is his girlfriend, Mummy," said James. "He doesn't like her."

"No, he really doesn't," said Rob, joining in.

"Okay, okay, you all like him. I get it. I promise to be nice," said Anna, holding her hands up in defeat.

The rest of the day was fun. As Rob had been unexpectedly nominated to cook a BBQ, they decided to just buy sandwiches from the visitor's centre, eating them down at the river bank instead of going out to lunch. It was still warm, even though it was breezy, and Anna found herself laughing in spite of her dream and her meeting with Calum earlier.

They then went for a drive north through Fort William, then another five miles up the A82 to the Glen Nevis Ski centre where the Lochaber Farm shop was situated. Rob picked up a huge leg of lamb along with some mint sauce, fresh garlic and balsamic vinegar for his marinade. They also got some local sausages, fresh salad and bread before they headed back to the cottage. The boys slept in the car on the journey home and Anna lightly dozed; the memories of her dream had faded away into the day.

As Glen pulled onto the one-lane road from Glencoe to their cottage, Anna jumped awake. She was sure she had just seen a blue Porsche pass them, going in the opposite direction. Maybe she just had that awful woman on her brain; hadn't Calum said she was gone?

The pulled into the drive, then Rob said, "The door's wide open."

"What?" said Anna, jumping out the car when it rolled to a stop. The front door to the cottage was wide open. She went to the entrance and shouted, "Hallo? Angus? Is that you?"

There was no answer. Glen suddenly grabbed her shoulders before she stepped inside. "No, let Rob and I go in first, just in case. You stay with the boys."

Anna went back to the car, the boys were still asleep, so she stood by the open car door waiting for Glen to call. Glen and Rob had gone in with Dexter, who didn't seem at all worried. She knew her dog would have barked if there was someone else in the cottage; he didn't like strangers being near his family unless he was introduced to them. Sure enough, Glen came back out to say there was no one there and it didn't look like anything had been touched. Maybe she hadn't shut the door properly and it had just blown open—it was a windy day.

Anna and Glen carried the boys to their beds. They were still fast asleep so Anna thought it wouldn't harm them to have a nap for a while. They had been on the go for the last few days and waking up very early in the mornings. No doubt they would be having another late night again tonight.

Rob brought in the shopping and no one mentioned the open door again, accepting it had blown open by accident. There was a very low level of crimes here in Glencoe, especially burglaries.

Anna threw herself onto the armchair, with her paperback that she was still trying to get into. She was not in the mood for a romantic novel; it had been a bad choice. Glen went for a swim while Rob set to work on butterflying and marinating the lamb's leg.

Chapter Ten

After their furious fight in the car park of the Onich Hotel, Helena had stormed into the hotel reception and demanded that she be moved to a different room. The young receptionist, who was an Australian backpacker hired for the summer season, took umbrage at being spoken to that way, so Helena had to change tact. She burst into tears, explaining to the pretty young blonde that she was getting hassled by Calum, and that he refused to take no for an answer. She said she had come up to Glencoe to escape him, but he had followed her there, and she just wanted him to leave her alone. She begged the receptionist to give her a different room and if Calum phoned to check on her, to tell him that she had checked out.

The young receptionist, not a stranger to unwanted attention herself, took pity on Helena, another comrade in the world of unwanted advances, so she agreed to find Helena another room, then pass the message on to the rest of the hotel staff.

For the next few days, Helena had seethed quietly to herself. She parked her car as close to Calum's parents' house as she could without being spotted by them. From there, she had watched Calum come and go, waiting to catch him with that woman. But he never left the farm much at all, and she saw no sign of him meeting Anna. Perhaps he had been telling the truth when he said they had just been friends, but then Helena would cast her mind back to that day at the Clachaig. She saw the way he looked at her; they were more than friends, she was sure.

Calum had checked at the hotel to see if she had left, and true to her word, the receptionist informed him coldly that Helena had checked out. When Helena returned to the hotel that evening, Carly, the Australian receptionist, pulled her aside to inform her. Helena thanked her with tears in her eyes; she had always been a good actress. Carly also arranged for her to park her car in the garage at the hotel, so that Calum wouldn't spot it if he came to check.

Now here she was, three days later, sitting in the hotel bar, finding solace in a glass or two of red wine. She was still at a loss on what to do next. Calum now thought she had gone home, which meant he wouldn't be looking for her. He hadn't sent her any messages, nor tried to call her mobile. How dare Calum dismiss her like that? Who did he think he was messing with? She wasn't some piece of trash to be picked up and dropped whenever he felt like it.

From the day Helena had first met Calum six months before, she had set her sights on him. He had been attending a venue thrown by the marketing firm she worked for, in a huge marquee set up at Leith Docks in Edinburgh. Her boss had introduced them, hoping that Helena could persuade Calum to be one of their clients. Helena was attracted immediately to Calum, regarding him as new meat in a town full of has-beens. She charmed her way into his life and managed to persuade him to use their firm to produce advertising campaigns for his business. From then on, as far as she was concerned, they were an item. Granted he needed some pushing every now and then, always so busy with work, he hardly had any time for her. But she could live with that, and she knew he wasn't seeing anyone else.

Helena had told all her friends they were a couple, dragging him out to parties where they could be seen together. Her friends were sceptical, as Helena's reputation with men was questionable, and she had often been accused of being unstable and possessive. She was known to stalk some of her old boyfriends relentlessly, ruining any chance of them meeting someone else.

On one such occasion, Helena had spent a week following her ex-boyfriend. He had finished with her six months before, but she had heard he was seeing someone new and she flew into a rage. Dave (her ex) lived in a stone apartment block, so one night she followed him and his new girlfriend back to his flat. She went and sat on the stairway one floor above, where she remained for hours before his girlfriend left the apartment. As the poor, unsuspecting girl descended the stairs, Helena ran down after her, throwing herself at the girl trying to rip her hair out. Dave heard the commotion and ran out to find Helena on top of his girlfriend, trying to smash her head on the floor.

The police were called, and luckily, Helena was finally let off with a caution. But she knew her reputation was in tatters, so she sought out counselling for anger management. It had been a waste of time; after three sessions, Helena stopped going. She didn't like the way the counsellor got her to 'open up' about herself, making her uncomfortable. However, as far as her friends were concerned,

Helena's attempt at finding help for her anger made it easier to forgive and forget.

They had all liked Calum but could see he was not as invested in Helena as she wanted him to be. Helena just laughed it off, saying he was too busy at work and they would soon be getting engaged. She didn't seem to notice that it was all one sided on her part.

This trip to the Highlands was supposed to be the icing on the cake, as far as she was concerned. Calum would introduce her to his family, and she would charm them so that he would be proud of her. He would realise that she was the one he wanted to spend his life with, and they would arrive back in Edinburgh ready to buy her an engagement ring.

But everything had come crashing down when he had told her in the car that he didn't want to introduce her to his parents, and that he had booked her into a hotel. He wasn't even staying with her. Helena felt all her plans slipping away from her, and she had blown her top. Calum had offered to leave her at some hiker's pit stop, where she could turn around and go back to Edinburgh. So, she had to pull herself together fast, burying her anger while she rethought her plans. Then after their first day out, he had had the audacity to leave her a note, telling her to go home.

Who the hell did that? And who was this little, dowdy, mumsy woman he was sniffing around? She couldn't possibly be his type. There was no way Helena was going to leave until she had discovered more of what he was up to. She had invested too much of her time into becoming the girlfriend of Calum MacAlistair, and she wasn't about to watch it all fall apart now.

She couldn't return to Edinburgh without him. He was not going to make a fool out of her, not this time. This time she was going to get her man, she would soon have him running back to her with his tail between his legs.

As she sat there in her cloud of disillusion at the bar, nursing her third large glass of red wine, she suddenly became aware of two elderly gentlemen deep in conversation on the table next to them.

It wasn't until she heard one of them mention the name Anna, that her ears pricked up. Wasn't that what Calum had called the woman earlier? She leaned back slightly in her chair, trying to catch more of their conversation.

"Anna told me that her wee laddie keeps blethering tae some invisible woman called Corri. When I showed the laddie the picture of Corrag, he kent who it wis. But what would she be daeng haunting Kirstin's Cot, Ken? It disnae make sense," said one of the men.

"Come on Angus, ye ken that Corrag wis living in the glen before the massacre. She must have kent Kirstin and Rab MacDonald. Maybe there is some connection," said Kenneth.

"Aye well, I didnae want tae come across like some blithering eejit, but the laddie definitely recognised her name, though he said she wis bonnier than they had drawn her in the picture. He's only six, Ken, he wouldnae be telling tales at that age," said Angus.

"Old Nelly never mentioned Corri tae me when she was alive. But she did ken the cottage was haunted, by Kirstin herself. I did look intae it fir her, when my Edith wis daeng that painting of MacIain MacDonald. I couldnae find much on Kirstin, except that she died frae exposure after the massacre. She had a wee boy that she got separated frae, maybe her ghost is still looking for her bairn," said Kenneth.

"That might explain some of it. Anna said her brother wis arriving at the cottage today. Perhaps we could arrange tae see them in a couple of days, and shed some light on the situation," suggested Angus. "If it is a haunting, then I dinnae ken what I'm gonnae tell the owners."

Helena's mind was working overtime. This Anna was staying at a cottage called Kirstin's Cot, and she thought it was haunted. That couldn't be too hard to find, perhaps she could find out some more about the woman that Calum seemed so interested in. Maybe she could actually scare her away. Helena decided to check out the cottage the next day.

The next morning, Helena set out after her breakfast of three cups of black coffee and two paracetamol. She drove over to Glencoe Village and asked directions in the local shop. From there she found the cottage easily, so she parked up at the Clachaig Inn, hoping her car would be less conspicuous there. She walked back up to the cottage, remaining hidden in the trees. She saw two cars parked up outside, so she waited for a while, watching for some movement. A few minutes later, she saw Anna appear at the door with her kids and the dog.

The dog ran towards Helena, who had crouched unsteadily on her high heels behind a bush at the bottom of a tree; she held her breath and was relieved to hear Anna call him back to the car.

Helena watched as two good-looking men followed Anna out the cottage, heading towards the Land Rover. They all climbed into the vehicle, then drove off, leaving Helena breathing a deep sigh of relief that the dog had gone with them.

She gave it another couple of minutes before she stepped out from behind the trees and bushes, then headed gingerly to the cottage. The door was locked, so Helena walked around the building trying to find another opening, she was determined to get in. She found an open window that led into the boys' bedroom and managed to open it wide enough so she could squeeze through.

Her heart was pounding, but nothing would deter her now. She explored the boys' room, turning her nose up at the untidy piles of clothing and toys that were lying around the floor. She pushed the door of their bedroom open and peered out into the corridor. The place was deserted, so she stepped out and started to explore the other rooms.

When she got to the kitchen she turned on the lights to look around. She found Anna's wallet, which held her driving license. Helena looked at the name and address, gritting her teeth with frustration when she saw it was an Edinburgh address. Did that mean Calum had met her before? Determined to find out, Helena put Anna's details into her phone. Someone would know who this woman was, and she would get all the dirt she could drag up.

She wandered back up the old hallway that led her to Anna's bedroom, watched by the inhabitants of the old portraits that hung on the wall. Helena opened the door and stepped into the room. There was a faint perfume smell in the air, and there was clothing thrown untidily over a chair in the room, something Helena would never do.

This woman was grubby and unorganised. Calum would hate that, she was sure. She then went over to the dressing table and picked up Anna's perfume, spraying some on her wrist. *Well at least she has good taste when it came to scents.*

Helena sat down on the bed, suddenly feeling emotional and not sure what she was doing there. This was crazy; she had no proof there was anything going on between Calum and this woman. But she had seen the way he looked at her—there was no mistake there. She needed to gather her thoughts and come up with a plan to frighten this woman off for good. If Anna really did think this place was haunted, that would be quite easy to do. But then if Calum knew Anna lived in Edinburgh, what's to stop him meeting up with her there? She would have to think of something that would make Anna despise Calum.

He was her man, she had worked too hard to let someone swoop in now, and this bitch needed to know that. Helena clenched her fists as her anger grew when she thought back to how Calum had spoken to her the other day. She would make him pay for that.

The room was becoming very cold, but Helena didn't notice, overwhelmed by her jealous rage towards Anna. The anger was simmering inside her, getting more intense, like a volcano on the point of eruption. The rational part of her brain was telling her she was behaving strangely, but she could hardly hear it. Seething still, Helena tried to stand up, but it felt like her limbs were all lead weights, and she couldn't pull herself to her feet.

Tiredness washed over her, extinguishing the burning flames of her rage and her eyes started to droop as her vision became blurred. Helena blinked rapidly, trying to regain her focus and clear her head, but she felt herself being pulled back onto the bed. Someone was beside her, she could sense a presence feeding off her anger. She found she was gasping for air, as ice-cold fingers reached out and grabbed the side of her face. She wanted to scream, but had no energy to do so. Helena tried to roll away and make one last futile attempt to get up, before finally allowing the entity to completely seduce her. A woman's voice whispered in her ear, "Yer rage awakens mine. I want my son. Yer gonnae help me find him."

Four hours later, Helena awoke with a start to find herself lying on the floor at the foot of Anna's bed. She had no memory of how she had got there, and she struggled to her feet, guessing she must have passed out. The anxiety of the last few days had been getting to her; well, Calum was to blame for that. Another thing on her list to get even with him for.

She looked at her phone and saw it was nearly three o'clock. She had been there for hours. What the hell was wrong with her? Thank God they hadn't come home yet; she wasn't sure how she would have explained herself if she had been caught.

Gathering her phone, she looked around the room feeling strangely calm considering where she had just found herself. Her eyes were drawn to the portrait of Kirstin MacDonald. Helena stood and stared into Kirstin's corn-blue eyes and felt them staring right back at her with an unnatural maliciousness that made her shiver. She tore her eyes away from the picture, then turned to make her way slowly out of the room and back down the corridor to the front door. Unlocking it from the inside, she stepped out, leaving it wide open as she walked through the pine trees back down to the Clachaig carpark to get her car. Helena knew she would be back at the cottage soon; Kirstin needed her.

Chapter Eleven

The lamb was on the grill when Calum arrived, his face weather beaten from his climb up Nevis. He handed Glen two bottles of Prosecco, then went to join Anna and Rob who were standing by the BBQ.

"Evening," he said somewhat nervously. "Where are the boys? It's very quiet around here."

"They're up that tree behind us, hiding from you," said Anna. "I doubt they'll be quiet for long; they want to surprise you."

As if on cue, there was a whooping sound from the tree that was obviously for Calum's benefit. Picking up on the game immediately, Calum shouted towards the tree, "What was that? Some sort of animal?"

"We're monkeys," cried Ollie from the branches in the tree.

"There aren't any monkeys in Scotland, we can't be monkeys!" hissed James from a lower branch. "We're lions!"

"Oh no, not lions! Are you going to eat us?" cried Calum, jumping to hide behind Anna. "I'm scared of lions!"

"No, hungry lions really like sausages, so I think they should come and get some," said Anna, avoiding looking directly at Calum. She couldn't understand why she felt so self-aware around him.

Ollie and James climbed back down the tree, and before long, they were munching on hot dogs. James wandered around the garden as he ate, in a world of his own. Dexter was at his heels, waiting for the scraps to fall; he'd already had two sausages, but he never missed an opportunity.

The dog suddenly began growling, and Anna looked over to where they were standing. Dexter had all his hackles up and was crouched low, growling at something next to James. He then started to bark angrily, causing James to shout at him.

"Quiet, Dexter, leave her alone!"

"Leave who alone?" said Anna, getting to her feet and walking over to her son. There was no one there.

"It's Corri; she has to tell you something," said James.

Calum had been chatting away with Rob at the BBQ when he heard Dexter barking. He looked over to see Anna approaching James and the dog. She looked a little rattled, so he walked over to see what was going on.

James was holding onto Dexter's collar, but the dog would not stop growling. "Stop it, Dexter, you'll scare her!"

"James I'm not sure this is a good idea. How do you know that Corri is your friend? Dexter doesn't seem to like her very much," said Anna, concerned over Dexter's reaction.

"Dexter just doesn't understand!" cried James in frustration. "She just wants to tell you about the woman who broke into our cottage today."

"What woman?" said Calum with a sinking feeling in the pit of his stomach. Surely not?

"When we got back to the cottage this afternoon, the front door was wide open. We don't know if a woman broke in, and nothing was taken. We just assumed we hadn't shut the door properly, and it blew open in the wind," explained Anna. "It was just very odd."

"How does she know it was a woman?" asked Anna crouching down next to James to talk to him on his level.

"Corri saw her come in; she climbed in the window in our bedroom," said James, still showing no signs of being worried or distressed. "Corri says she's really, really angry. Her anger let Kirstin in."

"Okay, that's enough!" shouted Anna to the space James was looking at. "You are going to frighten my children. Why can't you talk to me?"

"I'm not frightened," said James.

"I'm not frightened either," said Ollie who had snuck up on them.

"It doesn't matter; she shouldn't be telling you stuff like that. She needs to talk to an adult," said Anna, aware of how ridiculous she sounded.

"She doesn't want to talk to you. She doesn't like adults," James tried to explain. "She's gone now."

Calum put his hand on Anna's shoulder and could feel she was trembling. "Perhaps we should just go sit down for now, take a deep breath and talk about it."

Anna allowed Calum to lead her back to the patio while the boys looked at her with wide eyes, not sure if they were in trouble or not.

"You have to admit the boys don't seem in the least bit bothered by her. This Corri does seem to be their friend," said Glen after they told him what had happened.

"It's funny, but it's not her that I'm worried about—it's Kirstin. I had another vivid dream last night; it was so real it scared me," admitted Anna.

"Another dream?" said Glen. "What do you mean?"

"I was saving that story until after the boys went to bed," she said.

"We seem to be skipping over the point here; do you think a woman actually did break in to the cottage?" asked Rob.

Anna turned to Calum and could see he was worried. "Do you think Helena would have done that?"

"I don't know. I wouldn't have thought she would stoop so low. But I'm learning a whole different side to that woman. I phoned the hotel yesterday and they told me that Helena had checked out. There is no reason for her to hang about, so I can't see her checking in anywhere else," said Calum, but his gut told him that he was wrong.

He pulled out his phone and found the number to the Onich Hotel, he dialled and minutes later asked to be put through to the hotel bar. He decided to avoid speaking with the reception desk in case Helena had got them to lie for her. Calum told the bartender he had found Helena's purse with a key card for the Onich hotel in it. He wondered if she was in the bar, as she was not in her room. The bartender knew who Helena was immediately, asking Calum to hold on while he passed the phone to her. Calum hung up.

"I don't know what to say, Anna. I feel completely responsible for this," said Calum miserably.

"I think perhaps I ought to pay her a visit," said Anna. "I'm not having her break into my house when I have my children here."

"Don't worry, Mum. We can look after ourselves," said Ollie appearing at her side, making her wish that she had put them to bed earlier.

"I know you can, but still, she is very naughty if she thinks she can just break into our cottage," said Anna, pulling him on her knee. "Look, let's just put her out of our minds for now. It's a lovely evening; your Uncle Rob has cooked some amazing dinner for us all. We can talk about all this tomorrow."

"Yes, lamb's ready, and I don't know about you, but I'm starving," said Rob.

They all conceded to drop the subject and went over to the table to eat. Calum dug into his lamb, but his mind was on Helena. She had deliberately got the hotel reception to lie for her. The woman was unstable and dangerous if she was breaking into Anna's cottage. It would probably be safer if he left Anna alone, but why should he? He was more attracted to her than he had ever been to any other woman in his life. Surely he was entitled to find some happiness. He had sorely neglected any emotional entanglements during the last few years whilst he built his business. It was something that his mother had nagged him about relentlessly. Helena had been a pleasant distraction, but if he'd only known how difficult she really was, he would never have entertained her in the first place.

Anna was trying hard to remain chirpy for the rest of the evening, but her thoughts kept turning to James and Corri. She had always been a methodical person, thinking things over thoroughly before she came to any decisions. Being spontaneous was not in her nature, but right now, part of her just wanted to get her children and go home.

She sat and listened as Glen relayed embarrassing stories about their childhood, smiling in the right places but not feeling part of the conversation. Calum laughed on cue, but Anna could tell he was as preoccupied as she was.

Ollie had crept back up onto her lap, and James had become very quiet while he sat there playing with his food.

"I think it's time I put these two to bed," she said, getting to her feet as Ollie snuggled into her shoulder.

Anna took hold of James's hand and the three of them went inside to the boys' room. She helped them into their pyjamas, then sent them to brush their teeth while she sorted out their clothes. She noticed the latch on their window was undone, and she wondered if Helena had climbed into their room. She slammed the window shut, locking it and shutting the curtains.

The boys both crawled into bed without an argument. She kissed Ollie, who had already rolled over and shut his eyes, then went over to James, who was lying on his back staring at her with big, brown eyes.

"Are you still mad at Corri?" he whispered.

Anna sat on the side of his bed. "I'm not mad, James. I'm just a little worried that she speaks to you and not to me."

"I know, but she's really nice and she likes me and Ollie," said James.

"I'm sure I would like her too if I got to know her," replied Anna. "James, don't you worry about it, I'm not mad at you. Have you thought about what you want to do tomorrow?"

"I want to swim in the pool," replied James instantly.

"Well we can do that first thing, just you, me and Ollie, before Uncle Glen and Uncle Rob get up, okay?" said Anna, kissing the top of his head.

"Okay," said James, satisfied, then he also rolled over to go to sleep.

Anna shut the door of the boys' room and started to make her way back outside. As she reached the old part of the cottage, she found Calum standing there, waiting for her in the dark.

"I need to talk with you," he said. "I just haven't had the opportunity to apologise properly, and I feel I need to explain."

"Explain? Really, there's no need. I'm sure your girlfriend will move on eventually," said Anna, instantly regretting that she sounded so harsh.

"That's just it. I never viewed Helena as my girlfriend," said Calum.

"Well, she doesn't seem to see it that way. Honestly, Calum, I'd be angry if my supposed boyfriend took me away, then started showing interest in another woman, and then, just dumped me," said Anna.

"I don't know how many times I can say this; it wasn't like that. Helena invited herself on this trip. I realised when we were halfway here that she was going to be a nightmare. I don't know why I agreed to let her come along. I guess it was just easier than arguing with her, but I didn't know you then. I had booked her in at the Onich Hotel without me, before we even set off. She was furious when she found out, and that was the first sign I had that she viewed our relationship as being more than what it was," Calum tried to explain. "Anna, I can't pretend I don't feel anything for you, and I think you must feel it too. From the moment we met, there's been some sort of chemistry between us, and I don't want to let you slip away from me."

In spite of herself, Anna softened a little. "Look, I don't know what to make of it all. I have just divorced a man who lied and cheated on me. I don't want to get dragged into some love triangle, Calum. I like you, and perhaps if Helena was not in the picture, then things would be different. But I can't go through another drama and neither can my boys."

"So, you like me," said Calum suddenly reaching out to put his hands on her shoulders to turn her gently towards him. "Well, that's a start."

"It's not as simple as that," she replied, frustrated that he seemed to ignore everything else she had said.

"It can be," he said and reached down to kiss her, taking her completely by surprise. She almost started to kiss him back when he pulled back abruptly, then held her at arm's length, looking straight into her eyes. "I am going to sort this, Anna. For the first time in my life, I've met a woman that makes me feel like a man should feel. I'm not going to let you go that easily."

"Hey, you two, we were wondering what had happened to you," said Glen, appearing in the doorway.

"I was just saying good bye to Anna," said Calum. "I'm afraid I have to get going now. I'm pretty bushed after my climb today, and I want to sort out this Helena situation early tomorrow."

Calum left shortly after, Anna suddenly said she was tired also and was going to get an early night.

"Oh, you don't get off that easily. It seemed very intense in there a minute ago between you two," said Glen. "And anyway, you haven't told us about those dreams yet."

"There's nothing to tell you about Calum. Glen, I just need some time to gather my thoughts. I tell you all about the dreams tomorrow," replied Anna.

She left her brother and Rob sitting in the garden, not even feeling a little guilty about leaving them to clear up. She'd make it up to them tomorrow. She just felt exhausted after this evening's revelations and needed to sleep. She glanced over at Kirstin's portrait as she took her clothes off. The eyes seemed colder than they had done before and they stared right through her, no longer carefree and happy. She was being ridiculous now; how could a painting change? She was letting this Corri thing really get to her. She got ready for bed, grabbed her paperback book and crawled under the duvet. She had been so tired when she hit the sack every evening that she still hadn't got past chapter three and tonight was no exception. Anna drifted off before she was three pages in.

***

The warmth of the fire did nothing to bring any feeling back to her feet. They had carried down the mountain and over the loch to Colla Stewart's farmstead in Glen Gour.

She had been barely conscious through the journey, awakening only to cry out for her son, Jamie.

Colla's wife Margaret had been taking care of her in the main house. It was three weeks since the massacre and her feet were already blackened and infected with frostbite. They had cut off two of her fingers in an attempt to save her hand, but they knew that her feet were well past saving. Kirstin had been living through days of agony as the warmth in the farmhouse attacked the nerve endings around the blackened, dead tissue of her feet and hands. She slipped in and out of consciousness as gangrene took hold, poisoning her blood and giving her a raging fever. Her hosts knew she was dying but did all they could to keep her comfortable.

Kirstin was in constant torment; even her pain was diminished by the anguish she was going through in her every waking moment. No one would tell her what had happened to her son. Kirstin had not seen Jamie since she had been brought here, and everyone was avoiding answering her when she asked where he was.

They had gently told her that Rab had been killed by the soldiers, so why would they not tell her about Jamie? She remembered handing Jamie over to Flora, and the young nurse had been with her when they reached Meall Mor, but Kirstin had not seen her since.

One night, Kirstin opened her eyes to find she was alone in the darkened room, the only light coming from the fire in the hearth. She was delirious with fever; her only thought was to find her son. He must be here, why were they not letting her see him? She gathered her strength and managed to roll from the bed, clattering down onto the hard floor. The fall winded her, and she gasped for air as she tried to pull herself up. Her feet had no feeling in them now and for a confused moment she stared down at what was left of her deformed, blackened toes. They were useless to her, she couldn't stand so she dragged herself towards the door and somehow managed to push it open, allowing the freezing wind and rain to rush in. Outside she saw a woman standing there, with a shawl wrapped tightly around her shoulder. The woman made no movement towards her, but just stood there watching Kirstin pull herself out the door.

Kirstin was screaming for Jamie, trying to be heard above the wind and pummelling rain. The woman then stepped forward to help, pity all over her face. But Kirstin suddenly recognised her, and her eyes filled with hatred as she recoiled from the woman's touch. It was Corrag the Witch. "Where's Jamie? What did ye dae with him?" Kirstin cried out to her.

The pity that had shown on Corrag's face was now replaced with hostility as she said viciously, "He's safe away frae ye. I told ye this would happen. Yer wee laddie will have no mammie the noo. Ye wouldnae heed my warning, Kirstin MacDonald. None of ye would."

"What have ye done with him, Corrag? Tell me! Ye'll pay for taking my son. I ken it wis you'se who turned the Campbell soldiers against us. Ye had the runes tae dae it. Those stones of black magic, and noo ye've stolen my son," ranted Kirstin hysterically as she lay there. She was soaked to the skin and trembling all over, but Corrag made no move to help the dying woman. "I'll come fir him, Corrag! I'll come fir my son; ye'll never take him."

Margaret Stewart, who had been awoken by the crash of the pots, ran to Kirstin's side. "Wheesht noo Kirstin, what are ye daen oot here?" she cried as she grabbed hold of Kirstin's thin body and hauled her back inside the house.

"She's taken Jamie, she has my wee bairn," Kirstin sobbed.

"Jamie is fine. He's being looked after until ye get well. Ye dinnae want him tae see ye like this noo?" said Margaret soothingly, her eyes full of sadness.

"Ask her," Kirstin mumbled weakly through her tears. "She's here. Corrag has my bairn."

"There's nae one here, Kirstin. Corrag hasnae taken Jamie," said Margaret, smoothing the wet hair back from Kirstin's pale face. "We had to send him away tae safety. It's nae safe roond here for MacDonald's the noo. Ye must ken that, Flora has him. We've told ye that, Kirstin, many times. Why dae ye no believe us?"

"Nae, the witch has taken him. She's here. I ken she's watching me. I just want tae see him. I just want tae see him," Kirstin wept, her heart broken and her strength fading.

Margaret laid her back down gently on the bed, her own shoulder wet through from the girl's tears. Kirstin's eyes were staring into the darkness and Margaret watched on sadly as the life dwindled from them. Kirstin was dead. But she had died broken hearted, still searching for her Jamie, and Margaret knew that was a bad omen.

***

Anna awoke to find her pillow soaked. Her face was streaked with tears and she had a sudden urge to check on her boys. She jumped out of bed darting down the hallway and into their room to find them both fast asleep in their beds. She felt shaken and drained, so she sat at the bottom of James' bed and let the tears come. She was crying for Kirstin, feeling the pain of losing her son. Who was Corrag? Why had she frightened Kirstin so much? Why would Kirstin think she had her son?

Anna felt a sight chill that made her turn towards the window. There was a figure of a woman standing outside, her face staring through the window. Her long, wild red hair was covering most of her face, though Anna could make out her eyes and they were cold and hostile.

Chapter Twelve

It was nine o'clock in the morning and the rain was coming down in torrents. Calum swung his dad's old Jeep Cherokee into the Onich Hotel carpark. He had phoned Helena on her mobile when he had got back to his parents' house the previous evening. She hadn't answered the phone. He was sure that she had guessed that it was him who phoned the bar. He would just have to hope that she was still at the hotel when he got there, which is why he had decided to arrive so early.

As he walked through the hotel lobby towards the dining room, the blonde Australian receptionist was giving directions to a young couple when she met his eyes and gave him a suspicious look. He recognised the accent as her being the one he had spoken to when he had phoned to check on Helena. He could only imagine what story Helena had fed her.

Calum had decided to try another tact. Anna had been right about the way he had treated Helena; he should have realised that she was more invested in their relationship than he was. He'd been selfish and he wanted to apologise, then hopefully draw a line under the whole sorry affair.

He found Helena seated at a table by the window. There was a coffee pot next to her, and when she saw him approaching, she filled a second cup, pushing it towards him as he reached the table. Calum reached down to kiss her cheek, but she sat still staring straight ahead, barely acknowledging his gesture. He sat down opposite her, and still she sat staring right through him.

"Are you all right, Helena?" Calum asked.

Helena's eyes focused slightly, and she smiled at him, "I'm fine, Calum. What did you want to see me about?"

Calum took a deep breath. He had rehearsed this speech all night long, but now he was here in front of her, he wasn't sure where to start. "Look, I'm really sorry the way things have turned out. I never meant to hurt you, Helena. I just didn't realise you felt that way about our relationship. I always assumed it was a casual thing between us."

"Did you really? Or is that just a convenient way to push me aside, because you think you've found someone better?" Helena replied, taking a sip of her coffee, her eyes frozen, staring ahead without showing any sort of emotion.

"It wasn't like that, you must know that. I had never met Anna until we were on the boat that day. I had already decided that you should head back to Edinburgh at that point. The Highlands are clearly not for you; you complained about being here from the minute you arrived," said Calum, trying to keep his voice level.

"You booked me into a hotel on my own. Of course, I complained," replied Helena, her voice also level and controlled.

"I never had any intention of staying at a hotel with my parents' house just down the road. I was coming to visit them and I couldn't expect them to put you up. It would have been very awkward, and we couldn't have slept together in their home. It was you who insisted on coming. You said you had never been to Glencoe and it would be a lovely opportunity for you to have someone to show you around," said Calum. "I'm sorry if you thought it meant something else."

"So, at what point did you decide to pursue mumsy? While we were on the boat?" asked Helena.

"No, of course not. As I said, I didn't even know her. Look, Helena, I'm not here to talk about Anna. She really has nothing to do with this. I hardly know her, and when you saw us at lunch the other day, I was simply thanking her for giving me a lift when I needed it," said Calum, trying to keep his voice low as the breakfast room was beginning to fill up with hotel guests.

"I don't like it when you lie to me, Calum, so don't test me. I saw the way you looked at her. Do you really think I'm going to allow you to treat me like a fool? I made you, Calum. I put you and your business on the map. You owe me," she replied, yet she seemed so detached from what she was saying, it was almost as if she was reading from a script.

"What are you talking about? You have nothing to do with my business. Your firm simply handles my advertising, and I can certainly stop that from happening. Helena, I don't need to be put on anyone's map," Calum whispered at her angrily across the table. "I'm really sorry if you think I've treated you like a fool. It was not my intention and if I could change things, I would. But I just don't have these sort of feelings for you. I never have done; I just thought we were close friends."

"Friends!" hissed Helena, her voice now getting louder which, strangely, Calum found to be a relief. This was more like the Helena he knew . "That's what you call six months of sleeping together. We are known as a couple all over Edinburgh. Are you telling me you didn't realize that?"

"I'm sorry, I don't know what else to say. We never discussed any relationship. I saw you maybe once a fortnight, if that. I never intended it to become a serious thing between us," said Calum, putting his head in his hands.

"You can leave now, Calum, but don't think for one moment this is over. People don't get away with treating me like this," Helena said calmly, leaning back in her chair to gaze out over the water.

"Helena, did you break into Anna's cottage yesterday?" Calum sighed.

"How would you know someone broke into her cottage if you haven't seen her?" asked Helena, still looking out over the loch.

"I didn't say I hadn't seen her. I was over at Anna's last night for a BBQ. Someone had seen you climbing in the boys' bedroom window. What the hell were you playing at?" said Calum, feeling himself losing his patience with her dismissive attitude.

"Now, who would have seen me, I wonder? No one was there; oh, unless it's Corri you're talking about. I can't believe that stupid witch is still interfering in my life," said Helena, her eyes now fully glazed over.

"What are you talking about? How do you know anything about Corri?" replied Calum, taken completely by surprise.

Helena turned to face him, her eyes once again coming back into focus. "Is there anything else you want, Calum?"

"I want you to get a grip. I've never seen you like this. You need to go home, Helena; I'm getting worried about you. You need to see someone, even if it's only your friends. You cannot hang out in this hotel on your own; it's making you crazy. Look, I'll phone you when I get back to Edinburgh, then we can chat again," said Calum.

"Oh, I'm not going home, darling. I'm just getting started. I was wrong about this place, and I'm certainly not alone, so don't worry about me, I really do like it here," she replied, smiling at him, her eyes unreadable.

Calum could feel himself start to tremble. "What the hell is that supposed to mean? What do you think you're going to do here?"

"That's for me to know and you to find out," Helena replied, getting to her feet.

"Sit down!" he growled at her through gritted teeth, aware that people were looking over at them now.

"Oh, I don't think so, darling. We have nothing else to say. So, I'll be seeing you soon," she said and walked out of the breakfast room.

Calum sat there, stunned and suddenly very afraid. He had never met anyone like this before; to say she was unreasonable was an understatement. But what really frightened him was what she could be capable of. He felt absolutely helpless, she had definitely threatened him, but did that mean she would be a threat to Anna also?

How the hell had she known about James's imaginary friend, Corri? Had she been spying on them the night before? She must have been hiding and watching them at the BBQ. Well, at least he hadn't lied to her about being there; she couldn't accuse him of that. It was obvious that Helena was unstable, and he would have to warn them at Kirstin's Cot. If she showed up there again, they would have to phone the police. He didn't know what else to do.

***

Helena left the hotel immediately. It was still raining as she went to her car. Kirstin was ever present in the back of her mind, guiding her onwards with a sense of urgency. She had to help Kirstin get her son back; that was all that mattered now.

She drove into Fort William and bought herself some hiking clothes and boots, which she changed into in the shop changing room after she had purchased them. She then bought some binoculars and a torch. By the time she had made all her purchases, the rain had finally stopped, and the sun was breaking through. Helena drove straight from the town back to Glencoe village, where she parked her car. She had chosen her route through the west of the Pap of Glencoe onto Aonach Eagach (The Notched Ridge) which stretched nine kilometres to the Devil's Staircase in the east. Helena was not planning on going that far though; she was climbing up its highest peak, Sgorr nam Fiannaidh (The Peak of the Giants).

She knew the way, Kirstin had shown her, and she could have found it blindfolded. Kirstin and Rab would always climb up here after kirk on Sundays when the weather was fine. It was early afternoon and she was about three quarters of the way up towards the peak when Helena veered off the track and made her way down a short, steep rocky incline hidden from view to the regular hikers. It descended down to a narrow ledge, about two feet wide, that led precariously around a hanging cliff face. Helena began to manoeuvre her way easily around the ledge, showing no fear considering how slippery it was from all the rain. It eventually led into a small cave hidden in the rocks, with a direct view down over Glencoe Village and Kirstin's Cot. Kirstin and Rab would spend many a day here, watching the people below in the glen and making plans for their future, before they made love. Jamie was conceived in this cave one warm September's day, and Helena could feel Kirstin's heart break as she thought of her son.

She pulled out the binoculars; she had a perfect view of the cottage from here. She lay down on her stomach on the damp, mossy floor of the cave, putting the binoculars to her eyes, then aligned them into focus directly on the cottage. There were three cars parked there now, and Helena knew that the jeep belonged to Calum. He must have driven straight back there after their conversation at the hotel. Obviously, the other car meant that Anna had guests staying with her. That would present a problem. Helena would have to find some way to get around that.

She continued to lie in the same position for the next hour, sharing her thoughts with Kirstin who was forever present in her mind. The level of Calum's betrayal threatened to overwhelm her, and as Calum continued to stay on at the cottage, Helena could feel anger rising inside her. Kirstin spoke to her soothingly, smothering her rage, keeping her calm and methodical. Now was not the time for emotions; that time had passed. Now, it is time to seek revenge.

The door opened and the two small boys came running out with that big dog of theirs. Helena watched as they played in the garden, the smaller one collecting a pile of sticks, then wrestling with the dog. The older boy was climbing up onto one of the small trees by the fence line. Helena focused her binoculars on him, feeling drawn to watch him.

"That's my boy," whispered Kirstin.

"But he is older," said Helena.

"Time may have passed, but I would recognise my Jamie anywhere."

Chapter Thirteen

"I'm sorry. I apologised and tried to reason with Helena, but she just wasn't prepared to listen. I just don't know what's going on with her. I've never seen her like this before; what she was saying didn't make any sense. We saw each other occasionally, not regularly, I had no idea she felt that way about me. I made a huge mistake allowing her to accompany me to Glencoe and now she is refusing to leave," said Calum as they all sat at the kitchen table. "She was completely calm, but in a scary sort of way."

"Do you think she will try anything else?" asked Rob. "She doesn't sound like she's got it together."

"I honestly don't know," said Calum miserably. "I think she must have been spying on us last night at the barbeque. She mentioned Corri, and I don't know how the hell she would have heard that name otherwise."

"Maybe we should contact the police, ask them to give her a bit of a warning. It might be enough to send her packing," suggested Glen.

Anna had been quiet since Calum arrived, she was still shaken from the face she had seen at the window the night before. "I don't know. I feel a little sorry for her. She obviously had strong feelings for you; perhaps once your words sink in, she'll realise it's pointless and head for home," said Anna. "I just wish she wasn't blaming me, but I guess she has to find someone to point the finger at, even if it is ridiculous."

Calum raised his eyebrows slightly at Anna's last comment, but she didn't seem to notice, and he saw she looked tired and a little drawn.

"Are you okay?" he asked her suddenly.

To her absolute horror, Anna suddenly burst into tears. She couldn't stop and was totally mortified at her lack of control. Glen immediately got up to hug his sister. "It's okay, it's been quite an emotional ride recently. You don't need all this on your plate too," he said, glaring at Calum.

"No, no, it's not that," cried Anna, trying desperately to gain control of her sobbing. "I haven't told you yet, but I had another dream last night, it was so real, and when I woke I saw what must have been Corri, watching me through my window. I ran outside, but she was gone. She did not look in the least bit friendly to me; in fact, the look in her eyes was murderous."

"God, Anna, why didn't you wake us?" said her brother. "You still haven't told us about those dreams."

"I seem to be reliving what happened to Kirstin on the night of the massacre. At first I thought it was my imagination, but when I awake from these dreams, I have the same physical symptoms that Kirstin was suffering from. The first time, my feet were frozen like ice; I could hardly walk on them. Then, last night, I watched as Kirstin died horrifically from frostbite and blood poisoning. I felt every bit of the pain she was suffering, but I also felt her heartache, as she never knew what happened to her son, Jamie. She never saw him again, and she was crying out for him when she died. It was so real; I could feel her desperation. It was awful," Anna told them tearfully.

"Perhaps you should think about leaving, Anna. This place is really affecting you; there is something not right about it," said Rob.

"I don't want to leave, I've planned this trip for too long and the boys are having a ball," said Anna, pulling herself together somewhat. She met Calum's eyes. "I'm sorry; honestly it's got nothing to do with Helena. I'm sure she'll just give up and go home."

"I hope so. I feel very responsible for this. I wish I could help more. I think I should contact Kenneth Macfie; I know you mentioned already that Angus was going to talk to him. Perhaps if I meet up with him he could shed some more light on what actually happened with Kirstin, and then we can finally lay this ghost to rest," suggested Calum.

"I'll come with you," said Anna turning to her brother. "That's if you and Rob don't mind watching the boys for bit?"

"Of course not. Why don't you take her out for the day, Calum? She could do with a break from this place," said Glen.

"It would be my pleasure," Calum replied as Anna went off to wash her face and freshen up.

She was very quiet as Calum drove them into Fort William, so he kept the conversation light, pointing out places he used to go when he was a boy. She listened with interest but he could tell she was still embarrassed about her outpouring of emotion earlier.

They pulled into the carpark next to the pier, the rain had started again, so Calum pulled out his father's huge golf umbrella from the back of the jeep. He walked round to cover Anna with it as she got out the car. They started to walk, awkwardly close as he was holding the umbrella high above them. Anna slipped her hand into the crook of his arm, then things became easier as they strolled down Fort William high street. Calum was almost sorry when the rain shower stopped suddenly and he could collapse the umbrella.

They had phoned Kenneth, who agreed to meet them at the Grog and Gruel pub, on the high street. It was difficult to get a table there during the summer months, but it was getting late for lunch now, so the bar was not so busy. They both ordered a beer and decided on some nachos to share as neither of them had eaten that day. They were half way through the enormous serving when Kenneth appeared, along with Angus traipsing in after him.

"I hope ye dinnae mind, but I brought this reprobate along. It sounds as though ye're having quite a time of it at that cottage of his," said Kenneth, plonking himself down on the opposite side of the table from them, while Angus went to the bar to get them both a beer. Kenneth held his hand out to Anna. "We havnae met, I ken young Calum here, though his accent has changed since he's bin living in the posh parts. I'm Kenneth Macfie, local historian, or local busy body, depending on which way ye look at it. If yer a Campbell, then I'm the latter," he said, shaking Anna's hand.

He was of medium height and medium build but had a huge shock of white hair that looked unbrushed and was in deep contrast with his enormous black eyebrows that hooded his wild, intense grey eyes. Anna could not begin to guess how old he was, nor whether he was joking or not about the Campbells.

Angus sat down, putting a couple of froth-topped pints of beer on the table. "Has he introduced himself yet?" he asked.

"Aye, he has," grinned Calum. "He's still scaring the shit out the tourists, is he?"

"I'm right here; I can hear ye," said Kenneth. "And that's all these tourists want half the time. A good scare tae tell their friends aboot when they get hame."

Calum laughed and Angus shook his head in feigned disgust. "So, I hear your still having problems with Kirstin?" Angus turned towards Anna, who was watching them with amusement.

"Yes, I know you'll think I'm crazy, but I've been having some terrible dreams, where I seem to be reliving what happened to her," said Anna, the smile leaving her face.

"I dinnae think yer crazy. I think Angus here is crazy allowing people tae come and stay at that auld cottage. Nelly would be turning in her grave," said Kenneth.

"Och Ken, it wasnae as if I had a choice. It was either me, or it would go tae some travel agents doon in Glasgie, they wouldnae even begin tae know the history of the place," said Angus.

"It's nae you'se I'm blaming. Nelly shouldnae have left that cottage tae her nephew; he disnae have a clue what can of worms he's opening letting the place oot tae the public," said Ken.

"Can you tell us more about the 'can of worms' it has opened?" said Anna. "Is the place safe? I have two small boys who absolutely love it there, but if it's not safe..."

"I've been trying tae dig up what I can on the cottage. Nelly had told me a while ago that the place was haunted with the ghost of Kirstin MacDonald, the young wife of Rab who wis killed in the massacre. Kirstin perished also, but it was a couple of weeks later due tae the frostbite that afflicted her when she escaped the soldiers. They had taken her over to the Stewarts at Glen Gour, and it wis said she died crying oot for her son, Jamie. She never got tae hold her bairn again after that night, nor kent what had happened tae him," said Ken.

"You just described the dream I had last night; the pain and anguish was so real. I can't imagine losing your child that way," said Anna.

"By all accounts, Kirstin and Rab's son lived. The nurse who carried him that night managed tae get the child tae Fort William, passing through the garrison stationed there. The Governor, Lt. Colonel John Hill, who led the garrison had some level of sympathy for the MacDonald's. Perhaps he felt a measure of guilt aboot what had happened tae them. MacIain MacDonald had come tae him before, and tried tae swear the oath, pledging allegiance to William of Orange. It was a Royal Proclamation, offering a general pardon to all the Highland clans providing they swore an oath of allegiance tae the King before 1st January 1692. However, Colonel Hill refused to administer the required oath, as he was not authorised to receive it. Instead, he sent the old chieftain on tae Inveraray, tae have the oath received by Sir Colin Campbell. Lt. Colonel Hill also gave MacIain a letter tae carry wi' him, stating that he had arrived tae sign the oath within the allotted time.

"However, the weather was particularly bad, and MacIain was an old man. It took him three long days tae reach Inveraray, and when he arrived, he found that Sir Colin wisnae there. He wis aff celebrating the New Year wi' his family, so the old man had tae wait another three days. It wasnae until the 6th January that Sir Colin Campbell finally accepted the oath from the Glencoe MacDonalds.

"It wis widely kent that there were other Highland Chieftains who didnae sign by the designated time, yet their oaths were accepted without question. MacIain had nae reason tae think that his would be any different. The MacDonalds of Glencoe were withoot a doubt targeted, and I think Colonel Hill kent that. So, taking pity on the nurse, he sent two of his soldiers to escort her and Kirstin's bairn north, tae family in Glenmoriston.

"It was said that Jamie lived tae a good age and led another clan during the Jacobite uprising over fifty years later, but Kirstin never kent that her son had escaped," Kenneth told them.

Anna could see what Calum had meant about Kenneth being a good story teller. "But Flora was with Kirstin when they arrived at Meall Mor. Why would she leave her?"

"I'm sorry, who's Flora?" asked Kenneth.

"The nurse, her name was Flora. Kirstin was with her in my dream," said Anna, realizing it was unlikely that the name of the nurse had been documented.

"Well I cannae answer ye that lass, all I kent wis that Kirstin died frae her frostbite. She wis taken tae Glen Luce where the Stewarts did all they could, but she wis tae far gone. She died two weeks after the massacre," said Kenneth.

"What happened tae Rab?" asked Calum.

"He died on the night of the massacre. He was captured by Captain John Lindsay when he tried tae get tae MacIain's hoose. He didnae ken the chief wis already deed until he found MacIain's wife, thrown naked oot intae the snow. He threw his plaid around her, she wis hysterical and rambling. Her hands were covered in blood, some say the soldiers had gnawed the rings frae her fingers. Lindsay and his men caught up wi' Rab, as he tried tae help Lady MacDonald. They shot him once wi' a musket, then finished him aff wi' their dirks," said Kenneth.

"That whole night was pretty barbaric if you were a MacDonald," said Calum.

"That still doesn't solve the problem of Kirstin," said Anna. "She is haunting the place and she's angry. I could feel it when she smashed the plates that day. How can we let her know her child lived?"

"I cannae help ye wi' that. I may tell a good gruesome tale, but I havnae a clue when it comes tae ghosts," said Kenneth, his grey eyes opened wider than ever.

"At least I understand it all a bit better now. And I know that her son survived. Maybe Kirstin will sense that if she tries to visit my dreams again. I could somehow let her know that Jamie survived," said Anna. "There was one other thing that seemed strange. In my dream, when Kirstin was dying, she tried to leave the house to find Jamie, but instead, she found Corrag standing outside as if she was waiting for her. I felt Kirstin's fear of this woman but then it turned to anger as she accused her of taking Jamie. Corrag didn't try to deny it. It was as if she was taunting Kirstin, even though the poor woman was obviously dying. She made no attempt to help Kirstin, nor set her mind at ease."

"Corrag the Witch, there is a famous legend aboot her roond these parts. It's in the National Trust book of Glencoe, called 'The Sword in the Water'. The story tells of the witch called Corrag, who warned the MacDonalds of the forthcoming massacre, but they didnae believe her," said Kenneth enjoying his captive audience." Corrag, realising it was useless, went and hid in the hills until the murderous deed wis over. She then descended frae her hiding spot tae find all the hooses burnt tae the ground, dead bodies strewn everywhere and the place deserted. She went over tae what wis left of MacIain's hoose and found his broadsword. She picked it up and took it tae the Glen of Narrow's, where she threw it in the water, casting a spell as she did so. She said that the men of Glencoe had suffered enough, and as long as that sword lay undisturbed in the water, nae mare men of the Glen would die in battle ever again."

"Well, she couldn't have been that bad if she cared enough to do that," said Anna. "Did any more men die?"

"Well, here's the funny thing. Nae one ever did die, in all the wars that were fought, not one man frae Glencoe was killed. Not during the Jacobite uprising or the Highland Clearance nor even at Waterloo or in the Crimean or Boer wars. Not until the 30th June 1916 when they had been dredging the loch to enable bigger ships in tae collect the aluminium from Kinlochleven fir the war effort.

"The Captain of the dredger arrived at the hotel that night carrying the hilt of an old sword he had dredged up frae the bottom of the Loch. The local men were horrified and rowed oot intae the Loch and threw the sword back in.

"The next day wis the 1st July 1916, the first Battle of the Somme in the first World War. Seven men frae the Glen were killed on the front line that day," said Kenneth, his eyes fixed intensely on Anna.

"Are you for real?" Calum interjected, breaking the spell Kenneth had created. "I've never heard that story told like that before."

"Well ye havnae been paying much attention then, have yae sonnie," said Kenneth with a wicked glint.

Anna couldn't help smiling at Calum's facial expression. "I'm just glad I know more about what happened to Jamie. Maybe we'll be able to let Kirstin know in some way that her son was saved. Then maybe she can move on or rest in peace or do what other dead people do."

"I hope yer right," said Angus. "Or I'm going tae have a real problem trying tae rent that cottage oot, if it's as haunted as yer all saying it is."

"Perhaps the answer lies wi' Corrag. It seems she's bin visiting yer wee laddie, so I'm told," said Kenneth, glancing over at Angus for confirmation.

"Yes, she seems to have been visiting James since we arrived. Ollie sees her as well, and I'm sure I saw her in the early hours this morning, staring through the boys' bedroom window," said Anna, shivering at the memory of it. "It's strange though, the boys seem to like her, they think she's nice, but she was staring daggers at me."

"Aye well, Corrag wis a bit of an outcast. Nae one kent where she came frae, and they just tolerated her living amongst them. The highlanders were more accepting of witches and healers than the towns folk. She probably had a hard life and wouldnae trust anyone," said Kenneth.

"Just listen to us, sitting here in a pub talking about ghosts all afternoon," said Calum. "If anyone had asked me what I was going to be doing this summer, this wouldn't have been on my list. Come on, Anna, I'm supposed to be cheering you up."

Anna smiled, "I know, it's like some old horror film. Still, you probably wouldn't have come up with crazy, stalker ex-girlfriend either," she said wickedly.

"Ouch, that hurt," answered Calum, rolling his eyes.

"Are we missing something?" asked Angus.

"Only that it seems an acquaintance of mine from Edinburgh has broken into the cottage for some reason we cannot fathom," replied Calum, ignoring Anna's raised eyebrows when he said 'acquaintance'.

"She didnae take anything, did she?" asked Angus, frowning. "Dae we need tae call the police?"

"We don't know what she was doing? Trying to find out about Anna, I would think. And yes, we will be calling the police if it happens again. I've had a word with her this morning over at the Onich Hotel, but she doesn't seem to be very reasonable at the moment. Nor is she making any sense. At one point, she mentioned Corri. That's what James and Ollie call Corrag. I couldn't figure out how the hell she knew about her, unless she has been spying on us," explained Calum.

"Is she staying at the Onich?" asked Kenneth.

"Aye, she is," confirmed Calum

"That might explain it then. I met Angus there the other night, after Anna had bin tae tell him aboot the ghost," said Kenneth, turning to Anna. "We were talking aboot what had happened, and aboot this Corri who wis talking tae yer wee boy. I noticed a young woman knocking back the wine and sitting at the bar next tae us. I wondered whether she wis trying tae listen tae us and thought it wis a wee bit strange her being on her own. She could have over heard us talk aboot Corri easily; I never thought much more aboot it until noo."

"That's somewhat a relief," said Anna. "I really thought she had been watching us; maybe she was just trying to scare you, Calum. She is hurt and angry, and you know the old saying, 'hell hath no fury' and all that."

It was after three o' clock when Calum actually managed to drag Anna away from Kenneth and Angus. The rain had moved on, allowing the sky to turn blue and the sun to warm the air. There was a haze over Ben Nevis as the moisture on its slopes evaporated in the sunshine.

"Come on, we have the rest of the day for me to show you some of my old haunts," said Calum after they made their goodbyes at the pub. He took Anna's hand and led her back to the car.

Chapter Fourteen

Calum drove them to Kinlochleven, a picturesque town set at the eastern end of Loch Leven. It was once Scotland's main producer of aluminium, but now it focused mainly on the tourist industry. The town looked like a quaint, picture postcard village surrounded on all sides by huge mountain ranges. It had village greens dotted around, with park benches and picnic tables. Calum parked his car next to the church and then led Anna into the forest behind it, where a track led them upwards through the thick trees and giant ferns.

It was quiet, late afternoon, so it was likely that most of the hikers had been and gone from this spot by now, Calum explained to her. As they carried on up the carefully carved track, Anna thought she could hear the sound of a waterfall; then, Calum suddenly grabbed her hand and pulled her off the route.

They walked over some very rocky terrain but soon arrived at what looked like a fairy tale woodland dell, with sunbeams shooting through the green, leafy trees. Running through the dell was a burn that was fed from a crystal-clear pool that stood at the bottom of a cliff face. There were more giant ferns surrounding the pool, whilst a huge waterfall splashed down into it.

"This is Grey Mares Tail, the highest waterfall around here, nearly fifty metres I believe," said Calum, then grinned as he said, "We used to come here as teenagers on weekends, drinking beer, or whatever we could get our hands on."

"It's beautiful. I'm not surprised you hung out here," said Anna, impressed that such a magical place remained so secluded.

"I had my first kiss here, with Shonand MacPherson. I'll never forget it, it was cold and wet, and I thought I had done it wrong. Shonand MacPherson had kissed just about every boy in my class and I think I was the last. She didn't want to kiss me again after it; I felt so humiliated," admitted Calum with a woeful expression.

Anna burst out laughing, her heart feeling much lighter in this place. "It's incredible, really magical, Calum. Thanks for bringing me here."

"Well, they do say it is magical. If local legends were to be believed, Merlin brought Queen Guinevere here to protect her from Mordred," said Calum, loving that Anna's beautiful face was lit up with humour.

"Aren't we a bit far away from Camelot, here in the highlands of Scotland?" she replied.

"Oh, that's just one legend. Another says the Pontius Pilot was born under this waterfall," said Calum, trying to spill the words out before he fell about in laughter at her sceptical expression.

"What! Really! You're not serious," cried Anna. "We're even further away from Jerusalem. This place is epic!"

Calum turned to face her. He loved the sound of her laughing, and he just couldn't help himself. Still holding her hand, he gently pulled her towards him, leaning down to kiss her.

This time, Anna had been expecting it and fell into his arms willingly. She kissed him back, her whole body alive with excitement and an overwhelming surge of passion.

She had no idea how long they stood there before Calum pulled his mouth away, looking into her face. His face was deadly serious now as he looked at her, his eyes were hungry with desire. "Follow me," he said as he led her, splashing through the stream to the other side and then up towards the waterfall.

There were rocks hidden behind the falling water, and Calum pulled Anna up behind them to where a natural small passageway led through the rocks and out into another little dell, completely hidden within the cliff face and covered by the surrounding plants and trees. It was dark and smelt of pine and moss, completely protected from the elements.

"How did you find this place?" asked Anna, but was silenced as he pulled her to him again, kissing her deeply. She felt her desire rise to meet his. Never in her life had she felt this way, and she didn't resist when he knelt on the soft ground, laying down his jacket, then pulled Anna on top of him.

He kissed her with an urgency now, the taste of her overwhelming him, threatening to make him lose control in a way he had never experienced before. Anna's passion met his; no words were needed as they clawed at one another's clothing. The roar of the waterfall rang in their ears as they made love hidden away from the world.

They emerged from their little hideaway a couple of hours later, feeling like children playing 'hide and go seek' as they checked around to make sure they hadn't been spotted. The place was deserted.

"I never knew I had that in me," said Anna, smiling coyly. "I've never done anything like that before. Have I lost your respect now?"

"Never," said Calum, wrapping his arms around her. "I want to do it again; you were amazing. No one has ever made me feel that way.'"

"But what about Shonand MacPherson?" teased Anna.

"What? No, we were only fourteen. I never even got to first base," laughed Calum.

They walked back down the path to Calum's car, his arm draped over her shoulders as she leaned into him. When they got to the jeep, Anna tried to phone her brother to check on the boys, but she had no reception.

"Glen said I was to take you out for the day," said Calum. "He won't expect us back until later."

"He wouldn't have expected us to do what we just did either," said Anna.

"Are you regretting it?" asked Calum, suddenly concerned.

"No, not at all. For the first time in a long time I just feel completely free," replied Anna, her eyes shining.

"Does that mean we can do it again?" Calum asked hopefully.

"Yes, I think that's exactly what that means," replied Anna.

Chapter Fifteen

Corrag watched James and Ollie playing in the garden. She knew Kirstin was watching them, but she couldn't quite sense whereabouts she was. Kirstin had managed to remain hidden ever since James and his brother had arrived at the cottage. Corrag had not expected that; she had been sure that the children's arrival would have drawn Kirstin out. The boy, James, had a sensitive power within him, enabling him to communicate with the other side. Corrag guessed that Kirstin had sensed him and would probably wish to claim him as her own.

If only Corrag had her beloved runes, she would have been able to stop Kirstin by now. But her runes were long gone, along with her earthly body. She would have to find another way to help Kirstin move on from the Otherworld. It was, after all, her fault that Kirstin was there.

Corrag had spent centuries trying to find Kirstin's spirit, but she could not cross to the Otherworld; she was trapped as an earthbound spirit. The final curse she had cast on Kirstin had condemned her also. Until she could put things right, she would have to walk the earth alone.

She did not wish James any harm, but she needed him to lure out Kirstin's spirit. James's mother was going to be a problem, for she would not leave her children on their own. James was watched constantly, and he would not follow Corrag without telling his mother first. She would have to think of another way to get him to Kirstin.

***

Glencoe, 1688

Kirstin's life here in Glencoe was a little tougher than she had dreamt it would be. She had always been a spirited girl who liked to push the boundaries. When she had first arrived in Glencoe as the wife of Rab MacDonald, her honeymoon was soon over, as she was faced with the chores and the hardships involved in living as a highlander's wife. She had never had to work as part of a community before, and was certainly not used to working outside in all weather. The great mountain range showed no pity, nor protected them from the deluge of rain and snow that often came upon them.

Rab was kind and patient with his young, pretty bride, still enamoured by her delicate beauty and soft-spoken tongue. But the MacDonald's were a brave and boisterous bunch, with Rab often out riding with the rest of the men. They had a reputation for being cattle thieves and raiders, a title that was not altogether unjustified. The MacDonalds were on constant alert, protecting their territory from reprisal raids.

Kirstin was lonely when Rab left on these raids during the first year of their marriage. She had not found it easy to fit in with the other women of Glencoe. The language was a problem from the start, as the women spoke in Gaelic around her, and Kirstin, who had been brought up as a lowlander, spoke only Middle Scots. Kirstin knew that most of them could actually speak her language, but they had thought her soft and spoilt and kept their distance from her. They were never cruel, nor unkind towards her, as their men folk would not have put up with that sort of behaviour.

A few months after she had arrived, Kirstin discovered that many of MacDonald's in Glencoe had expected Rab to marry one of MacIain's daughters, a pretty, mousy haired young girl by the name of Jeannie. Kirstin's unexpected arrival in the Glen had broken young Jeannie's heart, instantly alienating Kirstin from the other women.

Kirstin was the daughter of a farmer who lived in Auchincloich in Ayershire. She was the youngest of two surviving girls and one boy, and she was the apple of her father's eye. Three of her older siblings had died from the plague, and then it took her mother when Kirstin was a baby. Kirstin's oldest sister, Margaret, was left to raise Kirstin, but Margaret became bitter and angry at the amount of attention their father lavished on the young girl.

As Kirstin got older, Margaret complained regularly to their father about Kirstin's lack of obedience and discipline. She flirted openly with the boys from the village and mocked Margaret for being left an old maid.

Kirstin's father had ignored Margaret's complaining for the most part, until one of his neighbours complained that Kirstin was trying to persuade his son to run off with her. Her father realised it was time to take her in hand, so shortly before her seventeenth birthday, he took Kirstin to Glasgow with him whilst he conducted his business. They stayed at his old friends', and he watched on with amusement as Kirstin relished the excitement of being in a big, bustling town

Rab was in Glasgow with MacIain, buying some grain to boost their supplies for the harsh winter ahead. Kirstin had taken one look at the strong, handsome, tanned young highlander, with his sun kissed hair worn long in a warrior's tail, and his melting green eyes that flirted unashamedly with her. She knew she wanted him there and then, and Rab was of the same mind. Whilst her father negotiated prices for his barley crop, Kirstin negotiated the logistics of running away with Rab.

MacIain had not been happy when Rab had come to him to ask if he could bring Kirstin back with them. He insisted that the young Macdonald approach Kirstin's father for his permission. Rab did as MacIain told him, but Kirstin's father was not about to give up his daughter to a wild highlander.

Desperation drove the young couple, and Rab found a preacher, who for a small amount of coin would marry them, there and then. Her father's despair when Kirstin told him what they had done angered her. Surely, he knew that she would not be happy as some farmer's wife in a boring, small town.

MacIain MacDonald was equally unhappy with the rash decision these youngsters had made. But the deed was done and could not be reversed. So Kirstin rode off with her new husband and family, seething that her father had refused to give her his blessing.

Whatever fantasy Kirstin thought she was going to live up in the mountains with Rab, was soon dashed by the reality of living as a highlander. But she loved Rab, and he did his best to make life easier for her.

Loneliness had sent Kirstin walking in the mountains when Rab was gone, and it was there, near Loch Achtriochtan, that she discovered the small hut belonging to Corrag, the witch of the Glencoe.

Corrag was unmarried, in her thirties, although it was hard to tell her age from the harsh life she led. Her hair hung loose and long, covering half of her face. It was a strange colour, not the orangey ginger that was common in the Highlands but a deeper red, like the last moments of a setting sun. From what Kirstin could see of her face, it was lined and there was something branded on one of her cheeks. Corrag subconsciously pulled her hair over to hide it as she saw Kirstin looking at her. Corrag was very thin, her face was lined, making her look older than her age, and some of her teeth were missing. Her hair was her most striking feature, and she hadn't bothered to tie it back like most of the other women did. Corrag's grey eyes gazed at Kirstin with suspicion as the young woman approached.

The MacDonalds used Corrag as their hedge witch, buying herbs and medicines from her. They left her alone most of the time and they never questioned where she had come from. They would bring her eggs, bread and milk in return for her treatments. MacIain would never let someone starve whilst living under his watch.

Kirstin introduced herself to the witch, and for the first time since the young woman had arrived in Glencoe, Corrag spoke to her in her own tongue. She invited Kirstin into her home, and as usual, Kirstin's curiosity got the better of her, so she entered the small, dark hovel.

There was one candle burning, which gave just enough light to see by. There were bones of all different sorts of birds and animals hanging from the roof by grass twine. They jingled as Corrag brushed past them and pointed to a heap of skins on the floor for Kirstin to sit on.

It was the first of many visits for young Kirstin to the witch's hut, and they soon became friends. Corrag told Kirstin little of her life, but Kirstin did establish that the witch's life would have been different if she hadn't been branded with a large 'W' on the side of her cheek for all to see. She said she was once a beautiful woman, but was accused of being a witch, a crime she denied. She had managed to escape but not before they disfigured her for the rest of her life. From then on, she had always been accused of being a witch, so she took refuge in the Highlands.

Corrag had in her possession an old leather pouch containing some ancient and chipped runes. She tipped the runes onto the mat in front of Kirstin, who had never seen the likes before.

Corrag explained to Kirstin that these runes were carved by Sadbh, a beautiful young girl who lived at the beginning of time, in a cave high above Glencoe. An evil druid fell in love with her, but she spurned his advances so he turned her into a deer with his Hazel Wand. Sadbh lived alone in the mountains until she met Fionn Mac Cumhail, an Irish Warrior who almost killed her with his bow. She transformed back into a woman and Fionn fell in love with her. She soon became pregnant, but the druid, possessed by jealousy, transformed her again into a deer. Sadbh was cursed to live in the

114

wilds forever, but she returned to the cave to give birth to a son she named Ossian, meaning 'little faun'.

Fionn found his son, but never saw Sadbh again. His son wielded powerful magic and grew to be a great warrior, who could run faster and leap higher than any other man. He also wrote the most beautiful poetry that could bring a tear to the cruellest of men. Ossian travelled and lived for a while in a place of timeless beauty known as Tir na nOg, the Land of Youth, before he eventually returned to his homeland. When he stepped off the boat, all the years he had been gone caught up with him, and he instantly became an old man and died.

Corrag called the stones 'Ossian Runes' and believed them to hold ancient druid magic. She threw them on the ground in front of Kirstin, then told the young woman of her past life in such detail that Kirstin couldn't help but be astonished. Instead of being afraid, in a world where witchcraft was punishable in the most heinous of ways, Kirstin was instead fascinated and asked Corrag if she would teach her to read the runes.

As the days and weeks went by, the runes had a strange effect on Kirstin, feeding her with their power so that the young woman hated to be apart from them. So, Kirstin visited with Corrag almost daily over the next few months, pretending to her husband that she was being charitable by bringing the lonely woman food. Corrag taught her how to read the runes and how to make simple potions and spells. Corrag was enamoured with this beautiful young woman and came to look forward to her visits. She loved to watch Kirstin handle the runes, caressing them with her fingers in such a sensual way that it emphasized to Corrag how lonely she had been living there by herself. Kirstin was beautiful and fresh faced, untouched by the rough mountain existence. Her enthusiasm for Corrag and her runes was intoxicating, and Corrag found herself falling in love with this young woman.

Kirstin was in her second year of marriage and still had not become pregnant. She knew Rab was disappointed, so she begged Corrag for help. Corrag was reluctant at first, not wanting to share Kirstin with anyone else. But Kirstin kept pressing her and eventually the witch agreed. She used the rune magic and created a potion from moss and fungi, then told Kirstin to drop some of the potion into Rab's dram before bed, then to take a sip herself. Kirstin did this, the taste was foul, but Rab did not seem to notice, already having had his fair share of whiskey.

Meanwhile, it had become common gossip amongst the other women that Kirstin was spending so much time with Corrag, and before long, whispers around the glen reached Rab's ears. He was angry that his wife had been neglecting her work to go visit the witch, and he forbade her from going to Corrag's again. Kirstin may have been in more trouble had she not been able to tell her husband that, at last, she was pregnant.

Kirstin did not visit Corrag again during her pregnancy. She had no need of the hedge witch now, and the power of the runes did not hold the same attraction over her as it had done before.

Kirstin discovered that with the news of her forthcoming baby, she was now accepted by the other women in the glen. They befriended her, taught her their language and helped her with her chores. Rab worked hard on extending their cottage to make space for the baby, and Kirstin finally received a cart full of belongings and furniture sent from her father's house in Auchincloich. With it came a letter from her sister with all the news from Ayershire, but there was no mention of her father. Kirstin was disappointed that he had still not forgiven her for leaving with Rab. Perhaps when he knew he had a grandson, things would be different.

Corrag was heartbroken at Kirstin's betrayal. She felt used and empty and was angry with herself for putting her trust in someone again. She spent months living in a cloud of malevolence with her runes, her only true friends in this cruel world.

Kirstin's time for having her baby was drawing near when, out of the blue, Corrag came to visit her at her home. Kirstin was horrified when she saw the witch at her door, pulling her inside quickly, demanding if anyone had seen her.

"A've brought a wee gift fir the bairn," said Corrag coldly. "A've bin waiting fir yae tae come."

"I dinnae want yer gift, Corrag. My husband will nae allow it," cried Kirstin, desperate to get rid of her unwanted guest.

"Ye'll need this charm fir the bairn, it will protect him in days tae come," said Corrag, pressing a small necklace made of the tiny bones and beaks of small birds into Kirstin's hands.

Kirstin threw the charm to the floor in disgust. "Get oot of here, ye old crone, before my husband sees ye. I dinnae want yer old bones, just leave us alone."

"So that's how ye repay me. Does yer husband ken it wis doon tae me that ye are with child? Ye never told him that, did ye? Ye'll be sorry fir treating me this way when that day comes, Kirstin MacDonald. I have seen ye crying out and weeping and yer blood seeping intae the snow aroond yer frozen feet," hissed Corrag as Kirstin pushed her out the door.

"Get oot Corrag, before they come and throw ye in the stocks wi' all yer mad ravings," cried Kirstin.

Corrag disappeared quickly, not wanting to attract attention; she was cursing Kirstin under her breath as she left. Kirstin turned to go back inside her cottage, then she saw the charm necklace lying on the floor. She picked it up, and as she did, so she felt the first pain of a contraction spasm through her body. Gasping, she took the charm outside to her herb garden and buried it under the rosemary bush she grew there.

Jamie arrived a few hours later, a healthy, strong baby boy, with lungs that Rab said he could hear halfway up Meall Mor. Their son thrived over the next couple of years and never had a sickly day. Kirstin was content with her small family, very rarely setting eyes on Corrag, and then it was from a distance.

One week before the massacre, Jamie was playing outside their cottage with two of the Campbell soldiers, Archie and Wullie Tweedy, enlisted brothers from Inveraray. They had been staying with them for nearly two weeks now. Kirstin was stirring a huge pot of oatmeal that was hanging over the fire in their hearth. It was a cold day, but Jamie was wrapped up well and used to the snow by now. Wullie was helping build a snowman, and she could hear Jamie roar with laughter. It had been hard work having the soldiers stay with them, but MacIain had insisted that hospitality must be given. The Old Chief had had a difficult time the last couple of months trying to get the oath signed and delivered to the King's sheriff. It would be taken as good will that the MacDonald's were seen to be so accommodating to the Campbell soldiers. However, it kept Kirstin busy making broths and oatmeal; these young Campbell soldiers and their sergeant had healthy appetites.

As she stirred, she heard Flora cry out to her from the back of the cottage. She went through to see what wrong and found Flora was pointing out of the rear window. Corrag was just standing there, staring in at them.

"She fair gie me a fright," said Flora. "She's just bin standing there, nae moving."

"I'll deal wi' her," said Kirstin, feeling a shiver go down her spine.

She returned to the kitchen and grabbed her plaid; wrapping herself up, she stepped out to make her way around to the back of the cottage.

"It's a braw day today, Mistress," said Archie, waving at her.

"Aye, it is that, Archie. Watch Jamie fir me, just a wee minute," replied Kirstin.

"Aye, the wee laddie is fair enjoying himself in the snow," replied the soldier.

Kirstin made her way around to the back of their cottage. Corrag was still standing there, watching Kirstin with hostile, grey eyes.

"What are ye after, Corrag? I told ye nae tae step foot on my doorstep again," said Kirstin harshly.

"That's nae way tae talk tae someone who befriended ye when ye had nae one. Ye wouldnae have had yer wee laddie withoot my help," said Corrag, her voice hoarse with the cold.

"How dae I ken that? Just because ye say so disnae make it true," said Kirstin angrily.

"I'm here tae gie ye a warning, though ye dinnae deserve my council wi' all yer harsh words," replied Corrag.

"I dinnae want yer council; I dinnae want ye here. If Rab sees ye, ye'll be in the stocks by nightfall," said Kirstin, wishing the woman would leave. Corrag made her feel uncomfortable; as much as she convinced herself that magic was nonsense, there was something about Corrag that made her question that.

"Ye see these soldiers yer letting play with yer son. In a week's time, in the wee hours of the morning, they will rise up and slaughter ye all," said Corrag, pointing a dirty, gnarled finger at Kirstin.

"Stop yer havering, they're oor guests, they mean us nae harm," said Kirstin.

"I told ye ye'd be sorry, Kirstin MacDonald. Ye turned on me and noo yer guests will turn on youse. All the MacDonalds in this Glen will be brutally murdered, the snow will turn red with their blood, and ye will lose yer only son, ye'll never see him again," Corrag hissed at her, still waggling her finger.

"Get away frae here, ye evil crone, get oot before something happens tae ye," shouted Kirstin, now trembling at the witch's words.

"Dinnae say I didnae warn ye, Kirstin Macdonald. Ye'll be walking this glen fir eternity searching fir that bairn of yers," Corrag spat at her as she turned and left.

Kirstin was red faced and shaking when she returned to the front of the cottage.

"Are ye all right, Mistress?" Archie asked her as she scooped Jamie up into her arms.

"Aye, I'm alright noo, Archie," she replied and then stopped just before she entered the cottage. "Ye wouldnae be thinking of daeng us harm, would ye?"

Archie and Wullie both stood, shocked at her blunt question. They looked oddly at each other.

"Who would be putting thoughts like that in yer head, lassie. Of course we wouldnae harm ye," said Wullie.

"Aye, I ken ye wouldnae. I'm sorry, it's that old witch, Corrag; she's got my head all in a muddle wi' her accusations," Kirstin apologised as she took Jamie back into the cottage. She turned to invite them inside and again saw the soldiers glance sombrely at one another. Kirstin could swear there was something hidden in that look; it just didn't sit right with her.

Later on that evening, she told Rab about Corrag's visit and what she had asked the soldiers. Rab was angry with her for asking the soldiers such a question, so Kirstin just let it drop.

A week later, Corrag's prophecy came true. The witch had also tried to warn Lady MacDonald herself, for the woman had been kind to her, but MacIain had also sent her packing. Corrag took her runes and climbed the near-impossible, snow-covered slope to Ossian's Cave high in the mountains on the night of the massacre. She imagined she could hear the screams and musket fire above the howling of the wind, and she held her hands over her ears and wailed. Although the MacDonalds had not believed her, they had been her family for a time. They were kind to her, something that she had not seen much of in her life. She no more wished them dead than she did herself.

The next afternoon, Corrag came down from the cave and saw what remained of the MacDonalds' homes. There were still bodies lying in the snow, men, women and children she recognised and her heart was heavy. Corrag found the Chief's broadsword and carried it to Loch Leven. Using her Ossian runes, she put a curse on the sword, that would protect the clan for the years to come. As Corrag tried to help some of the survivors, she heard talk that Kirstin MacDonald had survived but was in a bad way, being cared for by the Stewarts over in Glen Gour.

Corrag took a boat across Loch Linnhe; the runes had told her that Kirstin was in anguish. Corrag felt guilty for cursing the young woman in her moment of anger, and she wanted to help her find her son. Corrag's visions were rarely wrong; she knew Jamie lived, and more to the point, where he was. Her heart had softened some after all the bloodshed, and her love for Kirstin was as strong as it had ever been. She was ready to forgive her for her cruel words and banishment.

When Corrag arrived at the Stewarts that night, there was a howling gale and driving rain. Corrag knew she would not be welcomed in the Stewarts' farmhouse, so she used the rune magic to awaken Kirstin and lead her out to her. But Corrag recoiled in horror at the sight of her beloved Kirstin. The creature that crawled out of the farmhouse bore no resemblance to the fresh-faced, pretty young girl that Corrag had loved. Her body was broken and skeletal, her hair was stuck to her head, soaked through with fever sweat and rain, but it was her eyes that frightened the witch. Kirstin was insane with grief, and the hatred in these dark-ringed, hollow eyes was intense.

Kirstin screamed at Corrag, accusing her of not only taking Jamie, but for bewitching the soldiers to cause them to attack.

Corrag's horror and pity grew to anger once again. Even though she could see Kirstin was dying, she cursed her once again, but this time her curse was all the more poignant and precise. She cursed Kirstin to live in the Otherworld, walking the ghost planes for eternity, never finding peace until she found her son.

Chapter Sixteen

James was sitting on their rock mound staring out towards the mountains, as Ollie was standing his sticks up against the pile of rocks. Corrag appeared.

"What are ye looking at?" she asked James.

"I think she's watching me," said James.

"Dae ye mean Kirstin?" asked Corrag, putting her hand on the boy's shoulder.

"No, that lady that Calum doesn't like and Kirstin. They're both the same," said James. "I'm scared, Corri."

"Dinnae be scared, James. I'm here fir ye," Corrag told him.

"James! Ollie! Are we going to hit the pool today or what?" shouted Glen from the doorway.

"I'm going in first," cried Ollie, running for the pool house, pulling his clothes off and tossing them into the garden as he went.

"Go and play, James," said Corri. "Let me worry aboot Kirstin."

She watched the boy run off. He was more intuitive than she had first realised, and she hoped that wouldn't be a problem. James had to trust her if she was to lead him to Kirstin.

***

When Anna and Calum returned to the cottage around ten o'clock that evening, the boys were already in bed. Glen and Rob were watching TV in the lounge in the new part of the cottage.

"Well, hallo you two. We were just about to send out a search party," said Rob cheerfully.

"Oh, I'm sorry, we didn't mean to be so late," said Anna.

"Nonsense, you look much better now. I think Calum has done you some good today," said Glen, then laughed when he saw Anna blush while avoiding making eye contact with Calum.

"Glen and I thought we'd walk down to the Clachaig if that's okay with you. There are some local bands playing tonight," said Rob.

"Yes of course. Go, enjoy, please," said Anna.

Glen and Rob left soon after, Anna checked on the boys, who were both passed out, then went to the kitchen to fetch a bottle of red. Calum sat down in front of the TV and started flicking through the channels.

"I don't miss that," said Anna as she came into the room.

"What?" said Calum.

"Having the man of the house thinking he's in charge of the tele remote," laughed Anna.

"Oh, so I'm the man of the house, am I?" said Calum, pulling her into his lap.

As he bent to kiss her, there was a loud thud, as if something heavy had fallen on the floor in the old part of the cottage. They both jumped and looked at each other as another thudding sound came from above their heads.

"Maybe something is on the roof, an owl maybe?" said Calum.

Then there was another thud, this time coming from the corridor. The thudding became more frantic, soon becoming a loud banging as if doors were slamming shut. Bang! Bang! Bang! Bang!

They jumped to their feet and walked warily into the old corridor; it was freezing cold in there and Anna tried the light switch, but it didn't work. They had to rely on the light from the new part of the cottage shining down into the corridor as they walked onwards, shivering in the icy atmosphere. The silence was deafening as they passed by the old paintings with the dark faces staring out at them. Anna's heart was pounding when they reached the portrait of MacIain MacDonald. As she turned to look at the old Chieftain, the frame swung outwards violently and crashed onto the floor.

She squealed with fright and Calum pulled her to him instinctively.

"What the hell?" he said, staring at the old painting that was lying face up, with the old man's eyes gazing up at them. It then started to slide along the floor away from them, flying suddenly in the air aimed right at them. Calum pulled Anna to him just as the picture crashed into the wall next to them.

There was more banging that started almost immediately afterwards, this time coming from Anna's bedroom.

"Kirstin, is that you?" cried Anna. "We know why you're here. It's about Jamie."

At the mention of his name, the banging got louder. Calum was the first to step into the bedroom, though he wasn't feeling particularly brave. Haunted houses had never been on his to-do list, and if it wasn't for Anna and the boys, he would have been out of there faster than you could blink. Silence fell as soon as they walked into the freezing room. Again, Anna tried the light switch, but it didn't work in here either. The moonlight did light up the room slightly, enabling them to see the steam from their breaths.

"Kirstin, Jamie didn't die. He lived a long and happy life. You don't need to search for him," Anna called out into the darkness, feeling a little stupid as Calum was standing there watching her.

"Do you think she can hear you?" whispered Calum. "I mean, do you think she can understand what you're trying to tell her?"

"I don't know; we can only hope," said Anna with a shrug.

Suddenly, the lights switched on and the whole room instantly began to feel warmer. As Anna blinked to adjust her eyes to the sudden light, she turned to Kirstin's portrait on the wall. She stared at it for a while, not understanding what was wrong.

"Are you okay?" said Calum following her line of vision. "Who is that?"

"That's Kirstin, but there's something different about the picture. I can't quite place it, but it doesn't look right," said Anna.

"Her eyes look really angry, like she is furious with the artist," said Calum. There was something about the picture that left him cold.

"That's it! She was smiling before in that picture; she looked happy," said Anna. "Now she looks like a completely different person."

They both stared at the portrait for a while. Calum was a bit sceptical about Kirstin supposedly changing her expression, but he said nothing and put his arm around Anna, leading her out of the bedroom. They hung the picture of MacIain back on the wall; thankfully, it was undamaged.

Anna checked on the boys again, who miraculously had slept through the entire incident, then went back to the lounge, where she poured them a glass of wine each.

"Well, it looks like she heard you," said Calum. "All the banging stopped just after you told her Jamie had survived."

"I know, but I'm still creeped out by that picture. I'm now questioning my own sanity, I'm almost positive that Kirstin was smiling in that portrait, but now, as you said, she just looks angry," said Anna. "I don't think I'll be able to sleep in that room tonight."

"Why don't I stay with you?" suggested Calum, then laughed as Anna raised her eyebrows accusingly. "No, not like that, just so you feel safe."

They sat sipping their wine, talking quietly for the next couple of hours. Calum didn't know if it was the fear of ghosts that made Anna sit so close to him, but he didn't care. He loved every little movement and gesture she made, the way her mouth tilted upwards at the corners when she spoke, and how her eyes melted into his whenever they made contact. She listened intently to his stories with no interruptions, nodding and smiling as if totally captivated. He would feel himself become a little self-conscious under her scrutiny, but then she would rescue him by telling a story of her own, and their roles would be reversed. Never had he felt so completely captivated.

The conversation started to dry up as they both began to wonder where this night would take them. Anna didn't want him to leave, she felt safe with Calum, and she could feel herself falling for him. What had happened this afternoon had been completely spontaneous, she should be ashamed of her wanton desire, but she had no regrets. She looked into his eyes wondering if he felt the same, she didn't want just a fling, she wasn't that sort of person. But then the niggling doubts would pop in; surely, neither one of them was ready for another relationship. Maybe this was some sort of rebound, but even so, it felt so comfortable, like they were meant to be together. Calum was everything Alex had not been. He was unaware of his own attractiveness, and slightly nervous around her, which made him endearing. He was also incredibly sexual, in a very manly sort of way, proven this afternoon at the waterfall when passion had claimed them both; he had made her feel wild, alive and, most of all, wanted.

Anna was lost in thought as he gazed down at her. She had not agreed to having him stay, but she had not declined the offer either. Calum decided to chance it so he leant forward and kissed her lightly on her forehead. She turned her face up to look into his eyes and he kissed her again, this time on her mouth, slowly and deeply.

Anna took his hand and led him to her room without saying another word. They fell onto the bed, Kirstin's picture completely forgotten as the night's passion took hold.

***

Helena watched them from the window, they hadn't bothered to close the curtains and the rage inside her was boiling over.

"She's taken yer man as her own," whispered Kirstin in her mind. "And she's taken my son as her own. We cannae allow her tae dae that tae us."

Helena walked around the cottage to the boys' bedroom window; this time, it was locked, and the curtains were tightly drawn. She pressed her face against the glass, breathing hard so steam covered the window. She drew a rune symbol onto the glass, a circle with a vertical line on each side of it, then another horizontal line across the top to join them together, so it looked like a gateway.

She then walked back around to the front doorway of the cottage, spat on her fingers, then rubbed them in the dirt. She drew the same symbol in wet dirt on the bottom of the door.

Helena heard the sound of voices coming up from the lane, so she quickly went to hide in the trees, where she stood and watched as Glen and Rob walked up to the cottage. They were both a little drunk and trying to sing some Scottish ditty they had picked up from the pub. Neither of them noticed the dark markings on the door as they let themselves into the cottage.

Helena stepped back out into the garden, her face expressionless as she stood watching the cottage.

"Finish the markings, so I may cross over tae claim my son," said Kirstin's voice in her mind.

As Helena took a step towards the cottage, a dark shape manifested in front of her. Her eyes could not focus properly on the shape, it flickered in and out of the darkness taking no form, but she felt Kirstin's apprehension grow inside her. Then a voice spoke: "I've bin waiting fir ye, my bonnie lass."

"Nae, ye leave me alone, ye hag!" Kirstin cried out through Helena's stolen lips.

"I mean ye nae harm, lass," said Corrag.

"You can't stop her," cried Helena, as Kirstin recoiled deeper into the back of her mind. "I know who you are."

"My business is with Kirstin, and she alone kens my power. I can help her find Jamie," offered Corrag, her magic fading as she struggled to maintain her presence.

"I have found her son. She doesn't need you anymore, Corrag. She has chosen me to help her now," said Helena.

Corrag summoned the last of her power and reached out to encumber Helena in a ghostly embrace that enveloped her whole body. Helena started to whimper, as icy tendrils probed her mind, searching for Kirstin's spirit. Then, Corrag reached in, driving Kirstin's essence from Helena's mind.

Helena dropped to her knee, grasping her head as she felt Kirstin being wrenched from her. She blinked in astonishment, then looked around frantically having no idea where she was at first. She was alone in the dark outside a cottage, that she suddenly recognised as Kirstin's Cot, the place she had broken into the day before.

What the hell was she doing? She tried to remember how she had got here, but everything since her meeting with Calum earlier in the morning was foggy and unclear in her mind. She vaguely remembered buying the clothes she was wearing and then climbing a mountain, but she had no idea why she had done that. She hated climbing, and it had started to rain; her clothes were soaked through. Helena began to shiver with cold and exhaustion. How long had she been outside? She became aware that she really needed a hot drink and her bed.

Leaving the cottage before she was caught seemed the sensible option, but where was her car? Then she noticed the jeep Calum had been driving parked up next to the cottage. Was this the reason she was here? Had she followed him? Still shivering, she quietly started to explore around the outside of the cottage, checking the windows. The lights were all off now, and Helena had no idea what time it was. When she got to Anna's bedroom window, she saw the curtains were open, and she looked in to see Calum in bed with that woman. She gritted her teeth to stop herself screaming, then picked up a rock with the intention of throwing it at them through the window.

"Nae yet," a soothing voice she recognised whispered. "There's time fir oor vengeance, but ye must wait until I can join ye." Kirstin had returned, and all at once, Helena began to feel calmer. She dropped the rock, turning away from Kirstin's Cot. She walked slowly back down the track to Glencoe Village. It was raining hard and she was soaked to the skin, but she no longer noticed. No one would know she had been at the cottage and she could bide her time now.

***

Corrag sat at the end of James's bed. She was greatly weakened from her encounter with Kirstin, but she had managed to release the young woman from Kirstin's possession, although it was short lived. Kirstin was stronger than Corrag had imagined. The young woman Kirstin had possessed was carrying a great deal of anger, just an open invitation to be used as a vessel by some vengeful spirit.

Corrag had felt Kirstin's evil when she had tried to cast her from Helena. The young woman's pain in losing her son had transformed her into a venomous and malicious entity that was beyond anything Corrag had ever come across. The Ossian runes had prevented Corrag from being dragged into the unknown void of the Otherworld on her death, but Corrag had sent Kirstin there with her curse. What was left of Kirstin's sanity had been sucked away and there was nothing left that bore any resemblance to the free-spirited young woman she once was.

It dawned on Corrag that if she attempted to hand over the innocent James to that dark entity, then she would never be released from her earthbound spirit. It was too late for Kirstin now; she had existed in the Otherworld too long, growing vengeful and foul. Corrag would have to find another way to move onto the afterlife, for she could never take Kirstin there. The only option was to destroy the entity that was once her beloved girl, but that would be nigh on impossible. She would have to protect James from Kirstin, and in doing so, would have to find a way of warning his mother. Adults were so much more closed than children where spirits were concerned. It would take a lot more energy than she held to speak with Anna. Appearing to Helena had been difficult, but the woman was already open because of Kirstin, and so, Corrag had managed to break through. That would not be as easy with James's mother.

Corrag watched the boys sleeping, and swore to herself that she would find a way to get stronger. They were safe from harm tonight, but it wouldn't be long before Kirstin would come again.

Chapter Seventeen

Anna nudged Calum awake. It was nearly seven o'clock in the morning. "Calum, we had better get up. I don't want the boys catching you in here with me. They usually come into my room around this time," she said.

"Too late, we caught you," Ollie voice rang out from somewhere.

They both sat bolt upright in bed, Anna pulling the duvet around her naked shoulders. "Ollie, where are you?" she said

"Down here" came his voice from the bottom of the bed.

Calum leaned over and looked down onto James and Ollie, who were both sitting on the floor, their backs leaning against the bed, with Dexter lying across them.

"Erm, hi," said Calum.

"Hi," said both the boys in unison, then started giggling.

"We didn't want to wake you, but we wanted to go for a swim," said Ollie.

Calum was still trying to clear his head. Early mornings were not his thing, but then he had never had any children. Anna had already somehow pulled her bath robe on and was out of the bed.

"Why don't we all go for a swim?" she suggested, winking at Calum who fell back onto the pillow that was still calling out for him to sleep on.

The boys ran out of the room to get their swimming shorts on. "You can lie in if you like," said Anna as she retrieved her bikini from the radiator it was hanging over.

"No, no, it's okay. I wonder how long these two were sitting there," he replied.

"Oh, not long, they're not that patient. I wonder how I'm going to explain this to them," said Anna with amusement.

Calum could not believe how good she looked first thing in the morning. He dreaded looking in the mirror and could only imagine what a state he must be in at the moment. "Give me five and I'll be right with you. I'll have to swim in my boxers though," he groaned.

He looked even more desirable with his dark morning stubble and sleepy eyes. Anna felt a tinge of regret that she had to get up and leave him so soon. "I'm sure they won't notice," she said as she left the room, deciding to put her bikini on in the bathroom, not altogether comfortable with standing naked in front of him in broad daylight yet.

The boys tore past her, yelling as she went to get changed. She grabbed some towels then went to join them. Anna stepped outside and shivered; the weather had definitely turned, there was a real nip in the air, and it had rained hard overnight. The boys had not noticed the cold and were already in the water as she entered the pool house.

As she took off her robe and put the towels down on the sunbed, someone grabbed her from behind, and before she knew what was happening, she found herself being pulled into the water. The boys screamed with delight as she emerged to the surface to find Calum's dripping wet face grinning at her.

Bedlam then broke out, with the boys both diving on top of Calum trying to pull him under the water. He caught them both, one after another, and threw them high in the air so they came crashing down into the pool. Then chaos ensued, with Anna getting pulled into the battle, as Calum grabbed her, holding her as a shield as the boys splashed mercilessly at him. The screaming and the laughter brought a sleepy, hungover Rob to the door. He peered his head round. "I take it you lot will be wanting a cooked breakfast," he said.

"Yes, please," shouted Anna over the noise.

Rob disappeared to go cook, and an hour later, they were all dressed and eating. Anna was grateful that neither Glen nor Rob mentioned that Calum was an unexpected breakfast guest. She knew they could have been brutal if they wanted to, but they spared her this morning.

"I'm going to have to head off and check my dad doesn't need his jeep back and get some clean clothes," said Calum after breakfast. "I don't know what you guys have planned for the day, but maybe we could meet up later."

"We were going to suggest going to the Devil's Staircase today and walking some of the West Highland way," said Glen, who was not feeling quite as rough as Rob was.

"That sounds like a plan," replied Anna enthusiastically. She felt light hearted and glowing with happiness; a walk in the hills sounded fun.

"Well, how about you let me treat you all to dinner at the Clachaig later this evening when you're back. I still owe you and the boys a meal, Anna, and after the dinner you guys cooked me the other night, it's the least I can do," Calum suggested hopefully.

"That also sounds like a plan, as long as you pick up the bill this time," said Anna, trying her best to look completely innocent. Calum gave her a pained look.

"That's good for us. Shall we say we meet you there at six, Calum, so it's not too late for the boys?" said Glen.

With it all decided, Calum gave Anna a quick kiss goodbye and headed off. Glen gave her a questioning look.

"Don't you say a word," challenged Anna.

"My lips are completely sealed," laughed her brother.

They all left the cottage just before eleven and drove to the Altnafeadh carpark at the foot of the Devil's Staircase. The weather was blustery, but it was dry and warmer than it had been earlier in the morning, and there didn't seem to be any immediate threat of rain.

After parking, they began the climb with Dexter tearing off in search of some imaginary rabbit. The boys were both bright-eyed and bushy-tailed as they set off up the trail. Anna was amazed at how much resilience they had shown on their previous climbs, and they seemed determined to get to the top this time. They had opted to do the shorter but steeper climb up Stob Mhic Mhartuin instead of walking the six miles to Kinlochleven. The boys maybe could have managed that if the trail was flat, but not over the mountains.

The blustery, cooling wind soon was appreciated as the sun rays were warm and they had already stripped off their jackets, tying them round their waists. The steep climb was hot work. They were grateful when the trail flattened out for a bit with even the seasoned hillwalkers, Glen and Rob, feeling the tightening of their thigh muscles as they climbed. There were quite a few hikers out, but the sheer size of the place never made it feel crowded and they were on their own for most of the time.

Soon, the views became spectacular, there were red deer feasting on the summer grasses, and they could see right down into the valley below. They reached the summit of Stob Mhic Mhartuin, just over two hours after they had set off, which was good going with the kids. The boys roared with victory when they reached the top, and Glen told them they would have to make a stone pile with a makeshift flag to mark the occasion. They ran off collecting what stones they could find while Anna took in the breath-taking views. Ben Nevis loomed in the south west while Buachaille Etive Mor dominated the east. The tops of the mountains danced in and out of clouds all around them, and the wind constantly reminded them of how high up they had climbed.

They decided to have lunch just down from the summit, sheltered from the wind, and found a good spot. "Boys to the left, girls to the right," announced Rob as he went off to find somewhere to pee, his hangover well and truly gone by now.

They lazed around for an hour as they ate, taking turns with the binoculars that Glen had packed. Anna decided to answer a call of nature before they packed up and headed back down, so she followed a narrow path down to a small crevice in amongst the rocks. She relieved herself, and as she was about to climb back up, she saw a movement close by. She walked towards the edge of the crevice, just as something huge leapt past her, almost knocking her to the ground.

Anna stood breathlessly still as an immense white stag trotted to a halt just below her, then turned to look directly at her. She didn't dare to breathe as she stared back at the huge beast that stood just feet below her. As they stared at each other, a white fog formed quickly around the stag's legs, swirling unnaturally around the animal, then spreading over the rocks and paths around them both. Anna had never seen a mist form so rapidly but began to recognise the danger so she turned to head back to the boys.

She was quickly surrounded by a wall of white mist, and she was truly stuck, unable to see anything. All she could hope was that this was a low cloud, that would eventually blow over in the wind; she would have to stay put as it was too dangerous to move.

Glen began to wonder where Anna had got to; it had been at least ten minutes since she had nipped off. He stood up and looked in the direction she had gone but couldn't see her. He wandered slowly over to the little pathway but still could see no sign of her.

"Anna!" he called. Nothing.

"Anna!" he called again, louder this time. Still nothing.

"Maybe she can't hear you because of the wind," Rob shouted over.

"Maybe, I'll give her five more minutes, then I'll go find her," replied Glen, frowning.

Anna stood shivering, still trapped in the cloud. She hoped that the rest of them had found somewhere safe whilst this cloud passed over. She also wished she had brought her jacket with her; she was frozen in her small tee shirt, and it seemed to be getting uncannily colder. The strange thing was that the wind had stopped. It had been blowing quite a gale before; maybe she was in a sheltered area.

"Witch!"

Anna froze. What was her imagination playing at now?

"Witch, crone!" The voice was as clear as a bell.

"What the hell?" said Anna. "Who's there?"

"Corrag, I've come for Jamie."

"Kirstin, is that you? I'm not Corrag!" shouted Anna. "I don't have your son!"

"Liar!"

"I don't have him. He lived that night, but it was hundreds of years ago. Corrag never took him," cried Anna as the festering mist thickened so much she could almost taste it.

"Liar, I've seen him. He's mine, witch!"

Anna started to cough; the mist was intensifying, so thick now it was choking her. She was completely blinded, and she couldn't breathe. Panic began to set in as she gasped desperately to get air in her lungs.

Glen sat for another few minutes as the sun beat down on them. The boys were still adding to their rock mound at the summit, and Dexter was removing the rocks one by one as soon as their backs were turned.

"I'm going to find Anna. It's weird she isn't back yet," said Glen.

"Okay, I'll stay here with the boys," replied Rob.

Glen made his way down the path Anna had taken. He found the small crevice easily enough and looked around. "Anna?" he called out. Again, there was no answer. He was about to follow the path downwards when he saw something move off to his right. There was a magnificent white stag watching him quietly. Its horns were massive, and it stood so majestically still that it didn't seem real. Glen cursed that he didn't have his phone or his camera on him. The stag started to walk away slowly. Glen followed quietly behind, not wanting to startle it. As he rounded the crevice, he saw the stag had stopped and was nuzzling something on the ground. Glen crept closer, gasping in shock as he saw his sister's body, lying unmoving at the edge of a small drop. He scrambled down to her, while the stag leapt away from them, running back up the mountain.

"Anna, are you okay?" cried Glen, pulling her into his arms. She felt frozen. "Did you fall?"

He checked her pulse and put his head to her chest. She was still breathing, at least, but he couldn't figure out what had happened. There were no marks on her to indicate a fall.

"Anna, what's wrong? Come on, love, wake up!" he said shaking her slightly.

Anna fell to the ground, the oppressive fog still choking her. She was beginning to lose consciousness, and she could hear Kirstin laughing vindictively. Tears began to stream down her cheeks as she realised at that very moment that she was close to death. She couldn't leave her boys; who would take care of them? She battled to stay awake, taking shorter breaths instead of gasping in the foul choking air. Then she heard Glen's voice, calling her from somewhere far away.

"Glen!" she called out to him as the fog strangled her.

"Glen, I'm here!" she called again.

"Anna, wake up, come on, what's wrong with you?" said Glen.

Anna opened her eyes into slits, the sunlight blinding her. She inhaled air greedily as her lungs opened again. "Glen, the fog, where did it go?" she gasped.

"What fog? What are you talking about? It's a beautiful, clear day, too windy for any fog," said Glen, frowning at her.

Anna sat up feeling a little shaken and lightheaded, but apart from that, she was fine. She gave an involuntary shiver, but she no longer felt cold. "Glen, I was trapped in fog and then I heard Kirstin. She was angry, she thought I was Corrag, the witch."

"That's crazy, how could she know you were here? We never saw or heard anything," said Glen, helping Anna to her feet, "except for a huge stag; he was white as snow and he led me to you."

"It was that white stag that led me into the fog in the first place. It was so weird, the wind stopped and everything became a thick, white mist. It was like stepping into another world," said Anna, looking around but seeing no signs of anything that might offer up some sort of explanation. Then, she started to panic. "Oh God, Glen! The boys, Kirstin said she would take her son back. I think she meant one of the boys. Where are they?"

"They're with Rob, still building that rock mound. Come on, he won't let anything happen to them," said Glen, taking Anna's hand and leading back up the trail. He was beginning to feel that his sister and his nephews might not be safe here in Glencoe. Maybe it was time to think about taking the boys home.

Anna sighed with relief when she saw Ollie and James playing, completely unaware that anything had been wrong. They sat back down next to Rob and Anna explained what had happened. She was shaken, but here in the warm sunlight and beautiful scenery, it was hard to hang onto such a horrible image. It almost seemed like a dream already.

"I wish I'd seen the stag. It would have been amazing," said Rob.

"Well, thanks for that. Not, 'Oh God, Anna, that's awful, you nearly died.' No, you just want to see the giant animal that led me to that fate," she accused him, shaking her head in mock disgust.

"Well you're okay now, and it looks like the killer fog has gone, so you can't blame me for wanting to see the magical white stag," laughed Rob, tousling her hair. "To be honest, Anna, it sounds like you had some sort of panic attack. You know, with not being able to breathe."

Anna rolled her eyes, but truthfully, she thought Rob was probably right. Had she imagined it? It didn't seem likely as it had been so terrifying at the time, but she supposed it could have been some sort of panic attack. If there had been a fog, the boys would have seen it. She hadn't been that far away from them; maybe it was the stag that triggered it when it leapt over her. That seemed more plausible.

They packed up lunch and headed back down the Devil's Staircase to the car. The wind was beginning to drop now, and they could see dark clouds in the far distance. It would probably rain tonight, but for now, they could still enjoy the sunshine. By the time they got back to the car, Anna had almost forgotten her experience on the mountain and she was sure Rob was right about it being a panic attack. It was just after four, so they had plenty of time to get back to the cottage, get showered and changed, ready to meet Calum. Anna could feel her anticipation mounting as the time drew nearer and she kicked herself for feeling like a lovesick teenager. She couldn't help smiling when she thought of him.

Both boys nodded off immediately in the car on the way home, so they let them sleep until half an hour before they went out for dinner. They awoke, a little groggy at first, but soon livened up at the prospect of going out again. Dexter got left behind, which he was not happy about, but they left him a huge dinner, knowing he would soon be sleeping after his day on the mountain.

After a glass of wine, they all strolled down to the inn, finding Calum had already arrived. He was nursing a beer on a table outside, in what was left of the sunshine, with Murdo. He grinned and got up as soon as he saw them, bending down to give Anna a kiss on her cheek. Murdo shook his head in feigned disgust. "Well, looks like he's beat me tae it again," he said, then joked, "Is he gonnae pay fir dinner this time?"

"I'm never going to live that down, am I?" said Calum.

Introductions were made, drinks were bought and food was ordered. They moved inside as rain threatened, but nothing could dampen their spirits.

***

Helena watched them from an old Ford Mondeo that she had hired in Fort William. Her Porsche stood out in the mountains too much, and she needed a car that was less conspicuous. She was still in the damp clothes she had been wearing the night before, her once perfect hair now dishevelled and in need of a brush. She wore no makeup, making her unrecognisable from the young woman who had first checked into the Onich Hotel just over a week ago.

She was parked in a layby down by the stream that ran alongside the A82. She could see them clearly with her binoculars, and her anger simmered quietly as she saw Calum sit closely to Anna, touching her frequently and smiling continuously. They moved inside when the first drops of rain began to fall, and Helena began to cough, a horrible rattling sound that reverberated around her chest. When she stopped coughing, they had all gone inside, so she started the car. She would drive to Glencoe, park up and head back on foot to where she could see them return to the cottage. All Helena had to do now was wait for her chance to help Kirstin cross over and reclaim her son, then revenge would be hers.

Chapter Eighteen

Angus was out in his garden dead-heading his geraniums. It was approaching the end of August and with that, more and more of his prize blooms were withering as the cooler nights drew in. He wasn't aware he was being watched at first; his cottage was secluded and surrounded by trees. Visitors were rare, but he liked it that way. Not that he didn't like to socialise, quite the contrary, but he was very precious about having his own space. It was probably the reason he had never married—he liked to live his own way.

He suddenly felt goosepimples raise on his arms and the hairs on the back of his neck stood up. He turned to see a white stag standing just inside the treeline, watching him intently. He had had many deer in his garden over the years, it was not unusual for deer to come down the mountains during the winter months, but he had never seen a white stag before.

The Celtic Folklore surrounding the sighting of a white stag was a bad omen. Seeing the white stag indicated that the way to the Otherworld had been opened, and a transgression had occurred. Angus was well aware of the folklore and he swallowed hard as the stag stood waiting in the trees. Angus put down his clippers on the table then walked very slowly towards the animal, half expecting it to take off at any moment. But the stag just stood, staring at the old man as he moved closer.

Angus was now nearly at the tree line, just a few feet from where the stag was standing. Still it remained unmoving, and once again, Angus felt a chill come over him that made the hairs on his body stand up. There was something about the eyes of the animal watching him that invited him to draw closer. On a whim, Angus reached out with his hand, laying it gently on the neck of the huge beast. The stag immediately started to nod his head in acknowledgement but stayed rooted to the spot.

"Are ye okay, laddie, are ye injured?" Angus spoke soothingly as he stroked the animal's neck. It was enormous, its head a foot taller than Angus's and its great antlers were spread out like immense white wings. It allowed Angus to stroke him, and the old man obliged with great pleasure. Never had he experienced anything like this in his life. The stag bowed its head, then looked directly at him, which unnerved him slightly. An animal like that rarely made eye contact. Then, Angus felt his mind grow fuzzy, as if his thoughts were being manipulated by some outside force. All he could focus on clearly were the eyes of the stag, drawing him into some sort of melancholy, magical ethos. He could now hear the stag's thoughts, and a new-found clarity seeped into his mind.

Within a minute, Angus took a step backwards, taking his hand from the stag, who bowed its head towards him. Angus was aware now of what he had to do, and he didn't like it. But the stag had been insistent that it was the only way to save the boys. He returned to his cottage and opened up his garage. It would take a little while to pack up what he needed.

***

Calum should have been returning to Edinburgh by now, he had already overstayed his visit by two days, but he just couldn't bring himself to leave Anna yet, not when things were going so well between them.

He phoned his PA, and was relieved to find that things had been running smoothly in his absence; he wasn't needed for anything urgent, and the meeting he had arranged could be postponed for a short time.

He was toying with the idea of taking Anna and the boys over to meet his family. He knew his mother would take to Anna and, like all good Mums, would love the boys. He had had quite a time explaining about Helena. Fiona had not liked her at all, so she was relieved to find that Calum had no interest in the obnoxious young woman that had banged on her door. He decided to spare his family all the ins and outs of what was happening with Helena at the cottage, hoping she would just eventually give up and go away.

He did tell his mother about Anna but kept it brief, not wanting to commit himself just yet, in case Anna changed her mind about him. But so far, things were going well. They had a great night at the Clachaig Inn, and after eating they managed to persuade the manager to allow the boys into the Boot Bar so they could listen to some bands. Children are generally not allowed in there, but the boys had loved it and danced their hearts out. It was after eleven when they carried the boys back to the cottage. James was draped over Calum's shoulders whilst Anna carried Ollie. Rob and Glen stayed on to party with the locals.

Their night together had been better than the previous one. Calum had not thought that was possible, but they were more comfortable with each other now, and their love making reflected this. The only thing that left him a little unsure was that they had not talked about the future yet. That Anna lived in Edinburgh was a wonderful stroke of luck as far as he was concerned, and he hoped she felt that way too, but she never mentioned it.

Rob and Glen were late getting up the next morning, and looked a little worse for wear yet again. They opted for a quiet day, which was fine with the rest of them. The boys had slept late also, but were now playing happily in the pool as Calum and Anna drank coffee by the poolside.

"I will have to get back to Edinburgh at some point and check my business is still running," said Calum, hoping to broach the subject of their future.

Anna pulled a mock sad face, "When are you thinking of going?"

"Not for another few days. I phoned Mac, my PA. He says everything is fine, and he's a good lad," said Calum. "I'll have to introduce you when you get back to the city."

Anna smiled. "Yes, I'd like that," she heard herself say. Could she really be falling so deeply, so soon, for this man?

Calum punched the air. "Yes!" he said, victorious.

Anna just laughed.

"Mummy, we're hungry," said Ollie, clambering out the pool.

"Okay, let's get you out then, and I'll make us some lunch," said Anna, getting to her feet with a stretch. "I must be getting old. I'm so stiff after that climb yesterday."

"Are you sure it was just the climb?" Calum asked wickedly, and Anna slapped his head lightly.

"You shouldn't hit people," said James with a frown.

"No, you're quite right, she shouldn't," said Calum, laughing as Anna scowled at him.

The boys were wolfing down their mac and cheese when there was a knock at the door. Anna opened it to find Angus standing there with a big cheery smile on his face. Dexter jumped up and started barking furiously at the old man.

"How are ye doing?" he said suddenly, looking down at the door. "I'd just thought I'd drop by tae see if that ghost of yers has bin visiting again. Did ye ken there wis some funny mud markings at the bottom of yer door?"

Anna looked to where Angus was pointing to. The boys must have been doing mud paintings on the door frame. She got a cloth to wipe it off, feeling irritated that Angus had spoilt the day reminding her of Kirstin. "Well, she's not my ghost, Angus, but yes, she has been making herself known."

"Och, she'll probably just bang a few doors, then disappear. It's not like she can dae much else," said Angus after Anna filled him in with the whole story. "I wis also wondering if ye'd let me take the boys doon tae the loch. I have some fishing gear that will suit them, and I thought I could give them a wee go at trying tae catch a fish."

"Yes!" cried Ollie from the kitchen table. "Please, Mum, can we go? I want to catch a fish."

"I'll have them back by teatime," said Angus, still smiling strangely, like he was the happiest man on the planet.

Anna was puzzled. She grabbed hold of Dexter's collar as the dog was still growling angrily at Angus. She had never seen Angus smile like that before, it was a little creepy, but by now the boys were jumping up and down with excitement. "Yes, okay, if you're sure Angus, they'd love it."

Half an hour later, she watched them drive off in Angus's pick up. She let Dexter out of her room where she had had to lock him in, as he wouldn't stop growling and barking. The dog tore out of the house, down the road and after the car.

"What the hell is the matter with him?" said Anna.

"I don't know, but I'm sure he'll come back," said Calum, pulling her into his lap. "Angus loves kids. He took me and my friends fishing when I was growing up; the boys will have a great time."

"Yes, maybe, but did you not think he was smiling a bit much?" said Anna, knowing it sounded stupid the moment it left her lips.

"How much is he supposed to smile?" asked Calum.

"I don't mean that," she huffed. "It's just, I've never seen that look on his face before; it was weird."

"It's all that hanging around with wild man Ken; it must be rubbing off on him," said Calum. "Now we have the afternoon to ourselves lady, what shall we do?" he said, pulling her in for a long kiss.

***

Angus swung his pickup down a narrow track that was almost completely hidden from the road; you certainly would have to know it was there to have any chance of finding it. The track took them to the edge of Loch Leven where he had a boat waiting for them. It was packed up with camping gear, as well as fishing rods, large water bottles and food supplies. He reversed the pickup into a hollow in the bushes, then pulled some more loose bushes over the truck that he had cut earlier to hide it.

"Get in the boat, boys," he said as he began to push the small craft deeper into the water.

"Why are you hiding the truck?" asked James, looking puzzled.

"So's nae one follows us tae the secret island," replied Angus, and James accepted the explanation without question for a change.

James and Ollie both jumped in. "We didn't know we were going on your boat, Angus," said Ollie.

"Aye, I'm taking ye over tae the island fir a wee adventure," said Angus as he jumped into the boat and grabbed the oars.

"Is that the island with the human bones on it?" said Ollie, his eyes like saucers.

"Aye, ye'll find some bones of my ancestors there, all right. The MacDonalds' graveyard is on that island," said Angus.

"Who are the MacDonalds?" asked James.

"Who are the MacDonalds? Well, they're the greatest clan that ever lived in these lands. Hasnae yer mother told ye of the MacDonalds that lived here?" asked Angus as he rowed out onto the Loch.

"No, but can you tell us?" said Ollie, trailing his hand in the water.

"Well, they were my ancestors, great highland warriors that carried swords and dirks. They fought battles and lived off the land," said Angus.

"I've seen them on 'Horrible Histories' before. They drank their own wee," interrupted James.

"Nae, I dinnae think that wis them, they ate and drank good Scottish fare, made them strong," said Angus.

"They didn't drink it, they washed their hair in it. They called it Shampee; I watched it too," said Ollie, not wanting to be outdone.

"I think ye've bin watching the wrong programmes. The MacDonalds ruled all these here mountains and lochs, and then one day, they were betrayed by the Campbells—a group of soldiers that worked for the English king. The MacDonalds had given them food and shelter for weeks, and then one night, the evil soldiers got up and murdered all the MacDonalds while they slept," Angus told them.

"Why did they do that?" asked James.

"They were evil, he just said so," said Ollie, rolling his eyes at his brother.

"Well, all the murdered MacDonalds got buried here on this island. And their spirits will protect anyone from the same fate as them. That's why we're going here boys, tae stay safe," said Angus.

"Safe from Kirstin?" asked James. "Corrag said she would keep us safe too."

"Aye laddie, and that's just what she's daeing, she asked me tae bring ye here, tae keep ye safe," said Angus cheerfully. "So, we're gonnae set up camp here on the island, just for a few days, ye ken, until we get the all clear."

"But what about Mummy?" cried Ollie. "She won't be safe."

"Aye, she'll be fine. Corrag is watching her and so is Calum. Dinnae ye worry. She'll be glad yer both safe wi' me," said Angus as they pulled up next to a little beach on the island.

***

The afternoon sped by, they had stayed around the pool in the end, as Glen and Rob were flaked out on the sofas in front of the TV. Dexter had arrived back at the house an hour after he had run after the boys. His tongue was hanging to the floor and he passed out miserably on his bed.

Anna swam for a while as Calum watched her lazily from the sunbed. The rain had missed them today, and the sun appeared often between white fluffy clouds, though it was considerably cooler than it had been when they first arrived at the cottage.

By five thirty, Anna began to wonder how Angus was doing with the boys. They should be back any minute, so she went to stick a lasagne that she had taken out of the freezer earlier into the oven. The time passed by, and by six thirty, Anna was beginning to feel a little anxious. She phoned the number Angus had given her, but there was no reply.

"He'll be here any minute," said Calum, noticing she was getting restless.

By seven thirty, Calum was also getting worried. Where was Angus? He should have been back a couple of hours ago. This was really out of character for the old guy. "I'll just drive up to his house and see if they're there. He may have just lost track of time," he suggested, trying to keep his voice light.

"I'll come with you," said Anna, grabbing her jacket then saying to her brother, "Glen, phone me if they appear. Can you also phone Kenneth Macfie and check they are not with him?"

They arrived at Angus's cottage but there was no sign of his truck and his house was completely locked up, which was unusual for a cottage in the highlands. No one really locked their house up, unless they were going away somewhere for a time.

Anna was close to panic now and she rang Glen. "Any sign?"

"No, they're not here," he told her. "Kenneth hasn't heard from him either."

"Look, let's drive down to the loch. I know where they all go fishing down there. Perhaps he's got them gutting fish or cooking them on a fire," Calum suggested. He could feel his heart pounding as he spoke; this didn't make any sense. He had known Angus all his life. Perhaps he had been taken ill; they would have to phone the hospitals if he wasn't at the loch. He could tell Anna was trying hard to hold it together. It wouldn't be long before she fell apart.

Calum took his jeep down to all the places he knew around the loch. There was no sign of them, and after speaking to the locals that lived nearby, no one could remember seeing Angus with the boys at all that day.

"I'm phoning the police," said Anna, tears now beginning to form in her eyes.

"Yes, okay, let's head back to the cottage first, and we can call from there," said Calum. It was now just after nine o'clock and getting dark. They pulled into the drive, there was still no pickup, but Kenneth's car was in the drive. He came out with Glen and Rob, all their faces full of concern as they looked at Anna.

"I ken Angus, and whitever he's daeng, he has good reason. He'll no harm these wee laddies, dinnae ye worry," said Kenneth. Anna ignored him and went inside.

The police arrived half an hour later, two uniforms and the local sergeant they called Billie, who went to school with Calum and also knew Angus well.

"We're going tae call the hospitals just tae check, but I'm sure there must be a good reason for this. Angus wouldnae just take the boys," said the sergeant.

"Everyone keeps telling me that, but he has taken them. I said he was acting strangely when he was here. Even Dexter could tell something was wrong. I should never have let them go," cried Anna.

Calum put his arm around her, but she shrugged him off angrily and began to pace around the kitchen. Glen and Rob both looked stricken, Kenneth just sat quietly, all of them feeling totally helpless. No one seemed to know what to do next.

"We will locate Angus's car, meantime I'll leave PC Burns with ye just in case ye hear anything," said the sergeant nodding towards a female officer, who Calum knew happened to be Billie's wife.

When he left, Anna couldn't bear to be in the same room as the others, they didn't know how to react around her, so she got up and went into the boys' room to stare at their empty beds. She was shaking violently inside, and the pain in her chest was unbearable. She wanted to scream out, but her rationality told her it would do no good. She grabbed Buzz, James's rabbit that was tucked into his bed, then fell onto the mattress sobbing.

Chapter Nineteen

It was three o'clock in the morning when Helena parked her car in the Clachaig carpark. She had checked out of the Onich Hotel earlier in the day, then checked into the MacDonalds hotel in Kinlochleven under an assumed name. She wanted to be sure that Calum would think she had returned back to Edinburgh this time.

It was mild but drizzling as she started to walk up the lane towards Kirstin's Cot. Helena had spent the day on the banks of Loch Leven, collecting large pebbles. She then used a pen knife and scratched an ancient Rune marking onto each pebble. She had been coughing a great deal throughout out the day, and her chest had grown tight and sore when she took a breath. She had a short nap at the hotel but woke up coughing painfully. Kirstin was in control of her thoughts now, so she had collected up the pebbles and put them in a small bag to take with her. If she could remain unseen, she would leave the runes around the cottage and this would enable her to open a porthole for Kirstin to cross over into the material world.

Magical runes were used by the ancient Celts long before the birth of Christ. The runes were passed down through the centuries to those deemed worthy of wielding them. But these Ossian runes were created for a much darker purpose. Even the ancient Celts punished those who were caught using them.

There were a group of Celts who lived around 800 BC who used these runes in raising-the-dead ceremonies, opening portals into what they believed to be the Otherworld—a place where those who had committed murder, or those who died violently, would be taken after their deaths. The Otherworld was a place devoid of colour and sound, the sun never shone, the wind never blew and the rain never fell. The souls imprisoned there would, in time, lose all hope of moving on. The Celts believed that the spirit of Ossian was in these runes, and by using them to free the trapped souls in the Otherworld, Ossian would grant them forgiveness and send them on to the afterlife.

However, opening these portals also risked releasing evil, malevolent spirits, creatures who had lived for eternity in the Otherworld. They would seek these doorways into the living world, then possess a vessel, either animal or human. They would turn the being they possessed into a destructive force of evil, causing mayhem and death.

The Ancient Celts knew how to lay down wards to stop this happening, but this was something Kirstin had neither considered nor cared about. Her control of Helena had been easy as the young woman was unstable and full of rage. It was not hard for Kirstin to manipulate Helena, but she still had no power in the world of the living. She needed to cross over from the colourless planes of the Otherworld and possess Helena's body fully, then no one could stop her, she would be too powerful and Jamie would finally come to her.

Helena's chest was wheezing painfully by the time she reached the cottage; there was a police car parked outside it. The lights were still on inside, and for a moment, she considered turning back. Kirstin needed her to do this. There was no moon tonight, making the ascension from the Otherworld an easier journey. The moon always interfered with the runes' power in some form or other, so tonight was perfect. Helena crept quietly to the side of the house and laid down her first rune stone, propping it against the side of the cottage. She continued to make her way around silently, leaving stone after stone around the entirety of the cottage until every stone was gone.

She heard something stirring in the trees and looked over to see a huge white stag watching her. She dismissed it immediately, then noticed the bedroom light in the children's bedroom was on. Curious, Helena crept over to the window, the curtains were open, and so she dared to peep inside to catch a glimpse of Jamie. But the children weren't there. Instead, there was Anna lying on one of the boy's beds, while Calum sat next to her stroking her hair. Helena gasped in annoyance and Calum looked up, meeting her eyes.

The night had gone by so slowly, every minute seemed like an hour. Calum had no idea what to do; he was furious with Angus but equally puzzled. What the hell was the old man playing at? He must have pre-planned it, by the way his cottage was locked up. Angus had not intended to return that night.

They had left Anna alone in the boys' room, hoping that she may get some sleep. After a couple of hours, Calum decided to go and check on her. She was awake, lying quietly on James's bed, hugging her son's tatty stuffed rabbit to her chest. Her face was swollen from crying, but she had stopped now and was just staring into space. Calum went to sit next to her, but she said nothing. So, he started to pull the wet strands of hair from her face and kissed her cheek. Anna still didn't move or speak, so Calum assumed she just wanted to be alone. He stroked her hair lightly, then was about to leave when he heard a noise from the window. He looked up to see Helena's crazed, red-rimmed eyes staring in at him.

"What the!" he shouted, jumping to his feet.

Helena disappeared, and Calum ran for the door; he was going to catch that bitch if it was the last thing he did. Anna shot up, not sure what had just happened, but sure it had something to do with her boys, so she chased after Calum out of the room, then out of the cottage. Glen and Rob, along with PC Burns, immediately followed suit; everyone was shouting after each other. No one seemed to know who or what they were chasing.

"Calum, hold up. What's going on?" shouted Rob who, being fast, had almost caught up with him.

"It's Helena. She was at the window. She may know something," cried Calum.

Helena was cursing herself as she fled. She hadn't intended to be seen; she needed to remain at the cottage to say the incantation to activate the runes. Now she was being chased from the cottage. It was not what she had planned.

Her first instinct had been to run to her car and get out of there, but Kirstin would not allow her to leave. Tonight had to be the night; it was all planned. So, Helena doubled back on herself, running into the trees just in time to watch Calum and Rob run past.

She made her way as quietly as she could back towards the cottage, but she made more noise than she intended with the twigs and pine cones from the trees snapping underfoot. Calum stopped in his tracks and turned towards the tree line. Helena ducked down out of sight, remaining perfectly still.

Anna had caught up with them and she started walking in Helena's direction, but Helena was sure she couldn't see her, and sure enough, Anna stopped, then as she began to turn away there was a huge crashing sound. Helena fell backwards as the white stag leapt out towards her, his head and antlers down, as if he were about to charge her. Helena screamed, then she crashed out of where she was hiding, looking dishevelled and scared. The white stag followed her slowly, still with its head low and threatening.

Anna ran towards Helena and the stag, her heart pounding in her chest. Was this woman responsible for the disappearance of her boys? It seemed likely now and Anna had bloody murder on her mind as she descended on the woman.

"What have you done with my boys?" cried Anna, pulling Helena to her feet by her hair and shaking her hard. "Where have you taken them?"

Helena shrieked with pain and fury. "Get off me, you bitch!"

But Anna was bearing down on her with a rage that frightened even Calum as he stumbled towards them. Anna still had hold of Helena's hair, and with the strength of a lioness, she swung Helena round by her head, then pulled the furious woman up close to face her. "Tell me what you've done with them!" Anna cried into Helena's face, her eyes incensed with rage.

Rob and Calum jumped in to release Helena from Anna's grip. Anna reluctantly let go, throwing the crazed woman aside in disgust. Calum tried to put his arm round Anna. "Come on, let her go. We'll question her when we get her back inside," he said, gently trying to calm her.

Anna didn't reply but stood with her body tensed as Glen and PC Burns ran up. The policewoman stepped in to take over, grabbing Helena by the top of her arm, then escorting her back to the cottage. Helena started to cough badly, and she stopped struggling. Then she turned and looked at Calum as they passed him, with a strange, smug look spreading across her face.

Kenneth appeared; he was slower than the others as his legs didn't bend that easily anymore. He looked at the scene in front of him and watched Helena as she was dragged back to the cottage. He turned to look at the white stag that was still there, remaining motionless in the trees, forgotten by the others now. Everyone else followed the PC and Helena back to the cottage, but Kenneth remained, watching the stag.

Helena was marched into the cottage and then thrown unceremoniously onto a chair. PC Burns, first name Kirsty, had no tolerance for this woman, especially if she was involved with the missing boys.

In all Kirsty's years of living in Fort William, there had never been a case of two small boys being kidnapped. Kirsty and Billie had two young children of their own, and so she could imagine how Anna must be feeling.

Calum pulled a chair up in front of Helena as Kirsty phoned her husband to fill him in. Helena looked a mess; he had never seen her like this. She was always so pristine; she would never have let anyone see her without make-up. But here she was, her hair was indescribable covered in dirt and ruffled from Anna's vicious attack. There was not a stitch of make up on her face with dirt smeared across it, and she wore hiking gear. Again, this was something he had no idea that she even owned. But what was more frightening than her outwards appearance was that her eyes did not seem to be her own. He was sure Helena's eyes had been a greenish-blue colour, but now they seemed to be a translucent cornflower blue that transformed her face, making her completely unrecognisable, as she continued to stare at him with a weird smirk on her face.

"Helena, what are you doing here?" Calum started, keeping his voice level and calm.

Helena didn't answer him but just kept staring from those haunting eyes. He could hear the rattle in her chest as she breathed.

"You're not helping yourself any. We need to know what you're doing here. Anna's boys are missing. Does that have something to do with you?" he asked in the same tone, although he could hear Anna getting angry behind him.

Helena's eyes showed a moment of confusion when he mentioned the missing boys but again she did not answer him.

"For God's sake, Calum, enough of the niceties, demand she tell us," raged Anna from behind him.

"I think we'd better wait for Billie...the sergeant," said Kirsty, correcting herself. "He won't be long."

Anna kicked the legs of a chair next to her in frustration, sending it clattering on its side. Glen, who had remained quiet until now, picked it up just as the door opened and Kenneth arrived, looking slightly bewildered.

"What's the matter?" asked Glen with a frown.

"I have something tae tell ye all, but it disnae make much sense, so ye'll have tae bear with me," said Kenneth, his dark hooded eyes scanning the room before he continued. "That white stag, the one that ye saw yesterday, Anna, he's here."

"I know, I saw it," said Anna impatiently. "So what, it's a stag. Wait, how do you know I saw a stag?"

"Nae, not just a stag. It's some sort of conduit fir Corrag, and it brought a message. She says that ye musnae fret aboot yer laddies. They're safe with Angus; he's hiding them frae Kirstin," replied Kenneth. "Kirstin wants James."

"What are you saying, man? You mean the stag spoke to you?" said Glen, with disbelief all over his face. "I don't think now is the time for old wives' tales."

"Nae, not like that. I just felt this urge tae touch him, and he let me. When I did, it wis like he wis showing me what had happened. Then he spoke tae me and told me Angus has taken them to safety, because Kirstin is coming. He's taken them where the clans of the deed can protect them frae her," said Kenneth shaking his head. "I cannae explain it any more than that. I wish I could. I can hear what it sounds like tae ye."

Helena started rocking in the chair, her eyes were glazed and she was muttering incoherently.

Anna stared at her for a moment, "She's possessed by Kirstin," she whispered under her breath. "Why didn't Angus just tell me what he was doing?"

"Wait, you're actually are going to believe what Kenneth's saying?" asked Calum with exasperation. "A talking stag?"

"I didnae say it talked," growled Kenneth. "I just said it showed me what had happened when I touched it."

"Is it still out there?" said Anna going to the window, but she couldn't see anything, it was so dark.

Helena suddenly threw her head back and started to rant. Her words were strange and it suddenly dawned on Calum that she was speaking Gaelic. Kenneth moved towards her and sat in the chair Calum had used in front of her. Helena did not seem aware that anyone was there as she ranted on.

"It's an old Gaelic, and her words dinnae make a lot of sense, but I can git the jist," said Kenneth as he listened intently.

"Mosglaidh thugain sula on bha's Kirstin. Eadh thu Peanasaich sineach ana-cothrom."

"She's calling for Kirstin tae awaken frae her death, tae avenge those who treated her unjustly," Kenneth translated.

"Eadh thu do aon-mhac Kirstin. Bi treun nad eug bhoi agus cradh sineach co slaidte Jamie. Theirig air ais trobhad."

"She's telling Kirstin tae come back fir her only son and tae be strong in her wrath against those who stole Jamie." said Kenneth. Then he shook Helena gently, but she continued on. Kenneth looked worried. "We should stop her. I dinnae ken what she's daeng, but I dinnae think it's safe."

The lights started to flicker, and Rob went to grab some tealights from the drawer. He lit them and started placing them around the room, just as the lights flicked out. Helena continued, her voice had levelled and the words spilled out of her tonelessly.

"Mosglaidh thugain sula on bha's Kirstin. Fuirich do m'anam a adhlacadh ansgleo."

"I'm nae sure of her meaning. Something about taking her body intae the mist. I think it's like she's offering herself tae Kirstin," said Kenneth, wild-eyed as he got up from the chair. "I dinnae like this. I can feel the magic in this room."

The others noticed also that the temperature around them had dropped, and the candles were flickering wildly as if in some invisible breeze. Then, Helena stopped speaking and sat bolt upright in the chair. No one spoke as they stood expectantly, waiting for Helena to speak or for something to happen.

The front door blew open violently, smashing against the stone wall and splintering. A gust of freezing air blew into the room, extinguishing all the candles at once. They were in complete darkness, unable to see what Helena was doing.

Anna felt someone cold and incredibly strong grab her and start pulling her towards the door. She screamed, trying to fight off whoever it was and heard Calum cry out to her. Things were smashing inside the cottage; glasses and mugs were flying off the counter tops. In the darkness, those trapped in the cottage couldn't see them coming and were battered in the onslaught of flying missiles.

Anna was still struggling but couldn't fight off whoever had hold of her. She was half carried, half dragged outside, and she could hardly breathe. There was no way that Helena had the strength to do this. She fought back as much as she could but found she was gasping for air, feeling like she was being smothered. Somewhere in what seemed like the distance she could hear Calum calling for her, but she couldn't reply to him. Then suddenly, she was dropped on the ground and she could feel the wet grass under her. Her lungs thankfully filled with air and she continued breathing deeply as she tried to get her bearings. The person who had taken her was gone, but she seemed to be some distance from the cottage. She struggled to her feet, feeling shaken, then saw the white stag standing a few feet from her. It watched her as Anna reached her hand out towards him, and he stepped forwards so she could touch his long neck.

It was like getting pulled into a vacuum, where there was nothing except her and another figure that she couldn't quite make out. It was blurred at first but as Anna watched, it began to take shape. Corrag appeared with her dark red hair flowing down her back. Her eyes were cold and green, gazing uncertainly at Anna. "At last we may speak," Corrag said.

"Corri, I presume," replied Anna, aware that her voice seemed to echo around the strange, silent vacuum they were in.

"Yer boys are safe fir now. I asked Angus tae hide them," said Corri.

"But why not come to me!" cried Anna. "They are my children!"

"Kirstin will nae rest until she reclaims her son. She has her sights on yer James, and she blames ye fir taking him. Ye'll nae be safe until we can send her back tae the Otherworld. She's here now, and I cannae protect ye all," Corrag told her. "She nearly had ye, I can only fight her fir so long; now she has crossed over, she is stronger than ever. I cannae defeat her."

"What can I do? I just want my boys back. Can you at least tell me where they are?" asked Anna.

"It's better ye dinnae ken that fir noo. But yes, they're safe. In a place where the ancient ancestors of the MacDonalds guard the spirits of their deed. Nae harm will come tae them there," promised Corrag. "Fir noo, follow the white stag back tae yer cottage, and dinnae be alone. I will try tae find a way tae take Kirstin away frae this place. She shouldnae be here."

"But wait, when will I see my children?" Anna cried out, but the vacuum had already gone and she was left standing on wet, marshy ground on the hillside. The stag was still with her, and it turned and started walking away.

Anna sighed deeply, then followed the huge beast down the hillside to the track that led to Kirstin's Cot. She felt marginally better, as she did believe her boys were safe now with Angus; however, she would rather they were with her. She hoped they would see it as some sort of adventure, though she wasn't sure how long she could cope without them. Surely, someone would know what to do about this situation. Maybe if she just took her boys back to Edinburgh now, they would be safe, but something niggled at her, telling her that wouldn't be so. If Kirstin was stronger like she said, there would be no stopping her.

"Anna!" cried Calum. He was not far away.

"Over here," she called back, and within minutes, she was in his arms. They walked back to the cottage, the lights were back on, and the police sergeant had arrived. Helena had escaped during the black out, and no one could find her.

Anna looked over to Kenneth, he sat with his head in his hands at the kitchen table. He looked tired and shaken. She went over and sat down next to him. "I spoke to Corrag. The stag came to me. I know the boys are safe. She told me," she said.

"Thank God, I couldnae have convinced ye otherwise. We are gonnae have tae dae something aboot Kirstin. I think she has full control of that lassie noo. Yer in a lot of danger," Kenneth said grimly.

Chapter Twenty

Daylight brought another low-lying, chilly mist that snaked across the landscape nestling in between the mountains. No one had slept and Rob was making a mountain of bacon and buttered bread, insisting they should all eat something. It was his thing; he always turned to cooking when he was stressed.

Anna sipped on her coffee quietly, the daylight bringing with it clarity and a stark reminder that her boys would not be getting out of their beds and charging into her room. She prayed that they were safe with Angus.

Sergeant Burns and Kirsty had left while it was still dark, still searching for Helena. The entire Fort William police force was out looking for her now. They had discovered her Porsche parked up in the carpark at the Onich Hotel, but they informed the police that she had checked out a couple of days ago. They couldn't understand why her car was there. None of the other hotels in the area had anyone listed under her name, but it was a busy season and she could have easily checked in under a different one. The police would have to take the photo of her they had acquired from her DVLA licence to the many hotels in the area to see if anyone recognised her.

Calum went to speak with Anna. She had been slightly off with him since the boys had gone missing. He knew she blamed him, even though it really wasn't his fault. Maybe if he had taken Helena home himself, then sorted their differences out in Edinburgh, he could have kept her away from Anna. But would that have stopped Kirstin? They would never know the answer to that.

"Look, I'm going home to change my clothes, then I'm going out to look for Helena with the police. I'm sure as soon as we have her in custody, Angus will bring the boys back," he said to her.

Anna looked at him thoughtfully for a minute before she said, "I don't think you'll find her, Calum. I think Kirstin has complete control of her now, and she is probably hidden somewhere in these mountains, watching us, waiting for her chance to take James. She's going to be angry when she realises he's not here."

"Do you want to come with me? I'll feel better if you did. At least I can keep you safe, while we look," said Calum, noticing dark rings beginning to form under her tired eyes.

"No, I'll stay here. If Kirstin wants me, then I'll be waiting for her. She's not going to take my son," said Anna. "Calum, please go, see if you can find Helena, I'll be fine. Glen and Rob are here anyway, and you can phone me if you find anything. Take Kenneth with you though, he's scaring the shit out of Rob with all his black magic talk."

She stood up and kissed him on his cheek, leaving Calum with a feeling that he had just been dismissed. He left with his heart heavy and sick with worry. Was this his fault? He couldn't help but wonder.

***

The boys had taken some persuading to go to sleep the night before. James was upset because Buzz wasn't with him, and Ollie suddenly wanted his Mum, bursting into tears. Angus wasn't sure if he could do this for another night. It had seemed such a good idea when Corrag had explained it, but Angus was no spring chicken these days, and a night in a sleeping bag on the hard ground was not doing him any good whatsoever. He was stiff as a board when he got up, his back ached still, even though they'd been up for a good few hours.

They had had a cooked breakfast as Angus had finally relented and built a fire. He hadn't made one the night before in case it was spotted from the shore, but he needed some heat in his old bones this morning. The fire wouldn't be so noticeable in the daylight. He let the boys cook their own sausages on long sticks, informing them that they were now properly integrated as highland warriors. Ollie seemed back to normal this morning and happy to be there, but James was much quieter.

Angus had brought fishing rods for both of them to use, with the idea of keeping them occupied trying to catch fish. He did not factor in the attention spans of a four and six-year-old boy, so when half an hour had passed with no fish in sight, the boys had lost interest. He realised he had no idea what he was going to do with them for the rest of the day.

***

154

Calum arrived at Fort William police station around eleven. Billie called him through to his office, filling him in on the police search.

The receptionist at the MacDonald's hotel in Kinlochleven couldn't be completely sure but had thought the photo did resemble one of their guests, a single woman who had checked in the day before. However, she was not at the hotel, and she hadn't appeared for breakfast. The Police had searched the woman's room, confirming it was Helena. Sergeant Burns had left a plainclothes police officer sitting in the hotel reception area in case she came back to collect her belongings.

Calum decided to take a drive to the hotel anyway; he would feel more useful if he was actually doing something rather than just hanging about waiting. He was driving the jeep along the road at the side of Loch Leven, deep in thought when he absentmindedly glanced at the burial isle Eileen Munde. He swore he could see smoke rising. It was not that unusual for some of the locals to go over there to fish, but then a thought struck him. Hadn't Kenneth and Anna said something about taking the boys to where the spirits of the dead can protect them. Calum pulled over to the side of the loch and pulled out some binoculars from the glove compartment. He searched the island, and sure enough, someone had lit a fire. He decided to go and get his dad's row boat to check it out.

An hour later, he was on the water heading to the island. As he got closer, he saw some movement from the eastern shore, so he rowed in that direction.

Angus stood on the shore, watching him row up. The old man waded out to help drag the boat onto the beach.

"Where are the boys?" asked Calum.

"Calum!" shouted James as he came running up. "Angus told us to hide."

"Well I didnae ken it was ye, did I," said Angus in defence.

"Well, who the bloody hell were you hiding from?" said Calum more harshly than he intended. "Do you ken the state Anna's in? Angus, what were you playing at? You ken the police are out looking for you."

"He's teaching us how to be MacDonald warriors," said Ollie, who had appeared next to his brother carrying a huge stick.

"Well, that's all well and good," said Calum. "But I think your mummy would like to see you now. She missed you very much."

"I'm nae supposed tae take them back yet," said Angus wearily. "Corrag told me…"

"I ken all about Corrag," snapped Calum. "But she can't tell you to just take Anna's boys. We can protect them ourselves."

"Protect us from who?" asked Ollie, and Calum noticed how pale and tired his little face looked.

"From no one you have to worry about, especially now you're a highland warrior," said Calum, picking him up to carry him to his boat. "Let's all head home now and see your mum."

Angus was about to argue but had second thoughts. He was too old for this, and Calum was right. He should leave it to the younger men to protect the boys; he hoped Anna and Sergeant Burns would understand why he did what he did.

Calum phoned Anna to tell her he had found the boys and was bringing them back to the cottage. He then helped Angus pack up the tent and all the camping gear, putting it all in Angus's boat. Calum put James in his boat next to his brother and took them back to shore. Anna had sounded a little distant on the phone, not the reaction he had expected; he wondered how she was bearing up.

***

"Who was that on the phone?" Glen asked as Anna walked into the kitchen.

"It was Calum. He's found Angus and the boys, and he's bringing them back here," said Anna with a worried look on her face.

"That's fantastic!" cried Rob, who had just walked in the room. "Why aren't you happy?"

"I don't know, I just have a bad feeling about bringing the boys back to this cottage," said Anna.

"This is all getting ridiculous now. I know we've all had a bit of a shock with all that's been going on. I'm not going to deny that it hasn't been strange and scary, but we're all here now. Nothing is going to happen to James and Ollie; we will all be watching them like hawks. The police will find Helena, and that will get rid of Kirstin also, hopefully," said Glen.

"Mmm, maybe, I just don't know. Corrag was very convincing about how dangerous Kirstin was. I can't just forget that," replied Anna. "I'm thinking about just packing up and taking them back to Edinburgh."

"I don't really blame you," said Rob. "Why don't we just wait until tomorrow, the boys will probably need some sleep, and you look like you could use some also. We can rest up today, lock the house up tonight, the boys can sleep with you, and we can decide what you want to do tomorrow."

Anna grimaced. "Yes, okay, that sounds like a plan."

Calum arrived an hour later with Angus following him sheepishly in his pickup truck. The boys came charging out of Calum's jeep, flinging themselves into Anna's arms. She hugged them and kissed them all over their faces until Ollie pulled away, wiping his face on his sleeve with a look of disgust. Dexter was trying hard to get in the middle of them, delighted to see his boys again.

Angus was out of his truck, watching them. "I'm sorry, Anna. I dinnae ken what came over me. I thought I wis daeng the right thing."

Anna looked over at the old man. She didn't feel any anger towards him. "I know, Angus. I'm just glad to have them back," she said gently. "I'll phone the police and tell them it was a misunderstanding."

Angus thanked her humbly, then got back in his truck, tired and ready for his bed. He headed home.

They all went back into the cottage, listening to James and Ollie describing their adventures on the island. They were certainly no worse for wear, and Anna sat back on the sofa allowing Calum to pull her close, as James acted out the story of the exploding sausages that they had been allowed to cook themselves. She was tired and allowing herself to relax again, although she was still haunted by Corrag's warning.

Was she doing the right thing by staying on here for one more night? Somehow in the light of day, with her boys back with her, it all seemed like a bad dream, nothing they couldn't handle.

***

Kirstin lay down on the cold cave floor, looking down on her cottage with the binoculars. She was aware of Helena's mind teetering there, nudging at the edges of her focus. She could feel her struggling to regain control, but Kirstin was too strong now. She had crossed over from the Otherworld now, bringing her dark power with her. Helena was simply a vessel for her, but Kirstin was irritated, as the young woman's body was weak and ill. It was taking more magic than she wanted to spare, just to keep Helena's body strong.

She would have succeeded in getting rid of Anna the night before, had it not been for Helena's weakness and the white stag, the beast that Corrag had used. Why was the old witch interfering in Kirstin's business? Surely, Corrag would have passed over to the afterlife by now. Kirstin had never sensed the witch's presence in the Otherworld. Corrag had been the curser, not the cursed, and she always had her Ossian runes to protect her.

Kirstin turned her attention back to the cottage. She had not seen the children, and she was not sensing them either. They had not been at the cottage the night before, so, where were they? They couldn't hide Jamie from her; she would find him. He was hers.

She lay there unmoving for most of the morning, gathering her strength from the dark power that flowed through her from the Otherworld. The cave was cold, and Helena's body had been soaked through. Kirstin could feel her body shivering as she lay there and cursed at the weakness of this woman she possessed.

It was lunchtime when she saw the vehicles appear, then two boys get out and run to Anna. Kirstin felt a surge of jealousy as she watched her son hug that woman, as if she were his mother. He would know soon enough who his mother was, and she would take him back with her into the Otherworld, where they could finally be together. But first, she would have to get rid of Corrag and the others that guarded him. As soon as darkness came, her power would get stronger, and she would have her chance.

***

Kenneth sat at his desk in his old library, a room he had converted when he retired ten years ago. His collection of books on Scottish history was vast, but just now his desk was covered with books on Scottish witchcraft and Celtic magic. Although he had numerous books in his collection covering these subjects, it was not something that had held his interest for long, and so most of these books had been unread. This made it difficult to know where to start, so he decided to try and find any information he could about Corrag. She had been the one who had cursed Kirstin in the beginning, according to Anna, so perhaps finding out something about where she came from, would lead him in the right direction.

His attempts on Googling her only led him to the legend of the sword in the lake story. He also saw that she had been the subject of a fictional novel, but there were no factual references to what had actually happened to her. He looked at the time, realising he only had a few hours left for it would be dark by about eight o'clock and Kenneth was sure Kirstin would return.

His eyes wandered over to a shabby looking hardback with the title, 'The Witch Confessions'. It was first written in 1707 by an author named Richard Stevenson, but it was a name Kenneth was not familiar with. This copy he had was a reprint of the book, published in 1847, by the Glasgow Printing Press. Its binding was very worn, as if it had been well read, and the pages were darkly yellowed, with very small print. Kenneth switched on his spotlight; even with his reading glasses he struggled, resorting to a magnifying glass every now and then.

The author had put together a collection of final confessions from condemned witches throughout Scotland. These witches were to be hung or burnt, or even both, having already confessed their crimes to a scribe, normally under extreme duress and torture. The records had been kept at the courts or prisons where the witches were held captive, and the author had gone to great lengths to interview the witches himself before they were executed, putting their stories together into this volume.

Kenneth had no idea when he had bought this book, but then, he was known to pick up old books from jumble sales and fetes if the book covers were interesting or Scottish related. He may never even have read it. Kenneth had always felt that there was something comforting about being surrounded with old books, even if half of them were unread.

Kenneth flicked through the pages, stopping every now and then to read some of the gruesome accounts of the demise of these poor women. Some were clearly touched in the head, and their wild confessions were utter nonsense.

But there were other more sinister tales of witchcraft that, if Kenneth was to believe in entirely, would undoubtedly convince him on the power of black magic.

One such woman was Isobel from Lanark. No last name was given. The witch was locked in Lanark prison and had confessed openly, without torture, to witchcraft. She calmly spoke of invoking evil spirits from the dead, to cross over and possess some of her neighbours. She had blamed the neighbours of passing on the plague to her family. Isobel's husband and daughter had died from the disease, but somehow her neighbour's family had survived and Isobel had sought revenge.

Her possessed neighbours had lost their senses, killing their animals brutally before turning on each other. Only the father survived; he had been enticed to murder his whole family and was now ranting and raving in another cell in the prison, his mind completely broken.

Isobel showed no remorse, even when she was told she was to be burnt at the stake for witchcraft. She declared that she was happy for she would be reunited with her family. When she was finally taken to be burnt, the prison guards found that her fingernails on each hand were torn and bleeding. They discovered stones placed around her cell with bloody rune markings scratched onto them. As the flames licked around Isobel, she looked almost serene, with a look of contentment on her face. She died silently in the fire.

Kenneth continued to read story after story, his eyes growing weary with concentrating so hard on the small print. And then his eyes opened wide in astonishment. Here on page seventy was the confession of Corrag, Witch of Glencoe.

Chapter Twenty-One
Corrag

May 1693

For months after the massacre, the mountains of Glencoe wept; its stream and waterfalls ran red in the sunlight. Corrag could feel the despair in the mountain grass under her feet and taste it in the fresh water that cascaded down the cliffs. Some of the MacDonalds had returned to rebuild, the old chieftain's sons amongst them, but everything had changed, and they were no longer as friendly to her as they had been in the past. Corrag kept to herself, tending her herb garden to make healing potions for those who required it, but not many came and life became harder for her. There were those who still remembered her warnings, and they feared her now. The mountains were no place to live without friends; it was time for her to move on.

On a mid-summers day, with her spirits low, Corrag packed up her belongings, bundling them into a small sack that she would carry on her back. Her runes had warned her not to go, that she would meet her end if she left. Corrag did not care; she had lost Kirstin now, the only person she had ever truly loved. She torched her home and stood watching as her little hut burnt to the ground, erasing any trace of the time she had spent there. If any of the neighbours saw the smoke, no one bothered to come and check if she was all right. MacIain's sons had not forgiven her for taking their father's sword, and rumours of her role in Kirstin's demise were beginning to sprout.

Kirstin had accused Corrag of taking her son whilst on her deathbed, and now there were rumblings as people began to wonder if the witch had something to do with what had happened.

Corrag left the glen on foot, and no one uttered a kind word of farewell to her as she passed, not that she expected it now. Everyone was suspicious of everyone these days, the welcoming nature of the highlanders had been seriously damaged by the Campbells' betrayal. She arrived at the loch, and using what coin she had, she managed to get a boat down to Oban, a small herring fishing town.

From there, Corrag travelled on foot, begging for food or eating from the abundance of summer berries. She collected herbs in the hills and made tiny charms, selling them for bread. Occasionally, she told fortunes with her runes, but she didn't stay in one place for long, the branding on her face made many turn from her, and she was routinely spat on or thrown out of a village. She decided she would make her way to Dumbarton; she had grown up there and it was the closest thing she had to home.

***

1663–1680

Corrag had been used to being spat on and cursed for the most of her life. When she was very young, her family had lived on a farming estate in Dunbartonshire. She never remembered her father as he died when she was very young, leaving her young mother, Leana, to struggle to pay the rent on the farmstead. Leana had been unable to do all the manual work herself, her children being too small to help. She had a good knowledge of herbs, so she transferred her talents to becoming the local hedge witch. Even so, this did not cover the rent, and the landlord had no choice but to turf them out of their home.

Corrag's older brother was taken on as an apprentice by a kindly bootmaker and his wife when he was just nine years old while Leana, who was still an attractive young woman, managed to acquire a small cottage from a local landowner for her and Corrag to live in.

Corrag was still only six years old and her daily chores involved tending the herb gardens and helping her mother make the healing potions and powders from the herbs. Corrag enjoyed these days spent with her beautiful mother; they would braid each other's dark red hair as her mother told her stories of mermaids and kelpies. But on other days, Corrag was told she had to make herself scarce. These were the days that the landowner came for his rent, and Corrag was not allowed in the cottage when he was there. These visits became more frequent as time went by, and as Corrag grew older, she became more aware of the whisperings that occurred behind their backs in the kirk on a Sunday or in the village as she strolled through with her mother.

Her mother ignored it for the most part, but Corrag began to wonder why no friends would come to visit. Her answer came as she walked into the village one day to deliver some herbs. There was a group of children about her age playing with a puppy. Corrag wanted to go and look at the puppy, but as she approached, the other children got to their feet and circled her.

"Look, it's the witch's daughter," sneered one of the boys. "Look out, she'll gie ye the evil eye!"

"My maw's nae a witch," said Corrag.

"Aye she is so, and ye'll be one tae. Look at that red hair of yers, it's no natural, a colour like that!" said the boy. "My da says ye and yer maw have been touched by the devil hisself!"

Corrag had tried to walk away but the children started chanting at her. "Witch! Witch! Witch!" bringing a crowd of women out their houses to see what was going on.

The children quietened down when they saw their mothers, some even looked ashamed, but the boy who had started it just stuck his tongue out and ran off.

The following Sunday, as they walked to the kirk, Corrag was more aware than ever of the hostile eyes of the villagers on them. She became afraid and drew closer to her mother, who did not seem to notice. Corrag was relieved when the service came to an end and they could return to their cottage, but when they arrived, the landowner was there waiting for them. Corrag got sent away to play, so she scurried off to her herb garden; she liked to be alone there among the plants and the earth. She imagined she could almost hear the plants talking to her. Today, however, she could hear other voices, the distressed cries of her mother and the voice of the landowner shouting. It went on for a while, before she heard the door slam open and the landowner's horse riding off.

Corrag hurried back to the cottage to find her mother crying in a chair. "What is it, Maw?" she asked.

"We have tae leave here, Corrag. We nae longer have the means tae pay for this cottage," said her mother, sobbing into her skirts. "We have tae be oot by the end of the week."

Corrag was ten years old by now, and she loved her mother fiercely. If truth be told, her mother had been her only friend throughout her life, so to see her weeping and so broken made Corrag furious. She scampered out of the cottage running off through the trees, then over a footbridge across a small stream that led to a sloping wheat field, where she could cut off the landowner as he rode. She jumped out from the golden wheat in front of his horse, ready to confront the man who made her mother cry. But she startled the horse, so it reared and threw its rider. The landowner came crashing to the ground, then just lay there unmoving, his broken body in a strange position. Without drawing any closer, Corrag knew he was dead. She was horrified, then she heard the shouts of a man from the top of a hill nearby. Corrag dived back into the cover of the golden wheat field, crawling her way through the long stalks, until she reached the other side. Confident she hadn't been followed, she fled home to her mother.

The farmer who had seen the landowner fall was quite a distance away, but he would recognise that red hair anywhere, and hours later, soldiers rode up to their cottage.

Corrag screamed in terror as her mother was dragged from their home, chained, with a scold's bridle strapped to her face, so she couldn't utter a word. The soldiers couldn't decide what to do with the girl, so one of them hauled Corrag onto his horse behind him, and they both were taken to Dumbarton jail.

They clung to each other in a dark, damp cell. Her mother's face had been cut and marked by the bridle, and she was in shock, not understanding why she had been brought there. Corrag was too scared to tell her what had happened, so they just sat, huddled together in the darkness.

They were hauled up in front of the magistrate the following day. Corrag's teeth were chattering from cold, but her mother just stood quietly, pale and confused looking.

All Corrag could remember of that day was her mother collapsing to the floor in a dead faint when they accused her of witchcraft. A woman abandoned by her lover, out to seek revenge by the ways of dark magic. They dragged her mother off, back to the cells to get a confession from her. Corrag was taken from the court and passed to the kirk workhouse. Terrified from her cruel welcome, she escaped that same day and lived from begging on the same street as the jail that held her mother. There were other children begging there, all hoping to get a glimpse of their parents.

Corrag would always be haunted by the sight of her mother the day they finally dragged her back to the court house. Leana's beautiful red hair had been shorn from her head, her face was only barely recognisable, but it was her eyes that chilled Corrag the most. She was dragged past her daughter, unable to walk properly as her feet were so damaged, but her eyes flickered with recognition as they settled on Corrag. They turned to ice cold hate as they passed over her, and Corrag wilted away into the shadows in shock.

Her mother had confessed to murdering the landowner with witchcraft. Her sentence was more lenient; she was given the rope instead of the fire. Corrag went nowhere near the gallows that day, she was already tarnished with her flaming, dark red hair, although she tried to hide it under a shawl. She couldn't bear to see her mother's final dying breath, knowing it was for her crime that she died.

Corrag moved onto Glasgow, a larger town, with more chance of takings for the beggars there. She teamed up with a group of beggar children, and for the first time in her young life, she had friends her own age. They lived in abandoned buildings by the river Clyde, sharing their takings, so none of them went hungry. Corrag began to settle into that lifestyle, though the hate filled eyes of her mother were still firmly lodged in the deep recesses of her mind, giving her nightmares.

One of her friends was a boy called Duggie. He didn't know his real name, and Duggie just seemed to suit him. He was slightly older than Corrag and much braver. He was also a lot bigger than the other children, and in time, he became their gang leader. He was especially fond of Corrag, always making sure she worked the streets with him. Corrag was well aware of his attention, and one day when they were alone together down by the river, he grabbed hold of her roughly and tried to kiss her. She fought him off like a wild cat, drawing attention from the dock workers who laughed and hollered at Duggie, denting his ego. Duggie punched her in the face, and Corrag went sprawling onto some wooden crating, cutting her arm. He didn't even help her get up but just stalked off in anger.

Later that evening, when Corrag got back to their hideout, carrying her injured arm, Duggie was waiting for her.

"Ye want tae stay here wi' us, ye dae whit I tell ye. If I want a piece of ye, ye'll gie me it, understand!" Duggie told her viciously.

Corrag recoiled from him and went to sit alone in the corner. A small girl, new to the gang, came and sat by her. They called her Elf, which seemed to suit her as she was exquisitely elfin-like in her features. Elf looked at Corrag's arm, bringing out a clean handkerchief she had stolen from a merchant gentleman earlier at the docks. She wrapped Corrag's cut arm with it, then pulled out a leather pouch of what looked like stones at first. She poured them onto the ground in front of them and Corrag could feel the vibrations coming from them. They all had strange markings carved into them.

"They're runes," said Elf. "I can show ye how tae make them work. They can stop Duggie frae hassling ye."

Corrag soon discovered that she had a lot in common with the small girl. Elf's mother had also been accused of witchcraft, but she had passed on all her knowledge of these ancient Ossian runes to Elf. The girls spent the evenings alone in the corner, playing with the stones and casting minor spells. True to Elf's word, Duggie never went near Corrag again, and Elf said they could do a lot more than just that.

Corrag's face had been badly swollen by Duggie's punch, so the girls decided that his face should swell more than double its size. The runes worked their magic, and Duggie spent the whole week unable to speak or eat as his face was so swollen. Soon, Corrag found herself wishing every day was over, so she could rush back to hold the runes. Her connection to them was strong, and as time went by, she hated to be apart from them.

Elf warned her about getting too connected to them, for there was a lot of unharnessed power in the potent stones. It was better to have time away from them, but Corrag wouldn't listen, every day over eager to get back to the hideout so she may sit and talk with the runes as if no one else existed. Elf began to become a little wary of her, recognising the transformation in her friend and the desperate need she had to be near to the runes. The stones had wielded their power over Corrag, controlling her more than she controlled them. Elf's mother had warned her daughter that she must keep the runes under control or they would end up twisting her mind.

One day, when Corrag came back to the hideout, Elf was nowhere to be seen, and neither were the runes. As Corrag looked around frantically for them, she suddenly saw Duggie staring at her, with a strange look on his face. He got to his feet and started to wander casually over to her. Corrag got up and ran for the door, but another of the boys had blocked her way. Duggie grabbed her from behind and threw her face first to the floor, before straddling her. He hauled her skirts up as she screamed and tried to throw him off. The others just sat and watched silently as Duggie raped her in front of them all. When he got off her, he just laughed cruelly as she lay there crying in the dirt. She crawled to her feet, her body feeling like it had been ripped apart, and the humiliation burning on her face. Why would Elf do this to her? Why would she leave her unprotected? Corrag collapsed in the corner, sobbing.

The next day, she strode out of the building angrily, away from the smirking faces, and went to find Elf. She would make the girl pay for what had happened, and she wanted those runes. It didn't take her long to find Elf, working the streets near to the gallows.

There were always good pickings at a public hanging. Corrag, who was much larger than Elf, came up behind the small girl, grabbing her by the arm, then dragged her into an alley.

"Why did ye leave me? Duggie ravished me last night!" said Corrag, her eyes filled with anger. "I want those runes!"

"Ye cannae have them, ye dinnae use them as they should be used. They're tae powerful fir ye," said Elf, who was tearful and afraid. "I'm sorry aboot whit happened tae ye. I didnae think the spell would wear off that quick."

Corrag was past caring what her friend thought. "Where are they, dae I have tae shake them oot of ye?" she demanded. Then she saw the pouch hanging from a rope around Elf's waist. She snatched at it, but it was attached to the girl, so she pulled at it roughly. "Gie me it!" she cried.

Elf tried to pull away from her, which made Corrag all the more furious; she pushed the smaller girl to the floor. Elf started to crawl away, she was quicker than Corrag, but Corrag was stronger and still had hold of the pouch that was attached to Elf's waist. Elf kicked out at her screaming, and in a fit of rage, Corrag picked up a rock lying close to her, then, then, without a second thought, she brought it down hard onto Elf's skull. The girl fell backwards, blood pouring from her head. Corrag sat back in shock, then realising she may be caught, she gnawed at the knot that tied the rope to Elf's waist. Finally, she managed to loosen it, grabbing the bag of Runes to her chest, as if they were her long lost child.

Corrag then turned and stroked Elf's head. It felt warm and sticky; the girl wasn't breathing. She heard footsteps behind her, so she got to her feet and ran as fast as she could from the alley. She could hear people shouting, but Corrag was long gone before anyone could catch her.

She hadn't meant to hurt Elf. If the girl had just handed over the runes, then it would never have happened. Corrag returned to the warehouse where the children were living. Thankfully, Duggie and the rest of the boys were gone, so Corrag slipped into the corner that she had once shared with Elf and curled up in a tight ball, clinging tightly to the bag of runes. Tears would not fall; she felt nothing but the power from her Runes.

As darkness fell, she could hear Duggie and his gang coming back along the street. She sat up and poured out the runes onto the floor in front of her. She picked out what she needed and muttered the spell that Elf had taught her under her breath.

Duggie did not even look in her direction when he came in, and Corrag knew she was safe for the night, at least. She left the next day and never went back.

Years passed, and Corrag had managed to get herself some work with the fish wives at the fish market. They were a rough, no nonsense but kindly bunch, and they looked after their own. Corrag had not yet established herself as one of them yet, but she worked hard and earned an honest day's pay, enough to put a roof over her head and food in her belly. She had grown into an attractive woman, and it didn't go unnoticed with the local men. Corrag had her eye on one of the fishermen, named Tam. He always stopped at her stall when his boat came in, occasionally bringing her a colourful shell from the sea. One night, he asked her if he could take her for a walk after she finished work, and she agreed happily.

The walked along the banks of the Clyde, and Tam took her hand, which made her feel special. As they rounded a bend on the river, there was a group of men, obviously up to no good. Tam pulled her in the other direction, but it was too late; they had been spotted.

Corrag recognised the voice before she did his face. It was Duggie, and the years had not been kind to him. His face was gnarled and scarred from smallpox, and most of his teeth were missing. He recognised Corrag immediately, her dark red hair an instant give away.

"Well, lookie here, if it's no oor Corrag, all grown up," he said as he and his gang surrounded them.

"Back away laddies, ye dinnae want tae mess with the fisherfolk," said Tam, putting Corrag behind him.

"Och, oor Corrag is an old friend of oors," said Duggie moving closer menacingly.

"Leave us alone, Duggie. I'm no friend of yers," said Corrag.

Tam turned to her in surprise at her use of this vagabond's name, but as he did so, he was grabbed from behind by three of the gang and brought to the ground. Corrag screamed as they laid into Tam, kicking him senseless while Duggie grabbed hold of her. She wrestled herself free and ran as fast as she could, but the gang were in close pursuit, and soon she found herself surrounded again.

"Why dinnae ye just give it up, Corrag? Ye ken whit's gonnae happen, ye liked it last time," said Duggie, moving in. "Perhaps this time I can share ye aroond."

Corrag started chanting a curse, fishing in her pocket for a protection rune she kept on her person. Duggie halted in his tracks. "Whit's this witchcraft yer spilling oot?"

Corrag carried on chanting her curse, louder now as she stepped towards him, her eyes ablaze with fury. Duggie took a step back and looked at the faces of the rest of his crew. There was an uneasiness there, but he was not going to let this woman make a coward out of him.

Then, Tam appeared, beaten and bleeding, but he had his friends with him. They didn't hesitate as they attacked Duggie and his gang, with knives and wooden batons. Corrag continued to chant, lost in her spell now, as bloody murder went on around her. Duggie died with a knife in his stomach, and others lay wounded and bleeding. The town guard arrived, arresting everyone, including Corrag.

Corrag lay in the town jail for ten days before she was brought up in front of the magistrate. She did not know that Tam and the others had accused her of witchcraft. They had all seen her chanting her curse, and said she had put a spell on them, willing them to fight to the death.

The magistrate was not altogether an unreasonable man, suspecting that the two gangs had probably started the fight. But those from the fish markets were not to be trifled with, and they demanded that Corrag be tried as a witch.

Corrag was terrified; she remembered how her mother had been treated, so with tears pouring down her cheeks as she begged for mercy. The magistrate took some pity on the young woman but couldn't be seen to ignore witchcraft.

So, he sentenced her to branding, leaving a mark on her face to warn others of her sorcery. Then she was to be transported onto a slave ship to the American plantations.

Corrag screamed when the hot iron seared into her face, collapsing in a heap, sobbing more from anger than from the pain. They dragged her back to the dark cell that had become her home, and as she sat in that festering hole, she became vengeful and bitter. All she could think of was being reconnected with her runes, so she plotted her escape, scratching ancient rune markings on the walls; then she cast a spell. It was a simple spell, she put herself into a deep sleep, known as a death sleep. She had no heartbeat, nor did she take in air. When the guards checked on her they assumed she was dead, so they carried her body out to a cart, that took her to be buried in one of the town's mass graves, mostly used for the plague victims.

From there, Corrag awoke, escaping into the city once more, but this time she knew she would have to leave. Hiding her hair under her filthy shawl, she made her way to her old lodging, praying that no one would see her and that her belongings were still there. She was lucky. She found her bag of runes, rolled in her clothing, so she grabbed them, then left Glasgow and headed north, eventually arriving in Glencoe.

Chapter Twenty-Two
Corrag

1680–1694

The MacDonalds of Glencoe were a hardy bunch, surviving the harsh elements of the mountains, especially during the winter. A natural healer was welcome amongst them and they did not question where she came from, nor the brand on her face. They let Corrag set up home in an empty hovel on the lower mountain slopes, providing her with food in return for her medicines. They did not know that she used these ancient Ossian runes to help with their healing, nor would they have cared. Corrag lived there for twelve years, keeping to herself for the best part. She liked the MacDonalds but never again would she put her trust in another soul.

As time went on, Corrag became more powerful in the dark magic of Ossian, beginning to be able to see what lay ahead in the future. Although sometimes it was not always clear, this time Corrag knew she would befriend Kirstin, long before the lowlander came to the Glen.

When Kirstin appeared at her cottage that day, she did not realise it was because Corrag had called for her. There was a lot of natural magic in Kirstin that needed to be managed, and Corrag planned to do that. What Corrag did not plan was to fall in love with Kirstin.

Kirstin was eager to learn the ways of the runes, and began to visit with Corrag daily. Corrag found herself looking forward to Kirstin's visits; in a way the girl reminded her of Elf. She taught Kirstin how to take power from the runes and to use it for her own advantage. Most of the spells she attempted were small, spells to make the chickens lays more eggs or the cows produce more milk. But when Kirstin came to Corrag to ask if she would help her conceive a child, Corrag felt a surge of jealousy. She had not realised how much she had come to love Kirstin, and the thought of sharing her, of losing her to a child was unfathomable. But Kirstin continued to beg her for her help, telling Corrag that she would always be indebted to her and that Corrag would always be part of their family. Eventually, Corrag weakened and against her better judgement, made Kirstin a fertility potion.

When Kirstin came to tell Corrag she was pregnant, she was so happy she had hugged Corrag to her tightly, thanking her again and again. They sat together, talking about the baby and planning the life it would have.

But as soon as Rab knew, Kirstin's visits to Corrag stopped. Corrag waited and waited for Kirstin to come and visit with her, but she never did. Corrag was left bereft; once again she had dared to love and trust someone, and now, as had happened before in her life, she had been cast aside.

So eventually after many months, each month bringing a deeper sense of betrayal, Corrag took herself down the mountain side to Kirstin's Cot. She had painstakingly made a protection charm for Kirstin and the baby, using tiny bones from small birds that cut through her fingers as she weaved them together. Corrag had seen disjointed lines in her runes that surrounded Kirstin and her bairn. There was a darkness in the future for Glencoe, though what it was, she had no idea.

Corrag did not expect Kirstin's hostile reaction when she arrived; the young woman was not pleased to see the her at all. She cruelly demanded for Corrag to leave, and the witch felt her anger smouldering in the pit of her stomach. This was how Kirstin repaid her, by smearing her name and calling her a crone. Corrag was horrified as Kirstin callously threw the protection charm on the floor, then manhandled her out the door. The witch stood outside for a moment, her heart aching from Kirstin's treatment of her, then she turned and slowly returned to her hut.

The anger that took hold that day turned to vengeance and Corrag went straight to her runes, her only true friends in this world. Her rage was now bubbling over as she cursed Kirstin to have a painful and slow death and never to see her son grow to be a man.

The months went by, and Corrag remained in her lonely hovel, away from the other MacDonald', but still part of their lives. She tried to tell herself she enjoyed her solitude, but Kirstin had left an empty void in her now that could not be filled. She tried to forgive the girl, but she would see Kirstin with her baby from a distance, and the bitterness inside would bubble to the surface.

It was about six months before the massacre that Corrag's dreams about the impending fate of the MacDonalds started. At first, they were clouded and vague, like a shape in the darkness that she could almost grasp onto, before it slipped away from her. The dreams became more virulent; even during the day she would be stopped in her tracks by visions of blood and betrayal. She took to her runes, and soon enough, a picture began to form of what would befall MacIain and the Glencoe MacDonalds. When the Campbell soldiers arrived asking for shelter, Corrag was sure of the treachery that would follow.

She didn't know why she first went to warn Kirstin; perhaps she was subconsciously giving the girl a chance to make amends for her harsh treatment. But Kirstin's reaction was as hostile and cruel as the time before. She would not hear a word from Corrag, invoking the witch's anger once again. As far as Corrag was concerned, Kirstin deserved to be damned to the fate before her. But she did not feel that way towards the other MacDonalds in Glencoe, and she went straight to Lady MacDonald herself, to warn her of her visions.

The good lady was kind enough to offer Corrag a dram, but she would not hear of the witch's accusations against their guests. After all, it was a tradition in the highlands to give shelter to those who asked for it. These Campbell soldiers would not betray their hospitality, it would be an unforgivable breach of highland code. And so, Corrag was left to weep alone with her Runes in Ossian's cave, as the brutal massacre took place around her.

Corrag's attempt to make peace with Kirstin before she left Glencoe had almost pushed her over the edge. Kirstin was close to death and in a state of delirium, but her contempt and hatred towards Corrag was unforgivable. Corrag left Kirstin for the last time, reaffirming the curse she had placed on her a couple of years before.

Corrag eventually reached the town of Dumbarton in February 1694; she was ill from the harshness of travelling through the winter, with a cough that racked through her chest, almost crippling her when it struck. Dumbarton was cold, dirty and unfriendly, and Corrag slept rough for the first week, before finding a poor house to take her in. She kept the brand on her face covered, as witch hunting in Dumbarton, Paisley and the whole Glasgow area was prevalent. There was a grain famine in Scotland and everyone was hungry and on edge, with wild accusations flying around the town.

Corrag, as a newcomer, who was now very ill, would not to be tolerated. Eventually, her branding was spotted as she begged for food one day. Without further ado, she was dragged off unceremoniously to Dumbarton Tollbooth, where there were no less than five other women also accused of witchcraft imprisoned there.

Corrag lay on the filthy floor, ironically in the same dark cell her mother had been imprisoned in all these years before. She pulled out her runes, that were hidden under her skirts, still in the same little leather pouch that Elf had kept them in. She knew she was dying, and willed it to be soon, before she was sentenced to hanging or worse, the flames.

Her time spent in the tollbooth went by in a daze, with Corrag slipping in and out of consciousness as her fever spiked. Then, one day, she was dragged out of her cell and taken in a caged cart to Dumbarton Rock castle, where she was made to sit on a stool in front of a table where a large, overweight man sat staring at her with a lace handkerchief pressed firmly to his nose.

In his hand was a quill, and the table was littered with piles of paper. A prison guard stood silently behind her as the man began to speak.

He had a northern English accent, when he introduced himself as the Reverend Richard Stevenson, a scholar and investigator of witches. The Reverend told Corrag he was writing the memoirs for all the witches that were brought to the tollbooth, that her story may help prevent other young women from choosing the devils path.

Corrag stared at him uncomprehending, through long, grey strands of her filthy, lice-infested hair, her green eyes dead and hollow, surrounded in dark rings on her ravished face. She was only thirty-seven but looked nearly ninety. Her hands searched for comfort in the bag of runes that she had under her skirt, and as she grasped them, the guard stepped forward, ripped them from her hands. Corrag howled, begging to have them returned to her, as the guard handed the bag to the Reverend.

He tipped the runes out onto his desk, crossing himself as he did so. He looked in disgust at the pathetic creature who was wailing incoherently in front of him. "Madam, you may have these devil's stones returned to you when we are finished. For now, let us start at the beginning."

It took Corrag two days to tell her story. She became too weak to continue the first day, but a night in a new prison cell in the castle, without her beloved runes, spurred her enough to confess to all the next day.

The Reverend, true to his word, returned the little leather pouch of runes to her when she had finished her tale. He had pity for

Corrag, as he did with many of the witches he questioned, but his pity was diminished greatly when she confessed to killing Elf.

All of Scotland had heard of the brutal murders at Glencoe by now, and the Reverend thought that keeping Corrag alive for the time being, as a possible witness, would be advisable. He told the magistrates that she should be kept at Dumbarton Castle and fed properly whilst he sent letters onto his colleagues in Edinburgh. And so, it was ordered that Corrag be fed and cared for while she was their prisoner.

By the time the guards eventually got around to bringing a bowl of porridge to Corrag, she was long dead, her runes set out in a neat formation around her body.

**

Present Day

Kenneth sat back in his chair thinking. Corrag's story was tragic, but so were many others in these days. What stood out to him was the leather bag of runes that Corrag was so attached to, and he wondered what had happened to them.

The guards would probably have been afraid of them or not have understood what they were, so they were likely thrown away, or even buried with Corrag. Kenneth knew that Dumbarton castle had storage rooms crammed with centuries old artefacts, all of which had been put on an inventory.

Perhaps there was a chance the bag of runes had survived? It was a long shot, and probably ridiculous, but Kenneth decided he would go to Dumbarton anyway. He had been born in Dumbarton and knew the retired Curator of the Maritime Museum very well. He and David Bald had gone to Dumbarton Academy together, where they had spent their late teens impressing the girls with their boating skills on Loch Lomond. They had also attended each other's weddings. So, when Kenneth called him as a matter of urgency, David was immediately ready to help. Whether his old friend believed his story was hard to tell, but he said he would arrange for Kenneth to go through the inventory in the very unlikely chance the runes had been kept.

Kenneth left immediately for Dumbarton. It would take him a good couple of hours to get there, depending on the tourist traffic. He could be back in Fort William the next morning. Time was of the essence, for Kirstin was bound to attack again that evening. He hoped the boys were still safe with Angus.

Chapter Twenty-Three

"What's down there?" asked Ollie as he watched James use a little plastic spade to dig up the mud under a row of bushes.

"I don't know yet. Corri says it's for me, but I have to find it," said James, busily lifting clumps of soft, damp soil and dumping them unceremoniously on the beautifully mown lawn.

Glen and Rob were sitting on the garden chairs, both of them engrossed in a book of their choosing. It had been decided that the boys were never to be left alone, and as Anna and Calum had gone for a well needed forty winks, Glen had volunteered that he and Rob watch them.

"Can I help? How do you know where to dig?" asked Ollie.

"She said to dig by the big bushes that smell really stinky," said James.

Ollie pulled on one of the stalks of the giant rosemary bush and gave it a big sniff. "Yuck!" he said. "This must be it, it stinks!" He knelt down next to James and started using his hands to pull out the soil. Dexter started to join in, digging with his paws and sending a pile of soil soaring into a heap behind him.

Glen's eyes flicked over to them; they were there, safe and sound. It didn't register that they were now sitting in a pile of dirt, as his eyes drifted back to the thriller he was glued to.

"Look how long this worm is?" said Ollie, pulling the wriggling, slimy creature out of the soil.

"I found a bigger one," said James, picking up another. "Look."

The boys started stretching out the worms to see which one was the longest.

"Hurry, keep digging boys," said Corrag, who was standing over them. "Ye havnae a lot of time."

"But what are we looking for?" asked James, putting his worm down with a sigh and retrieving his spade. "Stop it, Dexter!" The dog still did not like Corrag's presence and was growling quietly under his breath.

"Just dig a bit further, yer almost there," said Corrag, unwilling to try and describe the charm she had made for Jamie all these years before. James would not understand the significance of it, but Corrag was sure it would protect him from Kirstin.

The boys dug deeper, piling the soil up behind them as they reached the roots of the ancient rosemary bush. James saw something with a yellowish tinge in the soil. He put his hand in and pulled out a piece of twine that was attached to many small bones and beaks of birds.

"Yuck! A dirty, dead bird necklace," said James, pulling a face of disgust.

"It's a special necklace, ye can clean the dirt aff James, then ye can wear it," said Corrag.

"What about me?" demanded Ollie. "Don't I get one?"

"Ye must let James wear this. He needs it tae protect him," said Corrag.

"Why don't I need protecting?" demanded Ollie angrily.

"I can protect ye, Ollie, but I cannae protect yer brother frae Kirstin. Ye want tae help him don't ye?" said Corrag.

"S'pose," said Ollie, still not particularly happy with the unfairness of the situation.

The boys ran back towards to cottage to clean off the necklace. Glen glanced at them as they sped by. "Where are you two going?" he asked lazily.

"To wash a necklace," cried James as they ran inside.

"Okay, then," said Glen still staring at his book.

Rob looked up from his book with a puzzled look on his face. "To wash a necklace?" he asked Glen, who just shrugged in response. They both returned to their reads.

Anna could hear the boys in the kitchen, and she could hear the tap running. She rubbed her eyes and sat up in bed, still feeling groggy and tired. She looked over at Calum who was fast asleep, so she slid out from under the covers and grabbed her cardigan. She still had her jeans and tee-shirt on, they had just collapsed in bed for a nap, but she had no idea how long they had been asleep. She smiled to herself as she heard the boys playing; they sounded happy and completely normal after their adventure on the island with Angus.

As she walked in the kitchen, she stopped, gasped and stared in horror at her boys and the dog. They were literally all black with dirt and mud from head to foot. There were pools of muddy water all over the floor, and the working surfaces were drenched also. James turned around to her beaming, a white smile showing through a blackened face.

"Look, Mummy, we got the mud off," he said, holding up a grotesque necklace of bones.

Anna heard an amused snort from behind her. Calum had followed her out and was staring at the scene trying to keep a straight face.

"Well, you got mud everywhere else, what on earth have you been doing? Where is Uncle Glen?" said Anna, unsure whether to be cross or not.

"He's in the garden reading his book," said Ollie, trying to work out if they were in trouble.

Anna rolled her eyes then turned to Calum. "Okay, your choice, you either bathe them or clean the kitchen," she said.

Calum laughed, "I'll clean the kitchen. I'll leave these little monsters to you."

Half an hour later, they went back out in the garden, the boys and Dexter now squeaky clean. The dog had been flung in the shower after the boys. James was insisting he wore that awful necklace that he had found. Anna was reluctant to allow him at first; she could only imagine the germs that lived on that thing. But when James told her that Corri had made them find it, she relented. Any sort of protection, however hideous, was welcome at the moment.

"You're awake," said Glen when they came out of the cottage. "It's been all quiet here, the boys have been playi..." Glen's eyes had drifted over to the bushes where the boys had been, all he could see were huge piles of muddy soil all over the once pristine lawn. "What the?"

"Yep, you and Rob are both sacked from watching the kids' duty," said Anna feigning disgust. "They had mud all over them, which they brought in and put all over the kitchen. Good job, bro!"

"Erm, well they seemed happy enough," replied Glen with a grimace, trying to make eye contact with Rob for some support. Rob was successfully hiding his face in his book.

It was just after six, and they were all hungry, so it was decided that the easiest thing to do was to go to the Clachaig again for food. James was fiddling with his bone necklace as they walked down the road, while Ollie scowled jealously at him. "It's not fair," he told Calum. "I want one too."

"We can try and find one like it in the gift shops tomorrow," whispered Calum. "Or something else, necklaces can be a bit girly." Ollie giggled.

Kirstin climbed down from the mountain in Helena's stolen body when she saw them all leave the cottage. She kept coughing and she could feel that the young woman's body was burning up. Helena was feebly trying to regain control but she was powerless and posed no threat to Kirstin.

Tonight, Kirstin would reclaim her son and take him with her into the Otherworld. Helena's body would be returned to her then, but she would undoubtedly be dead by then. It was the only way Kirstin could cross back over; she would have to kill her host. Jamie's host would have to die also.

Kirstin found the cottage completely locked up, including all the windows. They were obviously playing it safe. No matter, they would not be able to stop her when darkness fell. She tried the pool house, and finding the door unlocked, she decided she would wait there. She dared not stay out in the open as the police were looking for Helena. Shivering despite the warmth inside, Kirstin sat herself down on a sun bed, waiting for darkness to fall.

"Kirstin," Corrag's voice rang through the pool house.

"Why are ye here, Corrag?" replied Kirstin, her voice hoarse, but it did nothing to hide her irritation. "You havnae any power over me here, I'm in the world of the living now."

"Perhaps that's true, but yer as misguided noo as ye were back in the days before the massacre. I never meant ye any harm, Kirstin. I never took yer Jamie. He lived tae be a man, and he awaits ye in the afterlife. If ye harm this bairn, ye will never get tae see yer son again," said Corrag, materialising next to Kirstin.

"Liar! Dae ye think I dinnae recognise my own child. He belongs tae me!" Kirstin spat at her.

"I've protected the bairn against yer evil, Kirstin, and that's what ye've become—evil. Ye cannae harm him; he wears the charm ye should have given Jamie," Corrag told her sadly. "I never meant tae hurt ye. Ye were always my girl, and I would have helped ye if ye had let me."

"Yer feeble witch's magic is nae as strong as mine. Dae ye think a pile of bones will stop me? Go back tae yer wanderings, Corrag. Ye have no right tae be here. This wis my home, these are my mountains, and he is my son," cried Kirstin, then coughed violently. Her lungs were agony.

Helena's body was getting weaker; the time spent on the mountains with no nourishment had taken its toll. No matter, she would not need it for long. When she finished coughing, she looked around. Corrag was gone. No doubt her magic was too weak to allow her to stay for long. Corrag's interference just irritated her more than bothered her. That old charm the old hag had made would not prevent her from taking her child.

Kirstin could feel that Helena's body was shivering violently, so she pulled a towel that had been left from one of the other beds, wrapping it around her shoulders. She needed this body's strength to carry the boy. He wouldn't come willingly; his mind had been twisted too much for that. He believed that Anna was his mother, and Kirstin would not have time to convince him otherwise. He would soon enough understand, when she took him home.

Kirstin lay back on the bed, her eyes wide open as she watched the sky turn pink, then red and orange, and finally darkness extinguished the last of the colour and blackness fell. Soon after, she heard their voices as they walked up the driveway. Kirstin knew they could not see her, so she lay still, watching as they crossed the drive to the front door of the cottage and let themselves in. Kirstin still remained where she was as the lights of the cottage flickered on. She could wait until they had turned in for the night. It would be easier to grab Jamie then.

Chapter Twenty-Four

With nightfall came heavy rain, the clear sky that had been prevalent most of the day clouded over quickly with nightfall, and the wind rose to gale force proportions. The large glass windows of the pool house rattled as furious gusts battered them from all sides. It was almost midnight now and Kirstin watched as the last of the cottage lights were switched off. She sat up on the sun bed and let the towel slip off her. Helena's body was stiff and feverish, but Kirstin could ignore that. It was time.

Anna had insisted that the boys slept with her. There was no way she was letting them sleep alone with Helena still not caught. Calum had said he would sleep in the other bedroom in the old cottage across from Anna; he didn't want to go home for that same reason. He still carried some level of responsibility for bringing Helena here in the first place. At least Anna had seemed to forgive him, she had been snuggling into him when they were seated in one of the booths at dinner, and she allowed him to hold her hand on the walk back to the cottage.

No one had referred to Helena when they were out, mainly because the boys were there, and there didn't seem any point in frightening them. But everyone was still silently anticipating that phone call from the police to confirm that they had finally caught her.

James had been playing with the bone charm that hung around his neck throughout the meal. It was still a point of contention with Ollie, who scowled at him jealously. Calum didn't like the necklace at all. The bird's beaks, in particular, were putting him off his food, and he was thankful he hadn't ordered chicken.

Calum asked Anna quietly whilst they were walking back up from the Clachaig if she intended on leaving Glencoe the next day. Anna said she wasn't sure, but at this point it might be the safest option. He couldn't help but agree with her, so he suggested that he drive back with her. His car was in Edinburgh anyway, and he would feel better about her travelling, after all that had happened, if he was with her. At least he could then be sure that Helena wasn't following them.

They had sat up for a little while but the boys were sleepy and Anna didn't want them going to bed alone. She gave Calum a peck on the cheek and said goodnight to Glen and Rob before taking the boys off to bed. Anna was sandwiched in the middle of Ollie and James, with Dexter on her feet as she read them a couple of bedtime stories. They were soon fast asleep, and as uncomfortable as Anna knew this position was going to be in a few hours, she felt safe and content with her sons close to her.

The rest of the household had gone to bed a short time later, everyone exhausted from the previous night. Calum walked around the cottage and checked all the windows and doors before he turned in. The wind outside had picked up, and he could hear the beginnings of rain hitting the window panes. It was going to be a stormy night.

Glen and Rob had gone to bed; they both read for a couple of hours before switching off the lights. The wind was howling relentlessly around the cottage, a fierce summer storm battering its way through the mountains. Had it not been for the horrible night before watching Helena become possessed with Kirstin's ghost, they would have probably enjoyed the wild weather, but as it stood, they would both be glad when morning arrived and they could all pack up and leave.

The door of the pool house crashed open as it flew out of Kirstin's hand in the wind. She was buffeted fiercely as she made her way to the boys' bedroom window at the side of the cottage. As she expected, the curtains were drawn and the windows locked, but this wouldn't stop her. She started to cough painfully again, but the howling wind thankfully drowned out the sound. Kirstin bent down and checked the runes that Helena had placed below the boys' bedroom window, then carried on around the outskirts of the cottage, checking that the other runes were all still where they had been placed. They would be the source of her power.

Kirstin became aware that Corrag was watching, but she simply ignored her. She was no threat to her any longer. The rain was soaking through her, but she didn't notice as she finally checked the remaining rune was in place, arriving at the front door. How this cottage had changed, there was nothing left of the beautiful home Rab had built for her centuries before.

Kirstin muttered a spell under her breath, placing the rune on the lock. There was a faint tinkling sound from the other side of the door as the key fell out of the lock onto the stone floor. Kirstin tried the handle and the door opened. Careful not to allow the wind to gust in, Kirstin slipped in the doorway, quietly closing it behind her. Helena's stolen body was trembling violently as Kirstin made her way quietly through the kitchen. She cursed the weakness of this pathetic woman she inhabited.

She made her way down the corridor to the boy's bedroom, but as she reached their doorway, Dexter started to bark from Anna's bedroom. The stupid beast had woken and sensed her presence. Kirstin cursed herself for not dealing with the animal first; she would have to move quickly. She opened the door to the boys' room and sensed instantly that there was no one there.

Snarling angrily, she retraced her steps back to the old part of the cottage. She could hear Dexter's low growl coming from Anna's room. So, she tried the door to the bedroom opposite, and as she stepped inside, Calum sat up and switched on the light. He blinked while his eyes adjusted to the light and found himself staring at a crazed, dishevelled form of a woman that had once been Helena. There was no resemblance to Helena there now.

"Calum?" said Anna as she staggered sleepily out of her bedroom opposite. "Is that you walking around? Or is the dog barking at the wind?"

Dexter came tearing out the bedroom after her, barking viciously as he ran into Calum's room approaching Kirstin crouched low with his hackles up. But Kirstin's eyes were looking directly at Anna.

Then everything happened at once. Kirstin clapped her hands and the lights went out, plunging them all into darkness. Suddenly, Dexter howled horrifically, then fell silent, as Calum jumped to his feet, stumbling around blindly in the dark. He felt something brush past him and then his body froze to the spot. He struggled helplessly, falling to the floor, unable to move any of his limbs.

Anna had turned and ran back to her bedroom to protect the boys. Blinded by the sudden darkness and terrified of Kirstin, she screamed out for the boys to wake up. She then felt cold, wet hands grab her from behind and she was thrown by a powerful force into the wall. Anna banged her head hard, falling to the floor winded and panicking, trying to cry out between gasping for air. Somewhere in the distance, she could hear Glen's voice shouting for her, but her ears were still ringing from the force of the impact. She tried to crawl up the wall to her feet, but felt another blow come down on the back of her head and she fell unconscious to the ground.

Glen and Rob had awoken and ran to their bedroom door which was in the new part of the cottage, but it was jammed shut.

They could hear the boys screaming and Calum shouting, so they both put their shoulders to the door and tried to ram their way out. It was useless, the door wouldn't budge. They tried the windows but it was the same, some sort of force was trapping them inside the room, they couldn't even smash the glass.

Kirstin walked into Anna's bedroom and the lights flicked on. James and Ollie were both still on the bed, clinging onto each other in terror.

"Jamie, I'm here fir ye," said Kirstin in Helena's body.

The boys were almost apoplectic with fear. All they could see was this white-faced, soaked woman, with dark rings surrounding insane, colourless eyes. They couldn't understand what she was saying as she moved closer to them with a hideous smile. James grabbed the duvet and pulled it over their heads, and they lay there in each other's arms shaking with fear.

Puzzled at James's reaction to her, Kirstin waved her hand, and the duvet flew across the room, leaving the boys completely unprotected. She moved towards James. then stopped dead in her tracks when she saw the bone necklace hanging around his neck. Her eyes narrowed with anger as she recognised Corrag's handiwork. "Ye won't stop me noo, ye witch," she hissed, but an invisible force was stopping her from getting any closer to the boy.

In fury, she raised her arms and screamed unnaturally, the windows and light bulbs smashed in a million shards, spraying the entire room. The wind and rain raced in, catching hold of the curtains, making them flap wildly. James and Ollie were covered in glass and bleeding for tiny cuts, but they still hung onto each other on the bed.

Then Kirstin pointed at Ollie, fixing her eyes on him as she muttered another spell, willing him to obey her. He turned his face towards James, his face wet with tears as he reached out with his hand and pulled the charm from his brother's neck, throwing it across the floor. He then burst into tears, trying to hug James who was staring at him, not understanding what Ollie had done.

Calum was beginning to feel some movement in his limbs again and he somehow managed to pull himself to his feet. He tried to take a step forward but fell over. Determined, he hauled himself up again, this time finding it easier to move. Kirstin was losing her hold on him. He forced his feet to move into the hallway. It was as if he were marching through thick mud, the effort of every step exhausting. He kicked something on the floor and he bent down to feel warm fur. Dexter was lying there, still breathing, but his fur was wet and sticky.

He fought his way to Anna's room, he could hear the boys screaming and crying, but he couldn't hear Anna. He was almost at her bedroom door when he saw her shape on the floor. "Oh my God, Anna!" he cried as he fell with difficulty and pulled her into his arms. Her eyes were closed, but she was also breathing. He laid her back down gently, then got up again and staggered into the bedroom.

There was broken glass everywhere, and the wind and rain were blowing in wildly. The boys were on the bed, and Kirstin was trying to separate James from Ollie. Calum threw himself at her, grabbing her hair, trying to pull her to the ground. But she shrieked and spun around, reinforcing the spell that had held him immobile. She spat in his face as he collapsed against the bed, helpless once again

"Jamie, here!" Kirstin shrieked, now furious. Ollie was thrown backwards as James was pulled by an invisible force towards her.

She grabbed hold of his arm and dragged him from the bed, but he fought wildly against her. She'd had enough, so she snapped her fingers, and James fell limp in her arms. She picked him up as if he were a doll, and threw him over her shoulder. She then turned towards Calum, kicking him hard on the side of his head before she stepped over him and left the room.

The door to Glen and Rob's bedroom suddenly sprung open at last. They ran out as the lights came back on, illuminating the devastation in front of them.

Anna was beginning to stir and Glen ran over to her. The back of her head was caked in blood, but apart from that, there were no other injuries he could see.

"James?" she whispered as he sat her upright against the wall and went to check on the boys. Anna's room was a mess, glass everywhere, and the wind was still howling through the window. Calum was trying to stand up, although he was very unsteady, and he also had a nasty cut to his cheek. Ollie was lying on the bed with a pillow over his head. Glen could see he was covered in blood. Panicking, he ran over and scooped the small boy up to find with relief that it was just small superficial cuts from the flying glass, made to look worse as Ollie was now drenched from the rain streaming through the broken window. Ollie buried his little head in his uncle's chest, crying quietly. "She took James," he whispered through his tears.

Rob had found Dexter. The dog was badly injured but was awake and whimpering. "Where's James?" he asked Glen when he saw him with Ollie.

"James!" Glen shouted then saw the duvet in a pile on the other side of the room. He rushed over and hauled it up. James wasn't there.

"He's gone," said Calum, choking as he tried to speak. "The bitch took him."

Chapter Twenty-Five

Kenneth had arrived in Dumbarton around three o'clock in the afternoon. He knew the old town well as he was born in Dumbarton just before the second world war. He remembered the bombing of his home town as if it were yesterday. Dumbarton was a ship-building town situated on the banks of the river Clyde. It built many of the warships for the war effort and was therefore a prime target for the German Luftwaffe.

Kenneth's nostalgia always got the better of him as he drove into his hometown, so he took his usual small detour, driving past the old stone tenement block he used to live in with his parents. They were on the top floor, which meant a lot of climbing up and down the wide stone staircase when the air raid sirens went off. The building was still there, but it had been turned into modernised apartments now.

He arrived on time at Dumbarton castle and met his old friend David who, after greeting him, took him immediately down to a small room that could only be described as a broom cupboard. Kenneth had explained the urgency of his visit to David; he was given a brief lesson on how to operate the one computer set up on a small desk that looked like it belonged in some ancient school vault. It still had a stained inkwell carved in the top of it. Kenneth started to go through the massive inventory of artefacts that were still held in the castle.

It was after seven o'clock when he finally clicked on the last page of the inventory. There was nothing that remotely resembled a bag of runes. He had known it was a long shot, and now he was at a loss on how to proceed.

He phoned David to thank him and left the castle deflated, deciding to take a room for the night. He was too tired to drive back to Fort William now, and his night vision was not all that great anyway.

He needed a place with a bar, so he managed to get himself a room at the Premier Inn in Dumbarton, which had a comfortable bar where he could get good beer and some plain food. None of that fancy foreign muck they served everywhere now. David arrived when Kenneth was halfway through his second pint. He was accompanied with a very smartly dressed elderly lady, who Kenneth didn't recognise.

"I thought I'd find ye here," said his old friend while he held a chair out for the lady. "Let me introduce ye tae Margaret Duffie. She used tae work at the castle back in the late fifties and sixties. I've explained tae Margaret that ye havnae had any luck finding what ye were looking fir."

"I would have bin surprised if they were still there, they were probably buried along wi' the witch," replied Kenneth. "Nice tae meet ye, Margaret. I dinnae suppose ye ken anything about these runes?"

"Actually, that's why I'm here," said Margaret in a very soft-spoken Edinburgh accent. "David telephoned me earlier and told me about your search. When I worked at the castle, we didn't use computers, of course, but part of my job was to make inventories of the artefacts that were left after the war. Things had been moved around a lot, many of the items that were deemed to have no value had been packed in crates, with the intention of sending them onto the museum in Edinburgh. However, that never happened, so they were eventually stored in one of the dungeon cells that were sealed off in the castle. Part of my job was to go through the crates and make a list of what was in there. Most of the items were old clothing and shoes, of no value to the museum, but I do remember an old leather purse filled with stones. I remember them because they gave me the heebie-jeebies when I touched them. I put them back in the crate with all the old clothing, and I think they were most probably forgotten about. They had no value to the museum at the time, and I suspect they have not bothered to put them on their computerised inventory."

Kenneth breathed out heavily when Margaret finished her story. He felt his old heart racing with excitement. "So dae ye think the stones are likely to still be there?" he asked.

"Well, unless they decided to clear out the crates from the cell, I don't see why not. There were only three crates, and they were not in a part of the castle that is open to the public, so they were in nobody's way," replied Margaret.

Kenneth could hardly contain his excitement. David promised he would come and pick him up first thing and take him back to the castle. Kenneth didn't sleep much in the clean and pristine hotel bed, counting the hours until dawn.

The next morning, he was pacing the carpark, waiting for David to arrive, which he did on time. They arrived at the castle too early, so they took a seat on one of the wooden benches in the park that led to the castle entrance. The curator arrived at eight o' clock sharp as David had arranged for them. They made their way down some steep stone steps and through a door close to the French prison. The ancient steps were narrow and steep, and they led down to a very inhospitable, dark cell. Even with the old electric lighting, it was still very dimly lit, but David had anticipated this and brought a torch with him.

It didn't take them long to find the three crates stored up against the back corner of the cell. They were not particularly large crates, and on opening the first one, they found Margaret's description of the contents had been accurate. It was full of dirty old clothing, very dated, probably from the prisoners that were executed here at the castle. Kenneth had no idea how old they were, though he guessed they spanned the centuries. They pulled out the clothing of the first crate and found nothing that resembled the leather bag of runes. Again, the second crate was the same, so all hope rested on the third and final crate.

The runes were there, Kenneth saw them as soon as they had prised the lid off. The brown leather pouch sat on top of the clothing that had been stuffed in there. He reached over to pick them up, and as he did so, he felt an unnerving sensation race through his body.

He pulled at the drawstring on the bag, opening it, then he poured some of the stones out onto the palm of his hand. They were shinier than he had imagined, like polished granite, and the markings could be seen clearly on each stone, but still a dark menacing sensation reverberated within him as he handled them.

"It looks like ye've found them," said David, peering at the stones over Kenneth's shoulder. Kenneth suddenly found he had to resist the urge to snatch them away from his old friend. The power of the runes had already begun to take effect on him. He tipped them back into the pouch, disgusted by the feelings they stirred in him.

"Is there any way I can take these frae the castle?" said Kenneth his shrouded eyes intense as he looked at David. "Lives may depend on it."

"Aye well, I wis thinking aboot that. I thought we could dae a transfer note, fir ye tae take the runes back tae Glencoe museum. They dae belong tae Corrag of Glencoe, and I have already spoken with the curator of the castle here. He disnae see any reason why not. They have been hidden away fir years. Nae one's gonnae miss them," said Jeff.

"I dinnae ken how tae thank ye," said Kenneth. "Ye never cease tae surprise me."

"Well, I'm sure I'll think off something one day," said David, delighted by Kenneth's reaction.

Two hours later, Kenneth pulled his car into the Green Welly carpark at Tyndrum for a quick toilet stop. He bought himself a giant Mars bar and got back in his car. The bag of runes was sitting in the front seat next to him. He pulled out of the car park and onto the A82 to Glencoe. He wasn't sure what affect the runes would have on Kirstin's ghost, but they certainly had power; he could feel it radiate from the seat next to him. He hoped Anna and her friends had had a peaceful night at the cottage, but as he got closer to the Glencoe valley, a sense of dread began to fall over him.

When he finally pulled into the driveway of Kirstin's Cot shortly before noon, his heart sank. There were three police cars parked there.

Chapter Twenty-Six

Rob called the police as Glen tried to help Anna stand. Her head was spinning, and she couldn't focus, as her brother led her to a chair in the kitchen. She suddenly felt sick, so she threw herself at the sink to empty her stomach.

Calum had got movement back in all his limbs and he was sitting with Ollie, who was wrapped in a towel. Calum was tending to his cuts, which didn't look too bad once all the blood was cleaned off him. He put plasters on the deeper ones, whilst Ollie sat quietly, still shaking.

Sergeant Burns arrived along with his wife and five other police officers. He took one look at Anna and called for an ambulance. She had already refused to let Glen call for one. The paramedics arrived within the next fifteen minutes and they treated Anna at the kitchen table, as she refused to go to the hospital. The cut on her head wasn't too deep, so they used some paper stitches and glue to seal it. It was the concussion they were more worried about. Anna kept being sick.

They then turned to Dexter, who lay whimpering with his head on Rob's knee. His back leg was twisted and broken, and the emergency vet had already been called. The paramedics put Dexter carefully on a stretcher and carried him out to the ambulance, then they took him straight to the veterinary hospital where the vet was waiting for him.

Anna was pale and quiet, her head was thumping and she couldn't think clearly. With her focus returning, so did her fear for James. She knew he would be terrified, and she blamed herself for not leaving as soon as they had returned to the cottage with Angus yesterday. She had put her children in danger, and she couldn't fathom why she had been such an idiot. Her eyes drifted over to the walking boots in the corner of the kitchen. She got unsteadily to her feet. She was going to find her son.

"Anna, sit down," said Calum, firmly grabbing hold of her and depositing her back on her chair. He still had hold of Ollie, who was now strangely quiet. The little boy had both arms wrapped tightly around Calum's neck. "Come on, Ollie, go to your mummy, she needs a hug," Calum whispered into his ear as he prized the little boy's fingers from his neck and put him gently on Anna's knee. Ollie curled up in a tight ball as Anna hugged him to her chest.

"I need to find James," she said stubbornly. "I'm not sitting here while he's out there with that mad woman. He'll be terrified."

"The police are out in force, daylight is almost here and they will have helicopters in the sky searching. Helena won't get far with him; she looked like she was on the brink of collapse herself," said Calum.

"I need to be doing something," said Anna but her head was still spinning, and she started to retch again.

Calum brought her a bowl, massaging her back as she was sick again. "You must lie down, Anna, you have a concussion."

"I'm not going anywhere," said Anna.

Her brother and Rob appeared back in the kitchen. They were dressed in their hiking gear. "We're joining the search," said Glen. "Anna, stay here. I have my phone. As soon as I know something, I will call you. We'll find him."

"I should go with them," said Calum. "I know the area better. Can I trust you to stay here?"

"I'll stay wi' her," said PC Kirsty Burns. "And I think we should call Dr McKenzie tae come have a wee look at ye. He may be able tae give ye something for that sickness."

Anna nodded. As much as she wanted to go with them, she knew she would spin out as soon as she stood up, and she couldn't leave Ollie. Calum needed to be out there searching with the rest of them.

Calum was dressed and out of the door within minutes. Daylight had revealed a grey, wet morning in the mountains. The high peaks were covered with thick, low clouds, and a heavy drizzle soaked them through very quickly, but at least the intense wind from last night had gone. A police dog van arrived, with two German Shepherds inside, ready to join the search.

Sergeant Burns was leaning over the bonnet of his car with a map, coordinating the search. The heavy clouds were going to make it difficult for the helicopters, and so they were relying on the foot patrols and the dogs.

Glen gave the police dogs James's toy bunny, Buzz, to get the scent, and the animals were soon off in the direction of Sgorr nam Fiannaidh. Only the lower slopes of the mountain were visible, and

Calum had a bad feeling in the pit of his stomach that this wasn't going to be easy.

Anna was still vomiting when Dr McKenzie arrived, along with a woman who looked oddly familiar. The woman was probably in her sixties by the look of her steely grey hair that was tied up in a tight bun, but her face looked younger, smooth-skinned with a good summer tan. She wore a navy roll neck sweater with blue jeans and hiking boots, and her green eyes were full of compassion as she waited quietly until Dr McKenzie had given Anna an injection to stop her being sick, along with some sedative to make her relax.

"I'm sorry to intrude," said the woman in a soft accent, pulling a chair up next to Anna and Ollie. "I'm Fiona MacAlistair, Calum's mother. He phoned me and asked me to check on you. I'm so sorry this has happened to you here in Glencoe."

Anna tried a weak smile, but tears began to fall. "I'm so scared for James," she said.

"I'm sure Calum and the police will find him," said Fiona, putting her arm around Anna. "I think perhaps you should do what the doctor has told you and lie down until the sickness passes. Your other laddie is fast asleep there."

Anna looked down at Ollie still curled up on her knee. He was fast asleep; it had all been too much for him. She allowed Calum's mother to lead her to the boys' bedroom, were she and Ollie lay down together on James's bed. Anna closed her eyes but knew she wouldn't sleep. She just needed to get rid of this headache.

Fiona looked down sadly at Anna. She couldn't imagine how traumatised Anna must be feeling, but at least Dr McKenzie's sedative was working. He had been worried that her refusal to lie down would not help with the concussion, so Fiona had promised to get her to bed. She prayed they would find James before Anna awoke.

***

Kirstin was struggling as she made her way up the mountain. She hadn't managed a great distance as James was heavier than she anticipated, and Helena's body was in a very weakened state. The only way she could perform the spell to take them both across to the Otherworld, was to use the runes that Helena had left for her in the cave. But James was like a dead weight and Kirstin was using a lot of her power just to keep Helena's body from collapsing. She had James over her shoulders as she used her hands to help pull her up the wet, slippery slope, but the boy's limp body kept sliding off, time and time again.

She could hear the dogs barking in the distance and felt a moment's fear for the first time since she had stepped over into the material world. She would have to awaken the boy and make him walk with her. It was the only way. Helena's stolen body was no longer strong enough to carry him.

Kirstin laid James on the wet heather and tapped into her now dwindling power, muttering some words, then waited as James began to moan. She shook him and he opened his eyes, that suddenly became bright and alert as he stared in terror at Helena's deranged, sickly face. She was looking at him oddly, her milky pale blue eyes did not seem to belong to Helena's face. "I want my mummy!" James cried out, lashing out with his feet.

"I'm yer mam," hissed Kirstin angrily, trying to stop him kicking her. Her voice was rasping and broken, and she felt an excruciating pain in her lungs.

"No, you're not! I want my mummy!" screamed James, louder now, kicking and punching against Helena's frail body.

Kirstin grabbed hold of James's arm, but he continued to squirm, kicking out with his feet, struggling to get free. There was a crashing from behind them and a majestic white stag came to a skidding halt just uphill from them. It put its head down, snorting angrily, shaking its vicious-looking antlers in a threatening display. Kirstin loosened her grip on James in shock, and James bit her hard on her upper arm, then managed to pull one of his arms from her grip.

Kirstin cried out in pain as James bit her, then turned towards the stag, her eyes filled with cold fury, "You!" she snarled, but hardly any sound came from Helena's raw throat. Her breathing was laboured and painful.

The stag charged towards her and Kirstin threw herself backwards in fright, letting go of her remaining grip on James. The boy didn't hang around, his feet were bare, and his pyjamas were soaked through, but he was up and running before the stag reached them.

Kirstin lay on the ground, her hands reaching out towards the disappearing boy. She tried to cry out after him, but Helena's body started convulsing in a fit of coughing. By the time she stopped and could get her breath, she had lost sight of James. Kirstin tried to struggle to her feet, but the white stag stood before her, head still downwards, threatening an attack.

"Why?" cried Kirstin. "The boy means nothing tae ye!"

The white stag remained motionless, watching her every move.

Helena's body was shivering uncontrollably, it was taking all of Kirstin's power to keep the woman moving. She had no choice now, she had to let the boy go. She stumbled forwards, in the direction of her cave, desperate to get under cover and away from her attacker. But the white stag charged towards her, its antlers hitting the back of her legs, knocking her back down to the ground. All Kirstin could think of now was to get to the cave, but the stag was standing over her, stamping its feet, not allowing her to move forward.

"Why?" she began to weep helplessly. Then she collapsed back onto the ground, finally admitting defeat.

***

James was lost, soaked through and very cold, but he kept running. He could hear Corri's voice in his head, telling him which direction to take.

As he slipped down the grassy slope, he thought he could hear the sound of men's voices calling his name. He called back, but his small voice was lost in the vastness of the mountain. Suddenly, the white stag was at his side. It looked down at him, then galloped off towards the voices. The dogs sensed it first and started barking excitedly as they pulled their handlers towards the stag.

"What are they playing at?" shouted one of the officers as he wrestled with the dogs. "It's a bloody deer!"

Calum recognised the white stag. "Follow it!" he yelled, running in its direction.

The stag raced back up the slope towards James, and Calum's heart leapt when he saw the small boy running towards him. Calum grabbed James up into his arms, hugging him with relief, before handing him over to his tearful Uncle Glen. The boy was soaked and cold but remarkably brave. There were no tears, just a small determined face pointing in Helena's direction. "She's up there," he told them.

"I'll phone Anna," said Calum, surprised to find that his voice was choked with emotion.

"Use my radio link. Ye'll nae get a signal here," said Billie.

***

Fiona MacAlistair decided it would be better to tell Anna now, rather than let her wake up in despair. So she shook Anna gently awake to tell her the news. Anna stared at her, confused for a second, still under the effects of the strong sedative the doctor had given her. Then the realisation of what Fiona was telling her dawned, and she collapsed sobbing in Fiona's arms.

Ollie woke up. "Why are you crying, Mummy?" he asked groggily. "Where's James?"

"He's on his way home," said Fiona, smiling at the wide-eyed, sleepy little boy.

"Who are you?" Ollie asked her suspiciously.

"I'm Calum's mummy," she replied. "I've just come to look after you until James comes home." Ollie's face relaxed a little, and Fiona wondered at how resilient children could be. Ollie seemed to have got over what had happened last night and was taking control by hugging his mother and telling her to stop crying.

"Mummy, it's good news," he reasoned. "James is okay, the horrible lady has gone."

Anna pulled Ollie close to her. "Okay, I'll stop," she whispered.

"Why don't you go and give your face a wash?" said Fiona kindly. "You don't want James to see you so upset, do you?"

***

Glen and Rob had stripped James of his wet pyjamas and wrapped him in a waterproof blanket whilst they carried him back down to the cottage. From what the police and Calum could establish from James, Helena was still up in the mountain, so they resumed their search. There was no way Calum could relax now, without knowing that Helena was in custody. The white stag was a short distance away, watching them. It started nodding its head up and down and kicking one of its front legs forward. Calum stared at it for a second.

"I think it wants us to follow," he said to Billie.

"Aye, I'm sure it does," replied the sergeant with just a touch of sarcasm. Billie was not about to believe that Helena was possessed by the ghost of some long dead MacDonald, let alone follow a stag on the assumption that the animal knew what it was doing.

The police dogs carried on tracking, but with no particular scent to follow now, it was more difficult. Calum decided to follow the stag, ignoring Billie's request that they should all stay together. Soon, he was lost in the low cloud that covered Sgorr nam

Fiannaidh, but he could still hear the voices of the police officers behind him as he followed the pathway towards the summit.

The police were calling out Helena's name but had no response.

When the white stag had left her alone, Kirstin had managed to drag herself off the path and was close to her cave now. They would never find her in there. She was finding it harder to breathe, the pain in her chest making her double over when she started to cough. She knelt on the ground, clutching her chest until she stopped coughing. As she raised her head, she saw that once again the white stag was there, watching her.

"I hear something!" shouted Calum back down the slope to the others.

"The dogs can hear something also," shouted the police dog handler who held them on a lead. He unclipped their collars. "Go! Find!" The dogs ran off in Kirstin's direction, soon passing Calum as he sprinted after them.

The dogs found Kirstin within seconds. She tried feebly to pick up a rock to throw at them, but Helena's tortured body had no strength left. Kirstin relented, this was useless. She would have to leave Helena for now, so she released her hold of Helena's mind, to allow her spirit to mingle freely with the mists of Glencoe. As soon as she was free from Helena's vessel, the drain on the power she had been using to maintain the woman's strength was lifted. She could feel her energy grow, but she could not cross back to the Otherworld yet. She still had to get Jamie, so Kirstin would remain a spirit for now, watching and waiting for another chance to come. It would not be long, of that she was sure. As Kirstin looked down on Helena's sick body, she sensed another strong presence in the spirit world with her. It was close to her, and she recognised the essence immediately.

"Yer interference will nae stop me, witch. Ye have nae power over me!" she called out to Corrag.

"Come with me, Kirstin. Leave this madness behind. Ye've been in the Otherworld too long. It's affecting yer judgement, blinding ye tae the truth," replied Corrag.

"My judgement is clear, I see the path to my Jamie, and ye'll nae stop me!" Kirstin voice travelled with the mist, but only Corrag could hear her.

"Yer insane, ye will be cast intae eternal darkness frae the Otherworld if ye try tae take the boy there. He doesnae belong in that place," replied Corrag, but she could no longer sense Kirstin. She had gone.

197

Calum could see Helena lying on the ground a short distance away. When he reached her, he saw there was something seriously wrong. She was soaked to the skin, but her face was fiery red with a burning fever. She was barely conscious, and her breathing was very shallow. She coughed horribly, then, clearly in pain, she turned her eyes to look at him. They were Helena's eyes that stared up at him, and he thankfully realised that Kirstin was gone.

The police arrived just behind him. They unfolded their mountain stretcher, placing Helena onto it. She was rambling incoherently as they brought her back down the mountain to a waiting ambulance.

Calum walked beside the stretcher, yet again riddled with guilt, but this time over Helena. There was no denying that Helena had been her own worst enemy, but she had not deserved this to happen to her. At the very least, she would end up in a psych ward, but more likely prison for kidnapping James. No one would believe a possession story. He promised himself that he would find her a good lawyer; it was the least he could do.

When they reached the ambulance, an oxygen mask was placed over Helena's face and she was taken with blue lights flashing to Fort William hospital. The police had not read her her rights yet, so she was to have a police guard with her at the hospital.

Calum returned to the cottage to find James sitting at the kitchen table, with a blanket around him and a huge mug of hot chocolate. Ollie, who had also demanded a hot chocolate, was busy sharing out the marshmallows. Both boys were covered in plasters, and Anna rolled her eyes as she explained that they had tried to outdo each other with the number of cuts they had. She looked pale, but her eyes seemed relieved when she saw Calum.

"Is it over?" she asked.

"Yes, they have Helena in custody. She's very ill, though. They've taken her to hospital, under police guard, of course," he replied grimly.

"James has been telling us how he got away from her," said Fiona, who handed him a hot cup of coffee. "He was very brave, a real super hero."

"She couldn't catch me!" said James proudly.

"She wouldn't catch me either," scowled Ollie, jealous with all the attention lavished on his brother.

There was a knock on the door, and Kenneth stuck his head around the door.

"Everything okay?" he said, his wild eyes wide with dreaded expectation.

"It is now," said Calum. "You missed all the excitement."

"Coffee?" said Fiona.

Kenneth sat and listened to the whole story, without interrupting for once. He had suspected something like this would happen, and even with Helena under guard at the hospital, he couldn't be sure they had got rid of Kirstin. It seemed unlikely to Kenneth that this was going to be the end of it, but he kept quiet. He could see Anna had had enough, so he waited until he got a chance to speak to Calum on his own.

Anna gave James and Ollie a warm bath, then the three of them went to snuggle down for an hour or two. Glen and Rob drove over to the veterinary hospital at Fort William to check on Dexter's progress.

Chapter Twenty-Seven

Kenneth was acting weird, Calum decided. The old man kept making strange, urgent eye gestures towards him across the kitchen table. When Anna and the boys turned in, Calum and Kenneth went through to the lounge, out of earshot of Anna. Calum turned to him. "What are ye daeng, man? Yer scaring me half tae death wi' these weird eyes of yers, dae ye have something tae tell me?" he said, slipping back into his local accent.

"A've discovered something, but I didnae want tae scare the lassie. She's bin through enough. I want ye tae have a look at this book here, at the passage I've marked fir ye," said Kenneth, who handed him Reverend Stevenson's book on The Witch Confessions.

He was both fascinated and horrified at Corrag's story, and when he finished, he looked over at Kenneth with a frown. "So, you think that Kirstin's ghost is here because of Corrag's curse?"

"Aye, I dae. If ye had asked me a week ago what I thought aboot ghosts in Glencoe, I'd have laughed. In all the years I've kent Nelly, she never talked in any detail aboot the ghosts here. She kent me better than that, I wouldnae have put any stock intae it. But Nelly wis a lovely wee woman, close friends wi' my Edith, visited her every day when she was ill. She helped me come tae terms wi' losing her in the end, but when I think of it, I only ever visited Nelly here once, and that was tae see the paintings that Edith had done for her. I never thought much aboot it then, but there must have been a reason she kept folk away, fir she wis a sociable wee soul," said Kenneth.

"I remember Nelly, everyone in the town knew her," said Calum, remembering the small, silver-haired lady always with a smile on her face. "You said you had just driven back from Dumbarton. Does that have anything to do with all this?"

"Aye, I wondered if I could find out anything else aboot Corrag and her runes. One of my oldest friends used tae be the curator at the Maritime Museum, and he got me a pass intae the castle inventory. It's a wee bit of a story how we found these, but I'm sure these are the runes that Corrag had on her just before she died. The source of her magic, I believe," said Kenneth, pulling out the small leather pouch from his satchel."

Calum leaned over to take a closer look, thinking to himself that it couldn't be possible they had survived that long. "After all this time, they were still at the castle?" he said dubiously.

"Aye, they'd bin stored away wi' bits of old clothing and rags fir centuries, nae one had bothered aboot them, they didnae hold any value, except tae Corrag. Here, try taking a hold of the pouch they're in, it disnae feel right," said Kenneth, handing the runes over to Calum.

As soon as he touched the leather, an involuntary shiver ran through him. He dropped the pouch on the coffee table. "You're right, there's something nasty about it. What are we supposed to do with them, Ken?"

"I wish I kent. But if these have anything tae dae with the reason Kirstin's here, then surely, they should be able tae get rid of her, somehow," replied Kenneth. "I just dinnae ken how."

"You said you found Corrag's confessions in one of your old books. Any chance you've got any books on ancient runes in your collection?" asked Calum, grasping at straws.

"I dinnae think so," replied Kenneth.

Calum picked up Glen's laptop. The boys had been playing games on, so it was just left lying. He opened it up and thankfully there was no password lock. He went into Google and typed in 'Runes and their meanings'. The pages immediately went to Norse Mythology, showing chart after chart of Viking Runes and their definitions.

Calum reluctantly picked up the leather pouch and tipped out the Runes onto the small table. Touching the stones themselves was more disturbing than touching the leather pouch. He and Kenneth turned all the runes so they were facing upwards, then started trying to decipher them. But none of the patterns seemed to match any of the rune markings on the screen in front of them. Calum tried another page, then another, but it was the same. None of the rune markings seemed to match any of the stones they had laid out in front of them.

"Perhaps they're not Viking," said Kenneth.

"That seems likely, but what else could they be?" said Calum with frustration. He cleared the search engine and typed in 'Different types of runes'. The screen switched to lists of many different types of runes, Jewish runes from the Kabbalah, to black magic runes that could supposedly summon Satan. Still, nothing seemed to jump out at him as he scrolled down the page. He clicked on a heading titled 'ancient runes' and almost immediately the page opened to a chart that showed markings very similar to the ones on Corrag's runes, although there were subtle differences.

"Wait a minute. I might have something," he said. Kenneth leaned over him and they both stared at the screen. As Calum continued to scroll down, diagrams of the same Runes that lay on the table appeared under the heading, 'Ossian Runes.'

"That's them," said Kenneth. "What does it say? The writing is very small, I left my specs in the car."

Calum smiled and widened the screen to enlarge the writing.

"I never knew you could do that!" said Kenneth, leaning over Calum's shoulder to get a better look at the description of them.

'Ossian runes are ancient Celtic runes, recorded by the Romans as powerful magic used by the Picts in the 2nd century. It is likely they have been around a lot longer, but the first record of these runes were from the Roman's when Hadrian's Wall was being built.

The Ossian runes were not in wide use around Scotland, as they were associated with evil witchcraft, dark magic and the resurrection of the dead. One scholar wrote in the 11th century, 'There is no force more effective than the vibrations of an angry spirit, summoned by words and syllables of power, used in conjunction with the dark magic of the Ossian runes, to bring forth manifestations from the Otherworld into material being.'

Ossian runes became synonymous with dark magic and anyone found carrying them was tortured and burnt alive. Use of the Ossian runes diminished, and there are no records of them being used in Scotland after the early 14th century. The only known collection of Ossian Runes are kept at the Kings Museum in Aberdeen.'

"I think we found it," said Calum as he turned to see if Kenneth had finished reading.

Kenneth sat back. "So what noo?" he said with a sigh. "We ken what they are, but we dinnae ken how tae use them. There must be a way tae send Kirstin back."

"There must be more information somewhere. Perhaps the King's Museum will have some more information for us. Seeing as you're the museum expert, why don't you give them a call and I'll carry on looking online," suggested Calum.

"I can give it a try, but I dinnae ken anyone in Aberdeen," replied Kenneth.

"Just use that magnetic charm of yours," said Calum, then laughed. "But, don't let them see your face, you'll scare them."

"There's nothing wrong wi' my face, laddie," scowled Kenneth, his enormous, bushy eyebrows almost completely covering his eyes. Calum just grinned.

"Have ye checked on that lassie that they took away?" Kenneth suddenly asked changing the subject.

"I've already phoned Billie. Helena's not conscious, she has pneumonia, one of her lungs has collapsed, and the other is very infected. It will be a while before they can talk to her, that's if she pulls through," said Calum; again, a tinge of guilt went through him.

"Aye, well at least that gives us some time tae try tae work oot what tae dae about Kirstin," said Kenneth, then realising how heartless that sounded added, "I dae hope the lassie picks up, it's nae her fault this has happened tae her."

"Aye, I don't think the police are going to see it that way, but we can cross that bridge when she recovers," said Calum.

***

Two days later, Helena's eyes flickered open to find an oxygen mask was fitted over her face, but still her breathing felt shallow and painful. She had no idea how she had got here, but she felt so weak, that it seemed the least of her worries. There were machines bleeping and whirring all around her, there was a drip in one of her arms, while the other had a blood pressure strap around it that tightened every twenty minutes to take her reading.

In the corner of the room sat a young policewoman who was reading a book. Helena couldn't understand why she was there, and she hadn't the strength to ask. She knew she was very ill, but still she felt a strong sense of relief, like she had just been released from some sort of dark prison. She closed her eyes and drifted back to sleep.

***

Kirstin's spirit was watching the cottage. Her link to Helena's mind was still open, but Helena's body was useless to her at present. She would have to wait, or she would have to find another host. Kirstin could cross between worlds now, so finding another host was a possibility; however, finding the right host would be difficult. Helena had been perfect. She had a deep-rooted anger festering inside her, making her an easy conduit for an entity to possess. Kirstin would have to bide her time for a while. As long as Jamie was still here in Glencoe, she could afford to wait. She had to be stronger when she next attempted to reclaim her son. Kirstin would not stop until she had Jamie at her side.

Chapter Twenty-Eight

The next day, Anna and the boys were at the veterinary hospital with Dexter. He had had surgery on his cruciate ligament and stitches to a nasty cut that went the whole length of his stomach. He lay there looking at them sadly, with a large plastic cone around his neck to stop him from chewing the stitches. His questioning brown eyes were begging for them to take him home, but the vet wanted him in for observation for another two nights at least before he would release him.

The cut, from a large glass shard, had been deep in places, and he was worried about infection. Dexter's leg was going to take some time to heal, with short lead walks being the only exercise he would be allowed for the next six weeks. Anna knew he would hate that. James and Ollie were both sprawled on the floor with Dexter, patting him gently. Ollie had brought Dexter two of his stickmen to keep him company. Dexter didn't even sniff them when Ollie put them in front of his face. The dog was very miserable; even the boys couldn't cheer him up.

With Dexter in the hospital, it meant that Anna couldn't leave the cottage yet. The boys would scream bloody murder if they had to leave Dexter behind, she just couldn't do that to them or Dexter. He was an important member of their family. At least Helena was being kept at a safe distance from them now; she was in hospital but under arrest. Sergeant Burns had promised Anna that she would not be released until after the preliminary hearing, and that was not likely to take place any time soon. Helena was too ill to make a plea in court yet, and she had a police guard with her. Kidnapping a child was a serious offence.

When they got back to the cottage, Angus was there orchestrating the replacement of Anna's bedroom window.

"How's yer dog?" he asked.

"He'll be fine, after a while. They have to keep him in there for the time being," replied Anna.

"Does that mean ye'll be staying on for a wee while longer?" asked Angus.

"It would seem so," said Anna. "Though only if the boys feel safe."

"We're okay, Mummy," said Ollie, then stubbornly added, "We're not leaving Dexter."

"No, we're not going to leave him," James reaffirmed. "Anyway, the police have the bad lady now, and Corri says she is gone."

"Oh, she does, does she? Well, you can tell Corri from me that she didn't do a very good job of taking care of you when Helena took you," said Anna.

"Yes, she did!" cried James indignantly. "Corri made that big white deer come and make that lady let me go."

"You never told me that," said Anna. "I thought you had just run away.

"I did!" sighed James with a frown. "I ran away when Corri made her let me go."

"Well then, I suppose I should thank her," said Anna.

She had had a lot of time to think about the ordeal in the last couple of days. Calum had been very supportive, as had his mother, bringing up home-cooked food for them all. Luckily, James's disappearance had not been too long, and although the story made the Fort William Daily Record, it had not been deemed serious enough to make Scottish national news. Anna was relieved, as she didn't relish a difficult conversation with the boy's father, let alone her parents.

Her brother and Rob were due to leave today. Glen had offered to stay on, but Rob would have to return to their hotel in Devon. Anna convinced Glen that everything was under control now and he had nothing to worry about. Helena was in custody, Kirstin was gone, and as soon as Dexter was well enough to travel, they would all be heading back to Edinburgh. Calum had virtually moved in, so it wasn't like she would be on her own. Reluctantly, Glen agreed, so he and Rob packed up, planning to hit the road after lunch. They were going to stay in a hotel in the Lake district for a night, before carrying on to Devon.

Meantime, Calum had spent a lot of time researching then organising a top lawyer from Glasgow for Helena. He still couldn't be sure whether Helena's jealous behaviour was all to do with Kirstin or if she was partly responsible herself. Whatever the reason, she certainly wasn't responsible for kidnapping James, so Calum felt obliged to hire the best lawyer he could find for her.

The lawyers name was Ted Burnham, a hot shot lawyer in Glasgow, who had made his name in defending the supposedly indefensible. He wasn't cheap, but after hearing the story, he was sure he could get Helena off easily on grounds of instability. The only trouble was, he hadn't actually spoken with Helena yet, as she was too ill. The police were going to contact him when they were ready to interview and charge her.

The rest of that day went by quietly. Anna took the boys to the pool house while Angus sorted the window. Calum was working on his computer in the kitchen, catching up with some stuff his PA had sent him. The boys were a little more subdued than usual, but Anna thought they were worrying about Dexter more than anything else. She was playing in the water with them when Angus stuck his head around the door to tell her that the men had finished. The window was as good as new, all the glass had been swept up, and the bedroom was ready to use.

"I dinnae ken if this is significant or not," he said, handing her a stone about the size of an egg. "But it wis sitting outside yer bedroom window. It has some carvings on it. I've never seen it before."

Anna looked at the strange stone, it was a pale grey smooth rock, with some lines carved into it. Carved in the centre of the lines was a circle. "I wonder if this has something to do with what Kevin and Calum are looking into. Some sort of ancient runes they think have something to do with Kirstin being here. You found it outside the bedroom window?"

"Aye, just sitting on the ground below it. I've never seen anything like it aroond the cottage before," said Angus.

"Okay, thanks Angus. I'll give it to Calum and see what he makes of it," said Anna. "Come on, boys, let's get out the water now."

They all got out of the pool and headed into the cottage. No one had been in Anna's bedroom since that night; the boys stood nervously outside the door.

"Come on, scaredy cats!" said Anna, throwing the door to her room open. She was determined not to let the boys think she was afraid in any way, although she did have a certain amount of trepidation as she entered the room. Everything was exactly as it had been, except for Kirstin's picture; that was no longer on the wall. Anna had asked Angus to take it away.

"See, back to normal," she said cheerfully, and the boys ran in and jumped on her bed.

Calum appeared in the doorway. "Well, this looks better," he said, grinning at the boys. "Your Uncle Glen and Rob are leaving now. I just came to get you to say goodbye."

Anna's brother still looked apprehensive as they put their cases in the car. "Are you sure you don't want me to stay?" he asked Anna again.

"Glen, everything's fine now. The vet said Dexter could come home in a couple of days. Calum is organising a comfy crate for us to take him back to Edinburgh in, so we'll be home just after you guys get back to Devon. Stop worrying!" she assured him.

"We'll phone you tonight when we get to Keswick. We can turn back if we need to," said Glen.

"It's going to be quiet now," said Calum, putting his arm around Anna after they watched Glen and Rob drive off.

"It's never quiet with these two reprobates," she replied, nodding over to James and Ollie who were already dirty from digging up worms.

***

It was early evening when the doctor told the nurses they could take off the BP monitor and remove Helena's catheter. The intravenous antibiotics had worked well, and her temperature was stable. He wanted Helena to start moving around a little, going to the toilet on her own and sitting up in bed.

Helena still had her drip in for fluids and an oxygen tube in her nose to help her breathe. Her legs were in bandages from the damage inflicted by the stag when he attacked her, but all in all, she was improving. The policewoman had phoned over to Sergeant Burns to tell him, but he agreed to wait until the morning until they formally charged her. They would also have to contact her lawyer to see if he wanted to be present. Helena had virtually ignored the presence of the policewoman who was seated in the room with her. Her mind had been working overtime ever since her temperature had dropped.

She couldn't account for at least three days before she had ended up here, in the hospital. She remembered her anger at Calum and that woman, Anna. The nurses hadn't told her much more than the date. The last thing she remembered clearly was breaking into Anna's cottage, then everything else seemed to be in a fog lingering at the forefront of her mind, but just out of her reach.

Helena knew she was in some sort of trouble, but surely, they wouldn't have stationed a policewoman with her in hospital for simply breaking into the cottage. She never took anything, did she? She refused to acknowledge the policewoman, deciding instead to ask the nurses for a phone so she could call a lawyer.

When she asked, she was surprised to find that Calum had already sorted a lawyer for her and he had left the lawyer's card for her with the hospital staff. Helena thought it must be bad if Calum was trying to help her. The last time she saw Calum he was furious with her, but that was days ago. Why couldn't she remember? It was too late to call this Ted Burnham now, so she resolved to having to wait until the morning. She lay back on her pillow, staring at the ceiling still trying to figure out what had happened to her.

***

Kirstin sensed that Helena was awake once more. The young woman's strength was returning, which a few days ago seemed impossible. Kirstin had been sure that Helena was going to die. Still, she already had a strong connection with Helena; slipping back into her mind would be easy.

Chapter Twenty-Nine

Kenneth had no luck with the curator of the King's Museum in Aberdeen. No one seemed to know very much about where the runes had come from, or who had declared them to be Ossian runes in the first place. They were kept in a case, part of a collection of many different runes from the Celtic period.

Giving up that line of inquiry, he had poured over his books on Scottish witchcraft, but again, nothing had come up. He was at a loss, but the more he handled Corrag's pouch of runes, the more he was sure they were connected to what was going on at the cottage. He felt uncomfortable around the stones, something he couldn't quite put his finger on. Every time he touched the pouch, he had an overwhelming urge to hide them away and keep them for himself. He put the pouch away in his satchel and decided to drive over to Kirstin's Cot, to see if Calum had uncovered anything.

They were all sitting in the lounge in the modern part of the cottage. The boys were glued to cartoons on the television, which gave Anna and Calum a chance to talk quietly about what had happened. They had been so busy trying to sort out everything in the aftermath, they hadn't really discussed what they were going to do next.

"The hospital says Helena's awake, but doesn't remember anything. They are giving her a brain scan to see if she has any injuries that can explain it. I couldn't really tell them that she was possessed," said Calum.

"Have you been to see her?" Anna asked wondering how guilty Calum was actually feeling.

"I did, but she was still asleep. I arranged a good lawyer for her from Glasgow. I've offered to pay. I do feel a little responsible for what happened to her," said Calum.

"Well, you did tell her to go home," snapped Anna, then sighed when she realise how nasty that sounded. It wasn't Helena's fault that this had happened to her. She should have some compassion for the woman. The trouble was, she didn't have any. Every time she thought of Helena, all she could think of was how she had attacked them all and taken James. "I'm sorry, I know that sounded harsh, but I still can't get over what she did or what Kirstin did. I don't know, it all sounds so crazy when you say it like that."

"That kind of brings up the big elephant in the room. We still haven't talked about where Kirstin has gone," said Calum. "She seems to have left Helena now, but she must have gone somewhere?"

"That's why I want to get home as soon as Dexter is able to travel. I'm afraid of what might happen next," said Anna. "James doesn't seem worried just now, though. He says that Corri has got rid of Kirstin. That's the only reason I'm comfortable enough to remain here."

There was a knock at the door, and they both left the boys to go through to the kitchen to see who it was. Kenneth was already halfway through the door when they came through to the kitchen.

"I just thought I'd pop over and see if ye'd had any luck wi' these runes," he said, instead of saying hallo, or apologising for letting himself in.

"Oh, that reminds me," said Anna walking over to the counter where she had left the stone Angus had found. "Angus found this placed under my bedroom window. He spotted it when they were putting in the new glass."

Kenneth took the stone, studying the markings. "Aye, it looks like one of our runes, but it's nae frae Corrag's wee bag. This has bin newly carved."

"Maybe Helena carved it," suggested Calum.

"Aye, that would seem likely," said Kenneth with a frown. "Have ye looked tae see if there's any more."

They were soon all outside the cottage, searching the grounds around the cottage. They found stone after stone, all with the same markings on them. There were twelve in total, all placed against the walls of the cottage. After making sure there were no others, they brought them into the cottage and laid them on the kitchen table.

"These may explain how Kirstin managed tae possess Helena. Did any of ye notice the way they were laid. The one's I picked up all had the horizontal line at the top," said Kenneth.

"Aye, mine did also come to think of it," said Calum.

"Yes mine too, so what does that mean?" asked Anna fiddling with the rocks.

"Och I cannae be sure, but they look tae me like some sort of doorway, maybe letting something through," replied Kenneth then looked up as they heard a car come up the drive.

Anna went to the door to see that Angus had come back, "Have you forgotten something?" she asked him as he got out his car.

"Nae, I just had an idea when I got home, and sure enough it paid off," said Angus waving a scruffy looking notebook at her.

They went back into the kitchen and Anna got some beers from the fridge for them all. Angus sat down at the table with them, slapping down the tatty notebook.

"When we were getting the cottage ready, I found a lot of old scribbly notes, receipts, recipes and letters that Nelly had left behind in the cottage. I took them all, intending tae gie them tae her nephew, but he was here such a short time I forgot, and I wasnae gonnae pay for postage fir that lot. So, they've been sitting in my garage," explained Angus. "When I saw that stone yesterday, it jogged my memory, and so I checked when I got home. Nelly had a notebook wi' lots of drawings like the one on that stone. It didnae make any sense tae me when I first saw it, not until today when I picked up that rock outside yer bedroom window."

Kenneth opened the notebook and sure enough it was full of hand drawn images of the shapes that were on Corrag's runes. Even better, next to each image Nelly had scribbled a description of the rune and what it meant.

Her writing was not the most legible, but between them, they began to decipher the meanings. It didn't take them long to locate the image that was on the rocks placed around the cottage and Kenneth began to read out Nelly's description.

'*THE GATEWAY RUNE. This rune is of the most dangerous and darkest magic. It will open a gateway for the dead to cross over from the Otherworld to this realm. If placed correctly in conjunction with other runes of the same markings, the manifestation may cross over and inhabit a willing host. Beware of spirits from the otherworld, they are clever tricksters and manipulators. They will exploit weakened souls to release them, but in doing so, release evil into the world. To send them back, you must seal the gateway using the Black rune.*'

Anna let out a long, heavy sigh, "I think we have found how this happened now. It's really creepy thinking about this stuff," she said.

"Is there a Black rune in Corrag's pouch?" asked Calum.

Kenneth pulled out the pouch from his satchel and opened it, pouring the runes onto the table next to the marked stones they had collected from around the cottage. Immediately, as the runes hit the table, the stones with the gateway markings flew off onto the floor with a clatter, some smashing into pieces. They all sat and stared in shock.

"Well, I guess we know which stones are boss then," said Calum trying to make a bad joke.

Anna reached out to touch one of Corrag's runes, and as she did so, a pleasant sensation went through her. "They feel nice to touch," she said, caressing the rune between her fingers.

"Really?" said Kenneth puzzled. "I cannae bear tae have them near me, let alone touch them. It's like they want to seize control of my mind."

"Me neither," said Calum. "They make me feel really uncomfortable."

Anna picked up another rune and felt the same flutter of power tingle through her, making her feel empowered.

"I can almost hear them calling out for me to hold them, they want to protect me, to belong to me," she tried to explain, as she basked in the caressing warmth of the magic. "It's hard to put them down."

Calum was uncomfortable, so he reached over to take the rune out of Anna's hand. As his hand touched stone, he felt like he had just picked up a red hot coal. He yelled painfully and dropped the rune, grabbing hold of his injured hand. Anna grabbed Calum's hand to look at it; it was badly burnt, already blistering.

"What the hell?" cried Anna, dragging Calum to the sink to get cold water on his hand. "How did that happen?"

"I dinnae think they wanted Calum tae take ye away frae them. It's like they have a mind of their own," said Kenneth staring down at the runes, not daring to touch them.

"Nelly writes a wee bit aboot that here in this page," said Angus and then read.

'When handling the Ossian Runes it is important that you have performed the shielding spell to protect yourself and others in the vicinity, from being bewitched by them. The Shielding Spell is at the back of this book, and need only be performed once. Unprotected, the Ossian runes will try to possess the nearest female presence, by attracting her with a feeling of euphoria when handling the stones. If the stones are wielded by someone not chosen by them, they will

send out a destructive force causing harm and injury. The runes channel limitless amounts of forbidden magic; they are not to be used by the inexperienced."

"Maybe we should have read that wee note first," said Kenneth, stating the obvious as Calum soaked his burnt hand in a bowl of cold water.

"I don't want to touch them again," said Anna. "They're too tempting to hold."

"I think we should dae this Shielding spell Nelly has written aboot here. Maybe that will help?" said Angus.

"Aye, let me have a wee look," asked Kenneth and Angus passed him over the notebook. Kenneth read every word, "It disnae seem too complicated. A lot of stuff and nonsense if ye ask me, but we can gie it a try. We need to get these ingredients that Nelly has listed doon here."

Kenneth read out the list, "We need some soil frae aroond the place we are shielding and some fresh sage. Dae ye have that in the garden?"

"Aye," said Angus. "Plenty of herbs."

"Aye, well we'll need some rosemary and lavender also, then all we need is salt, but quite a lot of salt by the looks of it and some tealight candles," continued Kenneth.

"Aye, well I can pop oot fir some salt, that no a problem. I've got lavender in my garden, so I'll nip there on the way back and collect some. Why don't ye go and get the sage and rosemary while I'm away?" suggested Angus.

"Would you get some gauze and a bandage as well? This blister on Calum's hand is going to be sore," said Anna.

By the time Angus got back forty minutes later, the table was stacked with sage and rosemary. "Ye must have ripped oot the whole garden!" he said horrified.

"Aye, well we need tae be sure it's gonnae work," said Kenneth, unrepentant. "Noo, we need tae wrap the herbs in tae three bunches wi' the lavender and dry them oot in the oven fir a wee while."

Calum supressed his laughter, which started Anna off giggling.

"What are yoose laughing at?" demanded Kenneth unimpressed.

"Yer a right couple of auld wifies," laughed Calum. "It's like you're baking a cake."

"Aye, says the man wi' the big burn mark on his hand. We're nae taking any chances!" replied Kenneth, his hooded eyes glaring intensely.

214

When the herbs were still on the soft side of crispy, they took them out of the oven to cool. They then poured a substantial pile of salt in every corner and cranny of the kitchen, lighting tealights and placing one on top of each pile of salt.

Anna turned all the runes so they faced upwards on the table showing their markings, none of the men dared to touch them again. She could feel their power racing through her, enticing her to hold them to her. She reluctantly let them go. Kenneth lit one of the dried herb bundles. It immediately flared up and he tried to blow it out, so the herbs would burn slowly. However, the bunch was blazing fiercely, and Kenneth ended up dropping it in the sink before he burnt his fingers.

"Ye eejit!" said Angus. "Ye just light a bit of it, gie me a bunch."

Angus took hold of another bunch of herbs, lighting it at the very top, then blowing it out immediately. The dried herbs started to smoke, and soon, their thick, smoky aroma filled the kitchen.

"Right we have tae say some words noo," said Kenneth.

"Who has tae say them?" asked Angus. "Nae me!"

"It disnae matter who says them. It's a bloody spell, nae a wedding vow," said Kenneth irritated.

"Well, ye can say them, ye have the book!" said Angus.

"I think Anna should say them. She's the one the runes have chosen," said Kenneth.

"Right, I'll say them," said Anna, trying to contain her laughter. It was getting harder and harder to take this seriously. She took the notebook from Kenneth and began to read.

"Wait a wee minute! We have tae be flapping these herbs aboot when ye say it," said Kenneth who had successfully lit two more bunches, he kept one and handed one to Calum.

"Right, well let's start flapping," said Calum standing up and waving the smoking herbs around, trying not to make eye contact with Anna lest they dissolved into laughter and ruined Kenneth's moment.

Angus, Kenneth and Calum starting walking around the kitchen wafting their smoking herb bunches around until it was almost impossible to see through the smoke. Then the smoke alarm went off.

"Did ye nae take the battery oot of that thing?" said Kenneth to Angus over the piercing din. "Ye kent we were playing wi' fire."

"Just a wee minute," said Angus climbing on a chair to take the battery out the alarm. By now, the kitchen was filled with stinking smoke, and all of them were coughing and wiping their eyes.

"Can we dae this quicker?" said Kenneth. "My lungs cannae take much more."

Anna's eyes were watering as she read the words that Nelly had written. *'By the power of three. By the power of three. By the power of three. We summon you who guards the watchtower to shield us from these dark runes. We summon you who guards the watchtower to shield us from these dark runes. We summon you who guards the watchtower to shield us from these dark runes. Blessed be, we thank you for your protection against the darkness.'*

"Is that it?" asked Calum, choking as he still waved his smoking bundle about.

"I think so, that's all that's written," said Anna.

"Ye could have said it wi' a bit more feeling," said Kenneth, unimpressed.

"It's a spell, nae Shakespear," said Angus.

"Well nothing's happened," said Kenneth disappointedly. "Try to touch the runes and see what happens."

Anna picked up one of the runes and massaged it in her hand. "Nothing, I feel nothing," she said then picked up more of the runes. "No, absolutely nothing, it looks like it worked."

"Aye, well the real test will be if Calum can take them frae ye, withoot getting burnt," said Kenneth helpfully.

"Why don't you try to take it from her?" asked Calum. "I'm already injured."

"Aye well, there's nae point in two of us getting injured, and as yer already burnt, it won't make much difference noo," said Kenneth.

Calum turned to Angus.

"Dinnae look at me, I'm wi' Kenneth."

Calum gave up, rolling his eyes at Anna, he leaned forward to gingerly touch one of the runes in her hand. He laid his finger on it, and it felt cold and smooth. "Well here goes," he said, taking the rune out of her hand. Nothing happened; it was like he had just picked up a stone.

"It worked," said Kenneth, delighted with himself. "We did it! Noo all we have tae dae is work oot how tae get rid of Kirstin."

"Is something on fire?" asked James, coughing as he came into the kitchen.

216

"It stinks in here," said Ollie closely following him. "What are we burning?" he asked hopefully.

"We are burning nothing!" said Anna. "We were just trying to make the house smell nice."

"Well, you didn't!" declared Ollie with a look of disgust. "It smells like dog poo!"

Chapter Thirty

Ted Burnham had been with Helena for most of the next morning. Sergeant Burns arrived with another officer and formally charged Helena with kidnapping and assault. Helena hadn't said much as they read her her rights, and her eyes glazed over with confusion when she heard the charges. The hospital had said she would not be fit enough to be released for at least another day or so. She would then need respite care for a time, but they could organise that to happen at her home in Edinburgh. They didn't recommend that she be locked in a cell, so Ted was going to organise bail, inciting mitigating circumstances. He told Helena he would organise a psychological examination as she still had no recollection of what had happened. Her brain scan was clear, so there was no immediate explanation for her memory loss.

By the time Ted Burnham left the hospital, Helena was feeling even more confused than before. Why had she taken the boy? She didn't even like children. There was something niggling at the back of her mind, but she couldn't quite grasp onto it. The nurses told her that Calum had phoned while she was with the lawyer, but Helena had nothing to say to him and refused their offer of calling him back for her. She thought of calling her father but decided against that also. He would no doubt think she was guilty before she had a chance to explain anything. They never did get on.

Helena was almost bereft of any feelings as she lay in her bed. Her breathing had become much easier and her cough was almost non-existent; the meds had done their miracles. Although she still felt very tired, all she wanted to do was leave and return to her apartment in Edinburgh.

The policewoman had been allowed to leave now that Helena had been charged, and her bag and personal belongings had been returned to her, although no one could tell her where her car was. She couldn't remember where she had left it, any more than she could remember checking out of the Onich and moving into the MacDonald's hotel in Kinlochleven. Someone would know what had happened to her car. She checked her phone, it had been dead when they gave it back to her, it was now fully charged, so she rang the reception desk at the Onich Hotel.

The Australian receptionist was professional but frosty when Helena explained who she was. Her Porsche was still in their carpark; they had been trying to contact her. Helena told them she would pick it up later in the day, then she switched off her phone and lay back in the hospital bed. She would wait until it was dark and the night shift came on duty, then she would be able to sneak out. She was going to drive home.

Kirstin's spirit wandered aimlessly through Glencoe, she could see her cottage nestled there in the physical world, though she couldn't touch it. She had no way of knowing how much time had elapsed since she had left Helena's body, she could see that Jamie was still there at the cottage, but then so was Corrag's ghost. Her involvement infuriated Kirstin. Corrag had no reason to stop her reclaiming her son, yet there she was, befriending the boy and guarding him.

Soon, Kirstin would cross over again, she had felt Helena's essence grow stronger and she knew the young woman was healing. As far as Kirstin was concerned, Helena's swift recovery was a sign. She was ready and waiting to once again possess the young woman. She would wait for night fall; her power was always stronger in the darkness.

***

Dexter's tail began to wag as soon as he set eyes on Anna and the boys. They were at the veterinary hospital to pick him up and take him home. He managed to walk very slowly to the car, and they lifted him in to the waiting dog crate in the back. The vet had suggested that they spent one more night in Glencoe before they attempted to drive all the way back to Edinburgh. It would give Dexter a chance to settle back down with his family first, so that he was more relaxed when they travelled.

Anna lifted Dexter out of the car when they got back to the cottage. He was a big dog, but she was strong enough to lift him down gently. The boys were all over him, trying to hug him even though he still wore the giant plastic cone around his neck. They led him slowly into the house, then to his bed. Dexter sighed loudly as he lay his head down, staring at them sadly under the rim of the cone.

The boys put on the TV and settled in, one on either side of their beloved dog. Anna went to her room to continue packing. With a huge cage for Dexter in the back of the car, there was not going to be much room for anything else. Calum's mum had said she could leave some stuff with her until she was ready to collect it. It seemed like the best plan, so Anna was busily separating what they needed, from what they could do without. In all honesty, she would rather be leaving today, but the vet had been quite insistent.

***

Calum had driven over to the Belford Hospital in Fort William to see Helena. When he arrived, the nurses told him that she had left instructions that she didn't want to see him. He wasn't sure what to do about that, as he had decided to stay another couple of days to make sure Helena was safe to drive back to Edinburgh. The last thing he wanted to do was get in a car with that woman, but he felt he owed her that. He wouldn't forgive himself if something happened to Helena on her way back to Edinburgh. But if she didn't want to see him, then surely, he could stop worrying about her.

Calum was actually relieved when he thought about it, as it meant he could now travel back with Anna and the boys. She hadn't commented when he told her of his plan to remain with Helena, which left him feeling even more uncomfortable. He knew Anna was not about to forgive Helena for taking James, and he couldn't blame her, but it just made everything very awkward. Once Helena was back in the city, he would never have to see her again.

He decided to write a note to Helena, which he did. In the note he simply suggested that once she was released from hospital, he would like to offer to drive her back to Edinburgh. He would not visit her again, but would be waiting for her call.

A nurse took the note, leaving Calum free to head back to Kirstin's Cot. He hoped he would be there before Anna, so he could help her with Dexter, but her car was already there when he pulled in the drive.

Calum walked past the boys who were both seated on the dog's bed, glued to the cartoons on the TV. He found Anna in the bedroom with suitcases on her bed. She turned to face him, and he had a strong urge just to kiss her. He pulled her towards him putting his mouth on hers, kissing her for the first time in what seemed like days. She melted in his arms, returning his kiss willingly. They stood in their embrace for a time, finding comfort in the growing passion they felt towards each other. Calum let her go abruptly, holding her slightly away from him. "You know what I look forward to the most," he said hoarsely. Anna shook her head.

"I can't wait to get you back in Edinburgh, where we can put all this nonsense behind us and start again," he said.

Anna smiled, "Me too."

The sound of another car coming up the drive made them turn away from each other. Kenneth and Angus had returned, as they had promised to do the night before. For safety's sake, they had all decided to stay with Anna and the boys until they left the next morning. Kenneth was not sure what Kirstin could try now, but he was not going to take any chances. He and Angus had spent the morning going over Nelly's notebook about the Ossian runes. They had left the runes in a drawer in the kitchen at Kirstin's Cot, as Kenneth had not wanted to keep them after what had happened to Calum.

Anna got to the door to see Angus pulling out a crate of beer from the back of his old pickup.

"Hallo there, I'm just bringing in oor supplies!" he called over to her, as Kenneth had already made his way past her and into the cottage.

"I can see you've made sure you're not going to run out," Anna replied with a grin.

"Aye well, we dinnae want tae run short," said Angus carrying the crate past her, then plonked it on the kitchen table that Kenneth was already seated at.

Kenneth reached over, picked up a bottle of beer, flipped the cap off, then took a swig. "We've found something in wee Nelly's book," he said, wiping his mouth on his sleeve.

"Aye, we did," said Angus helping himself to a bottle. "We think we can get rid of Kirstin's ghost fir good."

"Well let's hear it then," said Calum, his eyes drifting over to Anna who had started to peel potatoes for the fish pie she had planned to make for everyone. She was so beautiful, but he had to smother his desire as he turned towards the two old, slightly insane codgers at the table.

"We didnae ken what we were looking fir, but here in the middle of the book, wee Nelly wrote doon a spell that would send unwanted spirits back tae the Otherworld, whatever that's supposed tae be," said Angus.

"I think it's some sort of Purgatory for the Celts. Ye ken like the Catholics send they're misbehavers tae Purgatory, until they can behave themselves," said Kenneth.

"I dinnae think the Otherworld is some sort of reform school for Celtic spirits," said Angus.

"Och I'm nae explaining it right," replied Kenneth. "Look here, this spell uses these Ossian runes, and if we dae it right, we can trap Kirstin back intae the Otherworld."

"I would be happier if she just never appeared again," said Anna, putting the potato pot on to boil. "If we could just get through tonight unscathed, then we will be gone tomorrow, and Kirstin can go back to hell for all I care."

"But we dinnae want tae take any chances," said Kenneth. "I think we should set up after dinner, so we're ready fir her if she decides tae pay us a visit."

"I'm nae gonnae be able tae rent this cottage oot again, unless we dae get rid of her," said Angus. "I dinnae think that I can persuade Nelly's nephew tae believe that the cottage is haunted."

Kenneth snorted in disgust, then took a long slug of his beer. "Damn Sassenach, couldnae even be bothered tae come and see the place finished fir himself."

"Aye, but he still pays my wages every month," replied Angus.

The afternoon drifted by, the smell of cooked cheese melting on top of Anna's fish pie brought the boys into the kitchen. They all ate dinner together at the table, and Ollie took Dexter some of the leftovers on a small plate. The dog licked it up gratefully; he hadn't eaten much over the last few days.

Anna put the boys to bed; they were back sleeping in their own room now. Angus had put padlocks on their windows for added security. She picked up a book to start to read to them when James stopped her.

"Mummy, we don't want a story tonight," he said, then pretended to do this enormous yawn. "We are so tired."

Ollie started fake yawning also, and Anna frowned at them. "I don't know what you two are up to, but I am coming back to check in half an hour, so you had better be asleep."

James started to snore very loudly, followed by Ollie who did exactly the same.

"I know you're not asleep," said Anna, wondering what they were planning. The boys kept on snoring, so she left them to it, leaving their door open so she could hear any noise from within. She had a feeling they were going to try to sneak back through to Dexter.

She joined the others who had moved into the lounge area, and were in a heated discussion about football. Anna groaned with feigned boredom and flopped down on the sofa next to Calum. It was nice to have normality again.

***

Helena was fully dressed under her covers when the nurse came in to bring her antibiotics. She took the pills, then lay down pretending to be tired. The nurse switched off her overhead light and left her in peace. Luckily, she had been kept in her own room, so she was away from the nurse's station that was situated on the ward. Helena sat up, pulling out the ventilator tube from her nose. She put her shoes on, then opened the door to her room to check the corridor was clear. Pulling her hood up over her head she sneaked out unnoticed. The taxi she had phoned under an assumed name was waiting by the kerb, and she was soon on her way to the Onich Hotel to collect her car. Her plan was to drive straight back to Edinburgh, at least she would have her friends around her there. The sooner she was away from this hell hole of a place, the better.

Retrieving her car, she noticed her Porsche was low on petrol. She remembered passing a garage in Ballachulish, so she decided she would fill up there, then just carry on home. It was eight thirty when she arrived at the garage and they were just closing, but thankfully they allowed her to fill up first. As she got back in her car, she began to feel strange. Her eyes couldn't focus and she shook her head to try to clear her vision. Helena felt there was something tugging in the back of her mind, something she recognised only too well. She tried to block it from her thoughts, but it was too strong and it slowly crept in, beginning to manipulate her mind. She drove her car out of the garage and headed back along the A82, still fighting with the presence in her head. The car started to swerve and suddenly Helena pulled off the road onto the track that led back to Glencoe village. Kirstin had returned.

***

Calum's phone started to ring. He had left it in the kitchen, so he jumped up and went through. The phone stopped ringing by the time he reached it. He picked it up and looked on the screen to see it was Billie's number. He was about to ring the Sergeant back when

Kenneth shouted through to him. "While yer in there, get these runes frae the drawer. We might as well set up that spell noo."

Calum phoned Billie pack and the police sergeant picked up immediately. "I was just on my way over tae Kirstin's Cot. Are ye there just noo?" he asked.

"Yes, we're all here. What the matter?" asked Calum, holding his phone with his shoulder pressed to his cheek as he rummaged through the drawer he thought they had put the runes in.

"It's Helena, she's left the hospital. Nae one saw her leave. I've checked with the Onich and her Porsche has gone. I'd thought I'd better warn yae incase she wis intending tae come over tae the cottage," said Sergeant Burns. "We have seen her on CCTV at the garage in Ballahulish just half an hour ago, but then she headed oot towards the main road. So she may just be going hame tae Edinburgh. Just tae be safe, I'm sending a couple of patrols over tae ye now. Just hang tight until they get there."

"Aye okay Billie, thanks for letting me know," replied Calum, swearing under his breath. What the hell was Helena playing at. Surely, she wouldn't be headed back here. He'd better find these runes, so he started searching in the other drawers. He was certain they had been in the first one, maybe Anna had moved them. Having no luck, he called through to the others.

"Have any of you moved these runes? They're not in the drawer," said Calum.

"What?" said Kenneth, appearing in the doorway with Angus and Anna close behind him. "They must be."

"Nope, I can't find them anywhere," said Calum then looked nervously over to Anna. "That's not the only news. Helena has run off from the hospital, that was Sergeant Burns on the phone. She was seen heading in this direction."

"How the hell did that happen!" shouted Anna furiously. "Weren't they supposed to be watching her?"

"They did until she was formally charged, but her lawyer organised that she should not be kept in custody because of her health," replied Calum.

"The lawyer you bloody hired!" yelled Anna. "I'm checking on the boys!"

She stormed towards the door but before she got to it, it slammed shut. "NOOO!" she screamed as she ran to grab the handle. The door would not budge.

Kenneth tried the main door out of the kitchen but it was also jammed shut. Anna started screaming, smashing her fists against the door like she was half crazed.

Calum tried to grab her, but she turned on him. "Get off me! This is all your fault!" she screamed, pushing him away from her. She ran to the table and picked up one of the wooden chairs, then hurtled it at the window. Glass shattered everywhere, and before Calum could reach her, Anna was already trying to climb out, blood covering her hands from the shards of glass around the frame.

"Get off me!" she screamed as he pulled her down from the window.

"Just let me!" he yelled at her, fending off her blows, but before he could move, a huge piece of wood flew off the from decking outside and slammed up against the open window. It was completely blocked, and would not budge. Anna screamed in bloody fury.

Chapter Thirty-One

"Are you sure Mummy won't be mad?" said Ollie as James quietly opened the back door to the cottage.

"I don't know," admitted James, but Corri says that if we do this we will protect Mummy and Calum and Dexter."

"Will it protect my stick people too?" asked Ollie.

"Stick people aren't real!" replied James.

"Yes they are. They're as real as Corri is!" said Ollie angrily.

"Shh, Mummy will hear us. We have to be really quiet," said James as they stepped outside.

They boys ran across the grass towards the pool house, then let themselves in. James was carrying the bag of runes in his hand. Corri had told him to take them from the drawer earlier.

Ollie stood on a chair by the wall.

"What are you doing?" whispered James.

"I'm putting the light on," said Ollie reaching up to the switch.

"No, you can't do that, we'll be seen. We have to stay hidden," his brother shouted over to him. Ollie jumped down with a sigh.

Corrag was waiting for them at the side of the water. James walked over to her and held out the leather pouch. "We've brought it," he said. The old witch could feel the power reverberating from her stones and she longed to be able to touch them.

"Tip them oot on the ground, James, so I can see them," said Corri. James knelt down and opened the leather pouch, then slowly tipped out the stone runes onto the side of the pool.

"They feel funny," he said as he picked one up.

"What do they feel like?" said Ollie, who knelt beside him and picked one up in his hand. "Oo, they tingle, like they're tickling my hand."

"Try tae find the black Stone," said Corrag as they both raced to pick it up. "That's the one, noo put that aside, then turn all the stones over so ye can see the patterns on them," said Corrag.

"It's too dark to see them properly," said James. "Can I switch my torch on?" He pulled out the small, yellow, minion shaped torch ha had got from his McDonald's happy meal from his dressing gown pocket and switched in on, shining it over the runes. They turned all the runes over so that they could see the markings on each one.

"You wouldn't let me bring my torch," said Ollie crossly.

"That's because the batteries don't work in yours," said James.

"That because you stole them," replied Ollie.

"Weesht now, find all the stones that have the shape of a small circle inside a square," said Corrag.

The boys started to scan the stones and managed to pick out four with these markings on them. Corrag nodded approvingly, "Now find two stones showing a circle with a cross through it."

The boys found the stones Corrag asked for. "What do we do now?" asked Ollie, then his eyes opened wide in horror as they heard a huge crashing sound from outside.

"Switch the light aff!" cried Corrag and James flicked the torch off. "Now place these four stones around this pool of water. One on each side."

James ran around the pool, putting the stones down. "Can't I do one?" whined Ollie.

"There's nae time, the two of ye get in the water. Each of you must hold onto one of the stones with the crossed out circle on them," instructed Corrag urgently. She could feel Kirstin getting closer.

"Mummy is going to be so mad that we went in the pool in our pyjamas!" said Ollie, taking off his dressing gown.

There was another crash from outside and then they could hear their mother scream. "Mummy!" yelled James and ran towards the door.

"James come back here, yer mother is safe, but it isnae safe fir ye," said Corrag suddenly standing by the door blocking his way. "Stay here in the water, she cannae hurt ye here."

James stood for a moment, unsure of what to do, then he heard his mother cry out again, and this time, Corrag was not going to stop him.

Ollie was already half way in the water. "James, what are you doing, don't leave me," he screamed as James pulled the door to the pool house open.

"James, Kirstin is coming, ye have to get into the water," said Corrag, drawing on what power she could from her runes.

James hesitated just as Helena appeared walking towards him. She looked better than the last time he saw her but only marginally. She reached for him and he ran back into the pool house.

"In the water, James!" Corrag cried out to him and the little boy threw himself in the pool after Ollie.

Helena stepped into the pool house and all the lights flickered on. She looked down at the terrified boys clinging to each other in the water, then started to walk slowly around the pool. She saw the runes at each side, but she couldn't touch them.

"Very clever, Corrag, but it won't stop me," said Kirstin thoughtfully as she spoke through Helena's stolen lips.

"The boy is protected, Kirstin. Even ye cannae defeat the power of Ossian. Leave him alone," said Corrag.

"Never!" screamed Kirstin. "Ye'll nae stop me!"

*　*　*

Calum was trying to hold onto Anna to check on the cuts or her hands. She threw him off her. "Get off me! This is your fault, Calum. If you hadn't come near me with that crazed bitch, none of this would have happened!"

"Calm doon, lass," said Kenneth, "We need tae keep oor heeds, and find a way tae get oot of here."

"Don't tell me to calm down!" screamed Anna, "That's my son who's in danger, and we are trapped!"

"Nae quite," said Angus, who was unscrewing the hinges to the inner door that led to the hallway. "We'll just take the door off."

"That's if she lets you," said Calum, shaken from Anna's furious accusation. He went over to help Angus, and within minutes, the hinges were off. Calum put his shoulder to the door, it groaned under his weight but still stood strong.

"We need something to ram it," said Kenneth looking around.

"What about the table, it's heavy enough," suggested Angus.

They grabbed the table and flipped it onto its side. Calum and Angus grabbed hold of a hefty wooden leg each, then ran at the door, slamming the table into it. They were both thrown across the floor as the table struck, and although the door didn't open, it shattered in the middle. Kenneth grabbed a hammer and started smashing the wood out of the door, making a gap big enough to climb through.

Anna pushed forward, but Calum grabbed her. "Not this time, lady. I'm going first. You get behind me," he said and Anna conceded it was pointless to argue.

They climbed into the hallway and ran through to the boys' bedroom. The boys were gone.

228

Anna ripped their duvets off in fury. "Where are they!" she screamed.

They all heard a whimper and turned to see Dexter hobbling towards them. He barked feebly then turned towards the lounge.

"He kens where they are," said Kenneth following him.

When they arrived in the lounge, they saw that the lights in the pool house were on and immediately recognised Helena's shape walking round the pool.

***

"Jamie, come oot the water, come tae me," said Kirstin as she still paced slowly around the pool.

"Leave us alone!" shouted James.

"His name's not Jamie," shouted Ollie. "Go away, you're a horrible lady!"

"Jamie, come tae me," said Kirstin ignoring their shouting. "If ye come wi' me, then nae one will get hurt. Ye don't want me tae hurt anyone, dae ye?"

"Stay in the water, James. She cannae hurt anyone if ye just stay put," said Corrag.

"Enough!" screamed Kirstin and she turned her fury onto Corrag. She willed Corrag's spirit towards her, and the witch found she was helpless against Kirstin's dark power. It was hopeless to try to pull away and soon she was within Kirstin's grasp. Kirstin reached out with her hand and rammed it down Corrag's throat, soaking up every bit of energy from Corrag's spirit, until her ghost simply vanished into nothingness.

James cried out in despair, but still remained in the water, holding Ollie close to him. Then his mother was there in the doorway. "Mum!" he cried out.

Calum and Anna were first to reach the pool house. They saw both James and Ollie standing clinging to each other in the pool. Anna immediately jumped into the water and went to retrieve her boys, whilst Calum turned to Helena. Helena was no longer present, and once again he found himself staring into Kirstin's milky blue eyes.

"Are you okay," said Anna grabbing both of the boys to her. "Come on let's get out of here."

"But Corri said we were to stay in the water," said Ollie. "She said Kirstin couldn't get James if we did that."

"I'm not going to allow Kirstin to get James or you," said Anna.

229

"Mummy, your hands are bleeding," said James, who hated the sight of blood at the best of times, and the water was turning pink around them.

"It's just some small cuts from some glass, water always makes it look worse than it actually is," explained Anna, trying to see where Kirstin and Calum were.

Then there was an almighty crash; the giant sun window had shattered as Calum went flying through it like a rag doll. He lay in a heap on the other side, not moving, just as Angus and Kenneth appeared, Angus carrying Nelly's notebook.

"Will ye never learn?" said Kirstin stepping towards them with an outstretched arm, her eyes ablaze with fury. Kenneth began to choke, he couldn't swallow, make a sound, nor take a breath and he fell down to his knees."

"Let him go," screamed Anna in horror as she watched the old man's face turn blue.

"Gie me Jamie, then I'll let him go," cried Kirstin.

Calum, who had been badly winded from being launched out the window, was back on his feet. He staggered up behind Kirstin and saw Kenneth on the ground struggling. Picking up a large rock, he launched at Kirstin, striking Helena's head hard with the rock. She immediately fell to the ground, and Kenneth managed to breathe again.

Anna started to climb out the pool with the boys, but Angus stopped her. "Nae, stay put. Kirstin hasnae gone and the runes are protecting the boys frae her," he said, pointing out the runes that were laid around the pool edge.

"We've got one too," said James holding up the rune that Corrag had given him. Ollie did the same.

"Jamie, come tae me, Jamieeeeee!" Kirstin's voice filled the pool house as the air went icy cold. Calum was next to Helena checking to see if she was still breathing when she opened her eyes. For a minute, he thought Helena was there, but her eyes changed, and Kirstin was looking back at him.

"We've got tae find the black rune," shouted Angus over everyone. Kenneth was back on his feet, looking a little worse for wear.

"It's by the pouch!" shouted James. "Corrag told us to put it there."

"Angus ran over to the leather pouch with the runes tipped out. The black rune was there and he picked it up, feeling the vibrations go through him as he did so.

Helena got to her feet, her face contorted and unrecognisable with rage, blood seeping from the wound Calum had given her on her head. She swept her hand to the left and Calum once again flew through the air, hitting the sunbeds at the side of the pool.

Kirstin then turned her attention back to Kenneth, taking control of the old man's body. Kenneth tried to struggle against her invasive intrusion, but he couldn't stop himself. Having no control of his movements, he started retrieving the runes from the side of the pool. When he had them all, he threw them aside, then went into the water to try to take hold of James.

"Kenneth, what are you doing?" screamed Anna, fighting the old man off. She threw James and Ollie to the side of the pool. "Run!" she yelled at them and both boys took off towards the door.

Meanwhile, Angus had the black rune in his grasp. He was reading the incantation in Nelly's book aloud, whilst holding the rune aloft. All the runes started to make a low humming sound and began to glow. Kirstin did not notice at first as she was so focused on stopping the boys from escaping.

As James and Ollie reached the door, it slammed shut on them. James turned, then found himself being pulled once again by some invisible force towards Kirstin.

"Not this time, you bitch!" screamed Anna who was trying to get out the pool but was held back by Kenneth.

Police sirens could be heard in the distance, and Calum managed to get to his feet once more. He had a few broken ribs for sure, but he ran towards Kirstin just as she grabbed hold of James. The boy started to struggle against her, but this time Kirstin was too strong.

Just as Calum threw himself at Kirstin, the lights of the pool house started to blow one by one, throwing a shower of glass over everyone. The water in the pool started to bubble and the Ossian runes cast out a light that blinded them all.

Angus still had the black rune aloft, and he found he couldn't let it go. It grew hotter and hotter in his fingers, but still he held on. Kirstin started to scream, dropping James at her feet.

Calum dragged James away, as Helena put her hands to her head. She could feel Kirstin inside her now writhing in agony. Kirstin no longer had control of her mind, but she was still there. Helena screamed, "Get out!"

Kirstin desperately tried to maintain her grip on Helena, but she could feel herself being pulled back into the Otherworld. Helena had gained control of her body and Kirstin was losing her power. She screamed out venomous curses at the forces that had a firm hold of her, but it was useless. The Ossian runes sent her now weakened spirit back to the Otherworld in an instant, then sealed the doorway forever.

Everything went quiet, apart from the sirens outside. Kenneth pulled himself out of the pool, baffled at the strength of the power that had controlled him against his will. Angus looked at the black rune in his hand; it now looked and felt harmless.

James ran to Anna as she climbed from the pool, and they sat together at the pool edge, James on one of her knees, then Ollie climbed on the other one. "Is she gone, Mummy?" James asked.

"Yes she's gone now," said Anna. She avoided making eye contact with Calum, unsure of how she felt about him. She just wanted to get her boys out of there.

Helena started to cry. She felt dreadful and her head was cut and painful. Calum went over to her and sat her down on one of the sun loungers, pushing a towel against the cut he had inflicted on her head. Sergeant Burns arrived shortly after, and after what seemed an age of answering questions, Helena was taken back to hospital. Calum went with her, he knew Anna didn't want him around, and truthfully, he did feel bad for Helena.

Angus and Kenneth went back to the kitchen to get a beer. The table was broken so they just sat on a chair holding their beer bottles in their hands.

"Well, that didnae gae exactly tae plan did it?" said Kenneth.

"Aye, well we did get rid of her, in the end," replied Angus, taking a deep swig from his bottle.

"Aye, in the end," said Kenneth following suit.

Chapter Thirty-Two

Three Weeks Later

It was Ollie's first day of big school. Anna stood in the primary school playground with the other mums, kissing her boys on the cheek as they wriggled free to run into class with their friends. She couldn't believe it was nearly the end of August and the summer holidays were over. She prayed that this year the boys wouldn't have to do a show and tell. Usually, the teachers got them to talk about what they did in the summer. She wasn't sure that the primary teachers would appreciate the boys scaring the other children with their ghost stories.

Anna walked to her car, Dexter was in the front seat again, though she still had to lift him into it. It was his seat and he deserved it, as far as she was concerned. She drove down to the carpark at Crammond Beach, lifted Dexter carefully down so they could start their slow morning walk along the sea front. He was still on the lead, and he looked mournfully out towards the sea, wishing he was running through the waves chasing his ball. "It won't be long now," Anna promised him.

As usual, her thoughts turned back to Kirstin's Cot as she tried to make sense out of what had happened. The pool house had been wrecked, along with parts of the cottage, so Angus had closed up the cottage for the rest of the summer. Anna had left with the boys and Dexter the following morning. She had no desire to see Calum, he had gone off with Helena, so he had made his choice as far as she was concerned. She knew she had hurt him when she blamed him for Helena being there, but she was distressed and he should have known that. To not even try to talk to her afterwards said it all. She felt hurt, but she brushed it aside. It wasn't as if she hadn't been down this road before. The men in her life had never been reliable or honest.

They arrived back in Edinburgh and life got back into a routine. Clare had got back from her holidays and she came around for a girly evening. Anna filled her in about everything, glad to get it off her chest with a girlfriend who could be as outraged as she was that Calum hadn't stayed around. Pouring yet another glass of wine, they toasted dead beat men and their bimbo girlfriends, and Anna started to feel better.

She made the boys promise not to tell their grandma about Calum, but she wasn't sure if that would happen. They had a tendency to let things slip out, and she couldn't ask them to lie.

Just last week, she was contacted by Sergeant Burns from Fort William police to say that Helena had just been released from hospital. The injury to her head had been severe and a blood clot had developed, so she had to undergo surgery. Calum had stayed around while she went through the treatment, the sergeant informed her. Helena had no recollection of any of the events at the cottage, and Angus had not wanted to pursue any charges for damage to property. He would put it down to the freak weather and get the insurance to cover it. What the sergeant wanted to know was if Anna still wanted him to charge Helena with the kidnapping. Calum had said it was all a misunderstanding, and Helena had been very ill and feverish. She didn't know what she was doing.

Anna felt a surge of anger that Calum had the audacity to make this claim on Helena's behalf. She said she would think about it, but after a sleepless night, she realised Calum was right. Helena was an idiotic bitch, but she was not responsible for her actions at the cottage. She phoned Sergeant Burns and told him that she just wanted the whole thing forgotten. He thanked her, and she could hear the relief in his voice. It would have been a complicated case, with many things left unexplained, if they had tried to take it further. Anna didn't ask after Calum, assuming he was back with Helena. They deserved each other.

As she walked, she watched the sea drifting out. Soon the tourists would be able to walk out to Crammond Island to explore, as long as they got back before the tide turned. The tide on that part of the shoreline was treacherous. Anna had once called out frantically to a family who were paddling in a tidal pool, unaware that the sea was almost upon them. By the time they heard her, they were up to their thighs in water. Thank God, they made it back safely.

The sun was warm and the breeze was light, so Anna sat down on one of the benches, while Dexter lay down at her feet. She loved people watching on the beach, and she could spare an hour before she headed off to do her daily chores.

Calum was in a particularly bad mood this morning, everything seemed to be going wrong. He had lost a contract and he suspected it had something to do with the fact that he had decided to no longer use Helena's company for his PR. The further he could get from that woman the better. And to top it all, his ribs were killing him still every time he moved. The doctor said they were badly broken and it would take a while for them to heal. He had been offered a back brace, but had refused to wear it.

He sighed, leaning back in his chair. His thoughts turned to Anna as usual. He wanted to contact her, but the last time he saw her, she had been furious with him. He supposed leaving with Helena in the ambulance had not done anything to improve the situation, but he felt a measure of responsibility. He had smashed a rock over the woman's head, so he had to check she was all right.

The following couple of weeks had been a nightmare. Helena needed surgery and blamed Calum for all that had happened to her. He had stuck around because it was the right thing to do, but neither one of them could bear to be in each other's company.

He was relieved when Billie told him that Anna was going to drop the charges. It would have made it very difficult if they were all dragged into court together. Helena was not in the least bit sorry, nor grateful to Anna for having done this. She threatened to 'sue the bitch' for defamation, but luckily for Calum, her lawyer (Ted Burnham) advised her that would be unwise as she had just escaped a bullet, by having Anna drop the charges.

Helena was seething when they shaved half her head for the operation, again blaming Calum for everything that happened to her. She threatened again and again that she would ruin him in Edinburgh, and true to her word, she tried. This contract had taken him a long time to get on his books, and Helena had obviously persuaded them to go elsewhere. The more distance he could get from this woman the better for him and his business. He would never be that stupid again.

He wondered again what Anna was doing and how the boys were. He missed them all but could not bring himself to pick up the phone. He wasn't good at handling rejection.

Then, as if on cue, his phone rang. He didn't recognise the number, so he answered it tentatively, half expecting a salesman, but it was Glen.

"Hallo, I'm just phoning to see how you are. Anna told me you had cracked some ribs," said Glen

"Did she? I didn't know that she knew that," replied Calum, a little surprised to have Glen on the phone.

"Yes, I heard you two haven't spoken yet. Seems a bit of a shame. You're not with Helena now, are you?" Glen asked.

"God no, I can't stand the woman. I had to stay with her, Glen. I smashed her over the head with a rock. I could have killed her, I couldn't leave her on her own up there," explained Calum.

"That's what I just told Anna. Of course you couldn't have left her. You did the right thing. But what I don't understand is why you haven't phoned my sister. I thought you two were keepers," said Glen.

"Aye, so did I," said Calum. "She made it clear that she blamed me for what happened."

"She was angry and scared; she was fighting for her son. She lashed out at you, but I know she didn't mean it," said Glen.

"Well, why hasn't she phoned me?" said Calum stubbornly.

"She didn't know if you went back to Helena. You have to admit it didn't look good, especially when you never called her. She's just been through a divorce from a cheating rat, she wasn't going to put herself in that position again. Give her a call, Calum," said Glen.

"I don't know," replied Calum. "When did you speak to her?"

"Just now. She's down on Crammond beach, walking with Dexter. He's still under the vet's care so she can't go far. She was sitting on one of the benches when I spoke to her. Crammond's not far from Leith, is it?" said Glen and Calum took the hint.

"No, it's not. Goodbye Glen, I've got to go," said Calum, hanging up and grabbing his car keys.

Anna was reeling after her conversation with Glen. Her brother had a way of making her look at thing differently. He had been right about Calum not being able to leave Helena, but still, he could have phoned her. She wasn't going to chase after him. He had her number and he knew where she was. If he had been that interested, he would have called.

She stared off into the distance, watching the seabirds feast in the tidal pools left by the receding waters. She wished life wasn't so complicated sometimes.

"Hello."

She jumped, startled by the sudden interruption. She turned her head to see Calum standing there awkwardly.

"Hello," she replied, feeling her heart beginning to race.

"May I sit down?" he asked. Then he sat, not waiting for an answer. Dexter's tail was wagging overtime and he whined with excitement to see Calum.

"Well, at least someone's pleased to see me," he said, fondling Dexter's head.

Anna smiled, "Who says I'm not pleased?"

"Are you?" asked Calum, beginning to smile.

"Am I what?" replied Anna, pursing her lips trying to hide her expression.

"Pleased to see me," said Calum, feeling more confident.

Anna bent forward and kissed him lightly on the lips, taking him completely by surprise. "Does that answer your question?"

He pulled her close, then kissed her, not caring about the passers-by, nor the pain from his ribs.

Epilogue

"This was a bad idea," said Angus as he slipped for the umpteenth time. They were near to Ossian's cave on the Aonach Dubh ridge, with Corrag's bag of runes. Kenneth had come up with the idea that they should bury the runes in the cave.

The climb was not as easy as they remembered it, but it was decades ago that either of them had attempted the climb to Ossian's cave, they were a lot younger and a lot fitter back then.

"Stop yer whining, Angus, we're nearly there," said Kenneth, who was sure he was struggling more than his old friend.

Finally, they got to the entrance and both entered the cave. The Ossian runes started to hum from inside the pouch. The vibrations were making their hair stand on end.

"Are ye sure we should have put the black rune back in the bag?" asked Angus. "We dinnae want Kirstin getting oot again."

"Aye, I'm sure. The runes will keep her locked away. Let's dig," said Kenneth, pulling out his small spade.

They chose a spot at the back of the cave. The ground was hard but they managed to dig up enough soil to cover the runes. They then covered the freshly turned soil in stones and rocks from the mountainside. No one would find them, the humming had stopped and the Ossian Runes were home at last.

Kenneth pulled two bottles of beer from his pack.

"Well let's drink tae Corrag," he said holding his bottle aloft.

"Aye, tae Corrag, may she rest in peace," said Angus, clinking his bottle to Kenneth's.

***

Corrag watched them in the cave. Her runes were safe and the curse she had placed over Kirstin had been lifted when Kirstin had escaped the Otherworld. Everything Kirstin did from then on was of her own accord. Corrag was finally free to move on to the afterlife.

She looked out fondly at the ancient mountain ranges, then saw the light awaiting her. She never looked back.

Notes from the Author

Those who have travelled through Glencoe will know how breath taking the mountain range is. When I was a child my parents would take us on holidays to many parts of Scotland, but driving through Glencoe was always my favourite. My dad would play The Corries cassette in the car and play the haunting melody of the 'Massacre of Glencoe' as we drove through the cliffs and waterfalls that led into the glen. I did the same for my own children and grandchildren years later.

The Glencoe massacre is infamous throughout Scotland and beyond and has always invoked my imagination. Kirstin and Rab MacDonald are purely fictional characters, but the story of Corrag the Witch is a true legend in these parts. There was not much I could discover about her, apart from the story of the Sword in the Loch, so I'm afraid her life story as written in the book is again purely from my imagination.

The Clachaig Inn is nestled in the glen surrounded by the mountain's majesty. I have had many a wild night there in my younger days, waking up in a tent with my face in a puddle being one of them. How I got to that state I'll leave for your imaginations, but Glencoe has and will always hold a very fond place in my heart.

CPSIA information can be obtained
at www.ICGtesting.com
Printed in the USA
BVHW042206030319
541685BV00016B/395/P